Lost

H. M. Sandlin

ISBN:9781080417025

CHAPTER ONE

I followed the path around the pond with my mom, watching the ducks swim lazily across the water. We walked around the trees and through the flower beds, talking about our plans for the day. I was so busy looking around, I didn't see the piece of wood sticking out of the flower bed and tripped, twisting my ankle. I yelped, and tears came to my eyes. I tried to take a step and almost fell over when pain shot up my leg. My mom helped me stumble over to a bench and sit down.

I heard people yelling and looked around, catching sight of the fountain in the front of the park shooting water into the air.

"What's happening?" I asked, trying to take my mind off the pain.

"I'm not sure. It looks like the fountain broke."

Everyone moved away from the fountain so they wouldn't get soaked. We watched as the water slowly stopped spraying everywhere.

My mom wanted to head home to make sure my ankle was all right, so I tried to stand up. I winced when I put weight on it and immediately sat back down. At the same time, the fountain started shooting streams of water higher than before. I had the weirdest feeling that the fountain breaking was my fault, but that was crazy.

My mom called for an ambulance so I could get my foot x-rayed. As we waited, the fountain once again returned to normal. When the paramedics arrived, they helped me into the ambulance so I wouldn't have to use my foot. At the hospital, my mom filled out paperwork while a nurse wheeled me into the x-ray room and asked what happened.

"I fell while I was out walking with my mom. I guess I wasn't watching where I was going, and I tripped over some wood."

"Are you sure you only tripped?" she asked after taking a set of x-rays.

"Yes," I answered.

"We are going to do another set." She walked out of the room after reminding me to stay still and took another x-ray.

"Let's get you to an exam room so the doctor can take a look at these." She wheeled me around, and we started back down the hallway. She didn't say anything else, but she seemed worried.

"Did the x-ray look bad? What's wrong with my ankle?" I asked.

"I have to let the doctor look at it. He will let you know," she said with a frown. I quietly let her continue wheeling me to the exam room. When we got there, my mom was waiting for me, and the nurse left to get the doctor.

"Are you all right, Sally? Does it still hurt?"

"Not much, Mom. I'm sure it will be fine."

The doctor knocked on the door and walked in. "Hi, Mrs. Abeneb. I'm Dr. Stevens." He turned to me. "You must be Sally. How are you feeling?"

"I feel fine."

"I was looking at your x-rays. That must have been a nasty fall."

"Not really, Dr. Stevens. I tripped on the sidewalk while we were out walking."

"Are you sure?"

"Dr. Stevens, what is going on?" My mom sounded agitated. "I was with her when it happened. She barely tripped. Frankly, I'm surprised it hurt her."

Dr. Stevens looked at us and reached into the folder he brought with him. He took several x-rays out.

"This is your daughter's ankle," he told my mom.

I stared at the pictures. Right across my ankle, you could see a huge break.

"Her ankle is definitely broken. She will be in a cast for at least six weeks, and we may have to do surgery if it doesn't set correctly," Dr. Stevens told my mom.

"How is this possible? Are you sure these are her x-rays?" my mom questioned him.

"Yes, we already double and triple checked. I think it would be best if we ran a few blood tests to see if something is wrong that could cause her bones to be so brittle."

"Of course," my mom agreed.

The next few hours were a blur as they put a cast on and told me to stay off my foot for a few weeks. At one point, my dad came with our neighbor to drop off my mom's car so she could drive us home. He left after making sure I was doing all right and said he would see me soon. The doctors did all their tests, gave me crutches, and told me I was finished.

"We will call you tomorrow when the results come in," Dr. Stevens told my mom. "Make sure she is careful until then."

My mom thanked him, and we left. "Are you alright, Sally? Honestly?"

"I feel fine, Mom. My ankle doesn't even hurt right now. It hasn't hurt since the ambulance ride. Did I really need all those tests?"

"It's only a precaution. Normally tripping like that doesn't cause bones to break."

"I know, Mom. I'm sorry if I'm a little grouchy. I'm tired."

"When we get home, you can lay on the couch and rest. Tomorrow we will see what the doctors say."

That night I fell asleep and dreamed I could control water. I could command it to do anything I wanted. I could make it rise into the sky and create spirals back down to the ground. It was a fantastic feeling. I woke up feeling refreshed and went to jump out of bed when I remembered the cast.

Carefully, I pulled my covers off and swung my legs over the side of the bed. I was waiting to feel some pain, but it never came. I put my foot down gingerly on the floor and tried standing up. Surprisingly, my ankle felt fine. I was able to stand and start heading toward the kitchen before my mom caught me.

"Sally. You shouldn't be walking. The doctor said you have to stay off your foot for a few days."

"I feel fine. My ankle doesn't even hurt."

"Let's see what the doctor says before you go walking everywhere."

"Fine. I will try to relax today." She helped me to the couch in our living room and started making breakfast. While we were eating, the phone rang.

"Hello," my mom answered. I didn't pay attention to the conversation until I heard her questions. "What do you mean, her bloodwork isn't normal? What's wrong with it?" I couldn't hear the doctor, but the look on my mom's face told me it wasn't good. "Of course. Send me the address. We will be there as soon as we can." She hung up the phone and stared into space.

"Mom, what's wrong? What did they say?"

"We need to go see a specialist. I'm going to call your father and pack a bag for us."

"Pack a bag?" I questioned. "Where are we going? You aren't going to leave me in the hospital, are you?"

"No, honey. I'm not leaving you, but the specialist is a few hours away. We are going to stay there for a few days while they run more tests on you."

"Mom, you still haven't told me what they think is wrong. It must be bad if we have to go that far away."

"Hopefully it's nothing serious, but we need to go make sure. Dr. Griffith specializes in cases like yours."

"Like mine?"

"When the hospital checked your bloodwork, there was something different about it. I didn't understand all of it, but something about your DNA breaking down. I'm sure everything will be ok once we go see Dr. Griffith. Rest while I call your father and get our clothes ready."

She gave me a kiss on the forehead and headed to our bedrooms to pack. When she finished, we got in the car and headed east, toward the shore. At first, my mom acted like we were on vacation, asking me about school, my friends, and the boy I liked. But as the day wore on, she became more and more agitated. I could tell by the way she kept drumming her fingers on the steering wheel.

"Are you alright?" I asked. Maybe she knew more than I did, or perhaps reality hadn't sunk in for me yet because I wasn't nearly as upset as her.

"Yes, I'm just a little concerned. Your father looked up the doctor and told me about him when we were at the rest stop. He specializes in rare blood disorders and is the best in his field. I'm sure he will be able to tell us what's going on."

She wasn't trying to convince only me. She was trying to convince herself.

"It will be fine, Mom. Besides, I feel great."

We fell into an uneasy silence. I must have fallen asleep because the next thing I knew, my mom was gently shaking me awake. I glanced out the window at a small hospital. It didn't look like a place that specialized in anything.

"Are you sure this is the right place, Mom?"

She looked around skeptically. "This is the address I was given. Let's go check it out." She pushed her door open and got out of the car. "Come on, honey. We have an appointment for three o'clock. We only have a few minutes, and I don't want to make them wait."

As she was speaking to me, I saw a man in a white lab coat walk out of the door to the hospital and start heading toward us. "It looks like they are already waiting," I mumbled.

"What do you mean?" She turned to see what I was looking at as the man came within a few feet of us.

"Mrs. Abeneb?"

My mom nodded. "Yes."

He put his hand out. "Hi. I'm Dr. Griffith. It's nice to meet you, though I wish it were under better circumstances."

My mom shook his hand, and I took the opportunity to look him over. He looked like a professor up close, not a doctor. He had on glasses that had a line through them. Bifocals, I think. My grandpa had a pair of glasses like that. His hair was starting to turn gray, and he had a few wrinkles, mostly around his eyes. When he turned to me and smiled, the lines around his eyes got even bigger.

"I know this must be a lot for you to handle, but my staff and I are going to try to make this as easy as possible. Why don't you follow me inside? We can get the preliminary tests out of the way so you can go rest in your cottage?"

"What cottage?" my mom asked.

"We keep several cottages in the area for patients to stay at when they have to be treated here for any duration of time. We want our patients to be comfortable and not stressed. Weren't you told about this on the phone?"

"I'm really not sure. I know the lady I spoke to told me she would handle our accommodations and gave me an address, but I figured it was a hotel nearby."

"I see," the doctor said. "I will talk with Emma to double-check."

"Thank you, Dr. Griffith," my mom replied.

We walked inside, and I immediately realized this was a different type of hospital. It had a very welcoming feeling and no sterile waiting area. It looked like a large living room with a desk set to the side. The lady sitting there stood up and shook my mom's hand.

"Mrs. Abeneb, it's a pleasure meeting you. My name is Emma. If you need anything at all, let me know."

"Emma," Dr. Griffith interrupted, "did you set them up in one of the cottages? Mrs. Abeneb is unsure where they are staying."

"Of course, Dr. Griffith. I have the key for them right here."

"Thank you, Emma," he said. "You are all set up, Mrs. Abeneb. If you need any additional directions, ask Emma. The hospital already sent over some test results, so we don't need to redo those. I'm sure Sally doesn't want to do any more tests than necessary."

We followed him down a hallway and into an office. Inside there was a large, round desk with three chairs and a blue folder sitting in the middle.

"Sally, why don't you look around the room while I speak with your mother and fill out your paperwork."

"She really should sit down," my mom said. "The other doctor told her to stay off her ankle as much as possible."

"Sally, how is your ankle feeling? Do you feel like you need to sit down?" he asked with genuine concern.

"I feel fine. My ankle hasn't hurt at all today. I don't think I need to sit down." I looked at my mom apologetically for disagreeing with her.

"It's all right, Mrs. Abeneb. I don't think her ankle is nearly as bad as you thought."

My mom didn't look convinced. As they started filling out paperwork, I decided to take the doctor's advice and look around. The room was much bigger than I first thought. As I walked away from the table, something caught my eye. Against the back wall was a small water fountain. It was coming straight out of the wall and running into a little basin on a small bookshelf.

I slid my hand over the shelf, and something sharp cut me. I let out a cry. Water bubbled over the edge of the basin and ran across the bookcase onto the floor.

"I'm sorry, Dr. Griffith." He came walking over to me with my mom behind him.

"It's all right, Sally. What happened?"

"I don't know. I slid my finger over the shelf and hit something sharp. Then the water started bubbling out of the basin. It must have gotten clogged. I don't think I touched anything that would have caused it."

"Well, it's all better now," he said, pointing to it. He was right. The water was flowing fine, and besides the water on the floor and bookshelf, you wouldn't even know it was clogged a minute ago. "It's nothing a few paper towels won't fix. Now let me see where you hurt your hand."

I held it up for him and tried to show him where it hurt, but there was no cut. Not even a red mark. "I guess I didn't actually get cut," I told him slowly. I really thought I had cut my finger.

"It's all right, Sally. Who knows, maybe you did cut yourself, and it healed very quickly," Dr. Griffith said, smiling.

I laughed again. "Thanks, Dr. Griffith."

He headed back to the table with my mom after cleaning up, and I walked toward the pictures on the other side of the room. All the photos were of a large mansion with different kids in front of it. As I looked closer at one specific picture, I saw something unbelievable. The kids were holding what looked like fire.

It looked so real, but that wasn't possible. It must be some kind of rock that looked like fire. As I looked at the other pictures, I saw each group of kids had something different in their hands. One group was holding a transparent ball with water dripping off of it. Another group looked like a mini-tornado was in their hands. The next group was holding what appeared to be a ball of dirt with flowers sprouting out of it.

I moved further down the wall and came to a group of glass vases. They were beautiful and filled with so many colors. I almost reached out to touch them but stopped myself before I ended up breaking one. The way my week was going, I would accidentally knock the whole shelf over.

I overheard Dr. Griffith tell my mom that I would be doing tests over the next few days, and she could drop me off if she wanted.

"Why won't my mom be staying with me? I don't think I want her to drop me off."

"That's perfectly fine, Sally. Your mom doesn't have to drop you off if you don't want her to. It will be a long day tomorrow while she sits in the front room waiting for you. I thought she might like to get some rest herself while you are here."

Now that he said something, I realized my mom did look tired. "I guess if she can't come in with me for the tests, there's no reason for her to sit in the waiting room." I looked at her. "What do you think, Mom?"

"Whatever makes you comfortable. I don't mind waiting."

"No, Dr. Griffith is right. You should try to get some rest too."

"Sally," Dr. Griffith said, looking at me. "Your mom and I are working on a schedule for tomorrow. I want you to be here by eight to start your tests. You don't need to do anything special. Wake up, have some breakfast, and come here. Does that sound good to you?"

"Sure," I replied hesitantly. "What kind of tests are you going to do? Will they hurt?"

"Nothing will hurt you, Sally. It's a few basic tests to see how you're doing."

"How long will I be here?"

"Probably until two o'clock. Then you can go back to the cottage to relax, and we will do any other tests that are necessary the following day. Why don't you let me see your ankle now?" Dr. Griffith asked me to move my leg around as much as I could and checked all the usual things doctors check, like my eyes and throat.

"Besides her ankle, Sally looks like she is in wonderful health. We will figure out exactly what is going on tomorrow," he told my mom.

"Is that it for today?" my mom asked.

"Yes, I think that's enough for today. You had a long drive to get here, and I'm sure you would like to rest. The receptionist will get you all set up, give you directions, and show you the best places to eat. I'll see you first thing in the morning."

Mom and I walked out front and got all the details settled as quickly as we could.

We got back in the car and headed up the road a few miles to the address we were given. In front of me was a small, beautiful cottage.

"Sally," Mom called. "Come inside and rest while I call your father." I followed her inside and down the hall to where my room would be and sat on the bed.

CHAPTER TWO

I woke up to my mom yelling for me. I sat up sleepily and shook out my long, blonde hair. Glancing to my left, I looked out the patio doors to an unfamiliar sight. I could see was wave after wave crashing on the shore, and I could smell the salt in the air.

In the distance, seagulls were calling to each other as they flew over the waves. Maybe if I sat here long enough, I would see a whale. Too bad I had to go to the doctors. I would enjoy the beach later. I dragged myself out of bed and got ready before my mom yelled at me again. When I finished, I grabbed a quick breakfast, and my mom drove me to the doctor's office.

"I love you, Sally. Call me if you need anything," my mom said.

"I will, Mom. I love you too," I said, getting out of the car. I walked through the doors and into the waiting room. The same receptionist was waiting and told me to follow her back to one of the rooms.

The doctor walked in a few minutes later. "Sally, how are you today? How does your ankle feel?"

"Hi, Dr. Griffith. I'm doing fine today. My ankle feels even better than yesterday. I really don't think it's that bad. Do you?"

"I'm glad you are doing well. I think you broke it, but you are a fast healer. We are going to do a quick x-ray and then get that cast off if it's all healed." He smiled and looked at his notes. I wasn't sure if he was joking about my ankle or not, but it did feel better. He did the x-ray, and when he showed me the result, I was stunned. I could see the break in my ankle, but it was completely healed.

"So the question is, how did you break your ankle so badly, and how did it heal so quickly?" Dr. Griffith asked.

"I don't know. Isn't that why we are running tests today?"

"What if I told you it was magic?"

"Magic doesn't exist."

Dr. Griffith shook his head. "Let's try something different. Sit in this chair and close your eyes. The nurse is going to put these electrodes on you so we can measure your heart rate, pulse, brain, and a whole lot of other things I'm sure you aren't interested in." A nurse walked in and came over to hook me up. As soon as she finished, she walked back out into the hallway.

"I'm going to tell you a story. I want you to relax and think about what I'm saying."

I sat in the chair and closed my eyes. "Why?"

"It is to help you relax and see what your reactions are."

"A long time ago, before the world existed, there were shadow kings. They traveled the universe exploring everything. One day they came upon a star and decided they would stay and live their lives. They combined their powers and created all the planets. They each took a planet as their own and named it after themselves."

"So Earth was the name of a shadow king?" I asked.

"Yes," Dr. Griffith replied. "One day on Earth, the shadow king was walking in his valley when a great flame fell through the sky. He ran to where the fire was burning. Standing around the fire, dragons encircled a group of elementals. They all bowed before him and asked if they could stay because their home was destroyed by a great evil."

"He agreed, as long as they stayed near the volcanoes. Things returned to normal, and they lived happily for many years. Again something fell from the sky. This time bringing ice and landing in a large lake. Sprites swam around a group of elementals, and they told a tale of devastation taking place on their homeworld and asked to stay. He granted their request, telling them to stay by the oceans and rivers."

"What are elementals?" I interrupted him.

"They are beings that can harness the power of the elements," he told me. "Now, try to relax."

I nodded my head, and he continued.

"Life went on, but many years later, something else came from the sky and buried itself deep in the ground. The shadow king made his way down into the Earth to see what landed. The dryads stood next to their own elementals. They told the same tale of a great evil taking over their home. He agreed to let them stay, giving them the freedom to move around the Earth as they saw fit, for they were no danger to him. It wasn't until hundreds of years later that the air elementals and sylphs came, though the tale they told was the worst.

"They came seeking a new home because the rest of the air elementals turned to dark magic. They were the last of their kind.

"The shadow king went to his brothers and told them what was going on and asked if they should help the rest of the universe. The brothers debated for days, but the decision was made to leave the universe alone.

They had their own matters to take care of and didn't believe anything could ever hurt them. So the shadow king and all the elementals lived peacefully for hundreds of years. At some point, humans came to be, but no one knows who made them or how they got on Earth.

"Elementals came to be seen as gods to the humans, and soon each element type had whole human populations worshipping them. The elementals taught the humans magic, and it was passed on to their children. Different elementals came across each other, and many great battles were fought. Each thought their abilities were the best.

"Finally, the shadow king became fed up with the elementals. He took their power away from all of their followers. He told the dragons, sprites, dryads, sylphs, and all the true elementals that they could stay as long as they never gave their power to anyone else. They also had to remain sealed in the areas he set aside for each. They agreed to the shadow king's terms, and life became peaceful. The people of Earth continued to spread across the land, slowly forgetting about the elementals. Since they no longer had magic, they forgot about it too. At least most of them did."

"Why did they forget about it?"

Dr. Griffith stood up from his seat beside me. "Let's talk. I can finish telling you the story later. What do you think so far?"

"It's an interesting story," I replied.

"It is the true origins of our world," Dr. Griffith said. I opened my eyes and looked at him. He seemed to believe what he was saying.

"I'm going to be honest, there is nothing wrong with you. You are an elemental. The elementals have been here since the shadow king separated people from the true elementals. Most live in havens, and some still don't know what they are. Sometimes, something like this happens. They break a bone, get sick, or try to donate blood, and the results come back that something is wrong. This is not true, it just means you have the abilities of an elemental. Most of the time, a family knows right away that a child has abilities and takes them to a special school like the one we have here."

I looked at Dr. Griffith as if he was crazy. "I think I would like to call my mom. I want her to come and get me." I started to stand up.

"I know you don't want to hear this. Most people would think I'm crazy, but how do you explain what happened? Bones don't heal that fast, and the cut you got in the office healed immediately too."

"The hospital must have confused my x-ray with someone else," I stammered, trying to come up with a reasonable explanation.

"You know they didn't. Plus, you are having incidents with water. The fountain at the park, the fountain here, whenever you get hurt, water starts to act differently." I thought back on it and shook my head. There had to be a way to explain it.

"I don't believe you."

"You have no choice. You are here because you are an elemental. There is nowhere else you can go. There are those out there who would like nothing more than to use your power for themselves. They will stop at nothing to find you. I'm sure they are already looking since you used a lot of power with the water fountain near your house. Using power, even unintentionally, always leaves a trace if you don't know how to conceal it, and calls other magic users."

I stepped away from him, not wanting to believe anything he said.

"Wait," he called before I left the room. I turned back toward him and stared. He was holding a ball of water in his hand. I reached forward to feel it, to see if it was real or if my mind was playing tricks on me. My hand passed through the water. I jumped back and watched as the ball of water moved away from Dr. Griffith and toward the sink in the room. As it splashed into the sink, I swayed on my feet.

"Relax," Dr. Griffith said to me. "Take deep breaths, and everything will be fine." He calmly led me to a chair, and I sat down. "Don't try to get up or talk until you are feeling better."

As I sat there, I tried to figure out how he did it. There was no way it was real magic. Maybe this was another test. "Dr. Griffith, I'm not sure what I saw," I started.

"What you saw is magic. I am a water elemental. I can make water do what I want, but it takes a lot of practice. There are also fire, earth, and air elementals."

"I don't understand. How is this possible?"

"I told you the beginning of the story. I think we should discuss what I think you are." I nodded, still not accepting magic but willing to hear him out.

"Obviously, you have an affinity for water, which we will test in a few moments if you are willing."

"What does that mean?"

"I will show you. Come with me."

He led me through the hall and out a door that opened into the most spectacular garden. In the center stood a sculpture of a mermaid playing in a fountain.

"Come sit down," Dr. Griffith said. "I want you to concentrate. Think very hard about how water moves. The shape of it, how it feels, what it looks like. Concentrate on making a ball of water rise from the fountain. Close your eyes, and see the water rising up into the air."

Closing my eyes, I decided it couldn't hurt to try. I wasn't magical, and when he saw that I couldn't do it, he would forget about magic and tell me what was really wrong. I thought about the water, how it felt when I touched it, the peacefulness that came over me when I swam. My thoughts formed the picture of the water rising from the fountain. Slowly, I felt something change inside me. It began as a tingling in my chest and moved down to my hands. When I opened my eyes, a small ball of water was floating above the fountain. I gasped, and it broke.

"Was that me?" I questioned Dr. Griffith.

"Yes, that was you." He smiled at me. "Now, let's see what else you can do."

"What do you mean?"

"I think you have an affinity for another element too."

"Why do you think that?" My mind was reeling, I couldn't believe I had done that. This was too much for me to take in. I needed my mom and dad. I didn't want to be a part of this. I went to get my stuff. "I think I want to go home," I told him.

"Sally, I know you are scared right now, but you can't go back to your old life."

"I disagree. That's exactly what I'm going to do. I will pretend this never happened."

Dr. Griffith shook his head as he spoke. "No, Sally, you can't. It's not safe."

"Not safe?" I laughed at him. "What? Are you worried I'll make a ball of water during class? Trust me, that's not something I will be doing."

"No, the Pulhu are going to be looking for you. They won't stop until they have you, or they decide you aren't a threat. They are not good people. They will use you or eliminate you if they can't use you. I'm sure they are already in your town. That is why I told your mother to get you here immediately."

"I don't believe you," I said, but a small kernel of doubt lodged in my heart. "Why would they be after me?"

"They come after all strong new elementals. They are a group that believes the prophecy must never be fulfilled. They would like to enslave the human race."

"What prophecy?"

"That is a story for another day. Either way, you must stay here where you are protected. Most of this small town is safe. Once you are enrolled in this school, no one should be able to get to you. It is protected like one of our safe havens."

"You mean, I have to stay here? I can't go home?"

"Yes, you must stay here where it is safe. I will speak to your parents. It is in your best interest."

A thought came to me that made me stop. "What about my dad? He was still in town when we came here."

"I already sent people to watch out for him. For now, you need to focus on staying safe. You will meet others like you, and we will teach you how to use your powers. Eventually, you will be able to hide your power from them, and then you can go somewhere else if you want to."

"Does my mom know what I am?"

"Maybe. Someone in your family had to be an elemental. The gifts are passed down through family, though sometimes they skip a generation or two."

"I don't even know how to tell her. What do I say?"

"You don't have to say anything. I will talk to her about it. Everything will be fine."

Dr. Griffith led me to another room. It was a kitchen, and the nurse that had helped me before was piling food onto two plates.

"Here, dear," the nurse said to me. "Sit down and eat. It will make you feel better." As much as I didn't believe anything could make my situation better, the food did smell amazing. "I'm Mrs. Habbot, but everyone calls me Nana."

As I ate lunch, I watched Nana walk around the kitchen, trying to figure out if she had powers too. From what I could tell, she was just an older lady who worked here, but after the day I had, I wasn't going to trust anything.

"Why don't we go finish up your tests for today and plan what will happen tomorrow?" Dr. Griffith asked.

I nodded at him.

"Goodbye, Nana," I said over my shoulder as Dr. Griffith ushered me out the door.

"Goodbye."

We walked down the hallway to another room near the back of the hospital. Dr. Griffith led me to a couch facing a fireplace. The fire was burning softly, so it didn't feel too warm. After sitting in my seat, I watched as Dr. Griffith took his folder out.

"What are we doing now?" I questioned.

"We are going to see if you have an affinity for fire. Tomorrow we will test you on earth and air."

"Is that all the elements?" I asked.

"At some point, another element slipped in, void. We don't know a lot about void. Some people think it is an evil element, but others say that void must be the balance of all things, and it can be used for both good and bad depending on the user. From what I understand, there has only been a handful of void elementals since the shadow king tried to take the elements away."

"What do you think of void? Do you think it's bad?"

"No. I believe every element has the potential to do bad things. They can all be destructive if the person with that power is bad. But if they are a good person trying to do the right thing, I think the elements will be used in good ways. You can study it more once you start school here and see what you think."

"How do you test me on fire?" I asked, changing the subject. I was getting tired and wanted to go back to the cottage and puzzle out all the new information I learned on my own.

"It is the same process as before. Close your eyes and listen to the fire.

You can hear the crackling of the logs and feel the heat of the flames. Make the fire grow warmer as if you were out on a cold, windy day and came inside to warm up. See the fire grow bigger in your mind."

I listened to Dr. Griffith talk and began to feel the warmth on my face. I could hear the fire growing larger. The snaps and pops of water escaping the logs increased in intensity. I turned the fire up in my head and felt a wave of heat push at me. I could almost see the flames dancing on my skin.

"Sally!" Dr. Griffith yelled from far away. "It's time to turn the fire down now."

I opened my eyes to see why he walked away from me and saw I was covered in flames. I started to panic.

"Relax, Sally. Turn the fire down in your mind now. You can do it," Dr. Griffith said, trying to calm me. I looked around and realized the fire didn't hurt me. I held up my arm and watched as a flame crawled across it and onto my chest. I only felt the slightest heat from the fire and an intense tingling sensation. "Sally! Turn the fire down," Dr. Griffith yelled again.

I tried to focus on the flames, but I didn't know what I was doing. The fear came back. I was going to burn the whole building down. The tingling grew even stronger, and my entire body felt like it was vibrating. I was shaking so much it felt like I would pass out. The dizziness grew. With a cry, I fell forward into the flames.

CHAPTER THREE

"Sally, wake up." I took a deep breath. It was all a dream. I could get back to my life. I tried to open my eyes. "Sally, come on. Wake up now, dear."

I tried to open my eyes again. I struggled to see, and when I finally brought the room into focus, my world came crashing down. I was in Dr. Griffith's office, and Nana was standing over me.

"I thought it was all a dream," I cried. Nana put her arms around me and held me while all my fear and anger came pouring out. "I want it all to go back to the way it was."

"I know, dear, I know," Nana said.

"What happened, Nana? Why am I in this office?"

"What's the last thing you remember?"

"I was trying to see if I could control fire and..." I gasped. "The fire was all over me, but it didn't burn. Oh no. What did I do? Is anyone hurt?"

"Everything is fine. No one was hurt, except you. You used so much energy creating your fire that your body shut down. You've been sleeping for almost two hours."

"Two hours?" I questioned. "Why? What do you mean I used too much energy?"

"When you use your element, it takes energy. Usually, that energy comes from you. If you use too much without knowing your limits, you could even die."

I didn't understand what she was saying. How was I supposed to know how much energy I had?

"We will talk about it later when the doctor is here. Let's try and get you up and see how you're doing." Nana helped me stand up and try to move around. I felt like any minute I was going to fall. I tried to remember exactly what happened, but could only remember the flames.

"Wait, Nana, what happened to the room? Did I burn anything down?"

"Everything's fine. Dr. Griffith is taking care of it right now. How are you feeling?"

"I think I'm all right." I continued walking slowly around the room. It felt like I was getting my strength back. "Can we go see Dr. Griffith please?" I needed to know how much damage I caused.

"Yes," said Nana. "As long as you are up for it."

I definitely wanted to see what was going on, no matter how tired I was. Nana led me down the hall. When we got to the room where I started the fire, I was surprised to see that it didn't look as bad as I feared. There were four burn marks along the fireplace wall, and the rug that was in here before was missing. Dr. Griffith was standing in the middle of the room.

"I'm sorry, Dr. Griffith. I don't know what happened."

"Don't worry, Sally. This is what we test for, and as you can see, no one was hurt."

"How is this possible? All I did was think about the fire."

"That is the power of an elemental. Don't worry. With some practice, you won't set anything on fire. How are you feeling? You used a lot of energy."

"I'm tired," I told Dr. Griffith. "Will it always be like this? I feel like I could sleep for days."

"No. You need to get used to it and find out your boundaries. I have already called your mom and talked to her. She remembers someone in her family, an aunt I think she said, that used to talk about using fire. She thought it was a fairytale and didn't believe any of it. After our talk, I think she is starting to understand that you need to stay here to be safe. She's in the other room right now waiting for you. Why don't we go out and see her?"

"Did you tell her what I did? Was she upset?"

"She's not upset, Sally. A little confused and definitely worried about you, but she's not upset at all." We headed toward the waiting room.

"What about my dad?" I asked Dr. Griffith. "Has he gotten here yet? Is he ok?"

"He has not arrived yet, but I'm sure he's fine. Our people are looking out for him."

"Do you know if Mom has talked to him?" I asked. He was supposed to be here hours ago.

"She hasn't heard from him yet," Dr. Griffith said.

We walked into the waiting room, and I saw my mom sitting with her head in her hands. My heart started to beat faster. I was so worried she would be upset. She looked up as the door opened, and as soon as she saw me, she ran over to wrap me in her arms. I held her tightly.

"I'm sorry, Mom. I don't know what's going on. Please don't be mad at me."

"How could I be mad at you? None of this is your fault. Dr. Griffith

16

assures me that everything will be fine, and you'll be safe here."

"What about you and Dad? What if they come after you? Where will you be? I don't want to be without you," I said, starting to cry.

"I know, Sally." My mom sounded upset too. "Until we figure out exactly what's going on, I think it would be best for you to stay here. And don't worry, we will stay close too. Dr. Griffith said we can use the cottage for a while. Dad can work from there. You are our first priority. Once we know you're safe, we can figure out everything else."

"When will Dad be here? I thought he would've been here hours ago."

"I'm sure he'll be here soon. He probably had some work stuff to finish up before he left."

Dr. Griffith walked over. "Mrs. Abeneb, why don't you and Sally go back to the cottage and spend the evening relaxing? We can meet again in the morning to go over everything that needs to be done. We can decide on a course of action at that point. For now, I think Sally needs to rest. She used a lot of energy today."

He was right. All I wanted to do was go back to the cottage and lay down.

Mom started to say something but looked at me and thought better of it. "I think you are right, Dr. Griffith. Sally does look like she needs some rest." I followed her out into the parking lot after saying goodbye.

"Are you all right, Mom? Dr. Griffith said you had an aunt that talked about being a fire elemental. Do you remember much about her?"

"She was very eccentric, and she was a lot older than my mom, maybe ten or twelve years older. When I was little, I went to her house a few times, and she always told me the most fanciful stories. I never believed any of them. I thought it was all made up. Now I'm not so sure."

"Is she still around? Maybe we can ask her some questions."

"I'm sorry, she's not. She passed away a long time ago."

"Do you know if Dad had anyone on his side like this?"

"He's never said anything."

"When will he get here?" I asked quietly. "I'm worried. He should have been here by now."

"I know," she said, "but I'm trying to be positive. There must be a reason why he's running late. Let's not worry about it until tomorrow. He will probably get here in the middle of the night and wake us up," she tried to laugh. I could see how worried she really was and decided to let the subject go.

Dad still hadn't shown up by the time we got up in the morning. I could see the worry on my mom's face. We returned to the doctor's office, and the receptionist told us to wait for Dr. Griffith. When he came out, he looked exhausted.

"Mrs. Abeneb and Sally, please come with me. I have someone you want to see." He walked quickly down the hall, and I almost had to jog to keep up with him. He turned into a room. Immediately, I could see this was a real hospital room, and someone was lying in the bed.

I looked at the person in the bed, confused and not understanding, but then my mom let out a sob and ran forward. I realized it was my dad, and I forced my legs to move. He was sleeping. I could see bandages all over his arm and shoulder, even his face was bruised. Anger replaced worry, and I yelled at Dr. Griffith.

"You said he would be fine. You said you had people that were looking out for him. What happened?" I accused him.

"I know, Sally. It was my mistake. I only sent two people to go look after your father. The Pulhu sent five people after you. Normally they would only send one or two. They must know something we don't about you. They caught up to your father as he was trying to pack bags for you and your mom. My people stepped in to help, and they were able to get away, but not without everyone getting hurt. Your father will recover. We need to be careful until we figure out why they sent so many after you. I need you to go to the school today. It is the safest place we know." Dr. Griffith looked worried, and that made me even more scared.

My mom looked up. "How bad is he hurt, doctor?"

"A few cracked ribs and some bruising. He is strong. I expect him to wake up sometime this afternoon. You must stay here until then. I think you should go to our strongest haven. I don't know if this town is protected enough for you to stay here. We have never seen them send so many people after one person before. It is very concerning, and I fear what they will do to get to you. You must stay safe, or they will be able to control Sally. I'm sure Sally would do anything for you."

"What is a safe haven?" Mom asked.

"It's an area that is protected with our strongest spells. We have many around the world. Many elementals live in a safe haven and travel into the nearest city for work, though some work directly at the haven."

"Where is the haven that you want them to go to?" I asked.

"Our safest haven is in Ireland. Your parents will need to go there."

No! I heard the scream in my head, but I didn't say anything out loud. They would be so far away. I wouldn't get to see them for a while. How was I supposed to do it? I had never been away from my mom and dad for more than a night or two. I could see the same desperate look on my mom's face, but there was also determination. She walked over to me and held my face in her hands.

"Sally, it will be ok. We can talk every day on the phone, and we can get on the computer to see each other. It will be like going to college or boarding school. I want you to be safe no matter what." We both had tears in our eyes.

"I don't like this, Mom, but I want you and Dad to be safe. Do you promise he'll be all right, Dr. Griffith?" I asked.

"Yes, he will be fine. You can even come and see him before they leave."

"They're leaving already?" I was surprised, but I realized I shouldn't be. The sooner they left, the safer they would be.

"How will they get there?"

"There is an airport close to here. Our people will stay with them and get them on the plane. People from the safe haven in Ireland will meet them when they land and take care of them. Someone will accompany your mom back to the cottage, and she can get everything you need and bring it back here," Dr. Griffith said. "Does that work for you?" he asked my mom.

"Yes," she said, trying to smile. "Thank you for everything you're doing. If the people you sent hadn't been there, I don't know what would have happened."

"It's not a problem, Mrs. Abeneb. This is what we do. We don't want to see anyone getting hurt," he told my mom.

"Sally, I will have someone drive you to the school and have one of the students show you around," he said to me.

I turned to face my mom and gave her a big hug. "I love you, Mom," I said. "Tell Dad I love him too. I will see you soon."

"I love you too, Sally. Please listen to everything the doctor tells you. I'll see you this evening, and you can tell me what the school looks like." She smiled at me. "Now, go with the doctor." I turned and followed Dr. Griffith out of the room. He led me to the back of the building where a car was waiting.

"Sally, this is Natasha. She will drive you to school. It is only a five-minute drive."

Natasha looked at me but didn't smile.

"Come," she said. I followed her to the car and got in. She took off immediately, and I said a silent goodbye to my parents.

"Thank you for driving me to school." Natasha's eyebrows lifted, but that was the only sign that she'd even heard me. I fidgeted in my seat. I didn't say anything else, and soon we were pulling up to what appeared to be a mansion. The place looked huge, but not at all like a school. When Natasha put the car in park, I opened my door and stepped outside. A lady came walking out of the front door and quickly stepped up to me.

"Sally?" she asked.

"Yes."

"I'm Mrs. Sullivan." She shook my hand. "Please come inside. Dr. Griffith called ahead to let me know you would be joining us sooner than we expected." She smiled warmly and led the way inside. "It's a pleasure to have you here, Sally. I'm sure you'll feel right at home in no time. I will have one of the students show you around while I work on getting a schedule ready for you. Please let me know if you need anything." Mrs. Sullivan stepped aside, and I got my first look at the inside of the school. I couldn't help staring at the entryway. It was beautiful. This was nothing like my old school.

Mrs. Sullivan smiled. "That's everybody's reaction when they first walk in. This used to be a house for royalty to stay in when they came to visit. Now we use it as our school. Near the back of the estate, there are cottages where elementals who are not students stay when they are nearby. That's where you stayed last night. That area is off-limits to students, so please don't go down there."

"I won't," I told Mrs. Sullivan. "How many students are here?" I asked.

"As of right now, we have about one hundred students."

"Sally!" I turned toward whoever was yelling my name, wondering if I should run. Maybe the bad people found me. As I was about to turn for the door, Mrs. Sullivan moved a step closer to me.

"As you can see, the students already know that you will be attending school here."

I smiled as the boy came to a stop in front of us.

"Johnathon, you know better than to run through the school. What is so important that you have to yell Sally's name and scare her?" Mrs. Sullivan asked.

Johnathon turned toward me, looking uncomfortable. "I'm sorry. I didn't mean to scare you. I heard there was going to be a new student, and I wanted to be the first one to meet you." He looked down at the ground kicking his shoe against the floor. I couldn't help but smile a little. He looked like he was around fifteen. He didn't seem to be threatening.

"It's fine, Jonathan," I told him, "but don't do it again." I smiled as he looked up at me.

"Ok."

He reminded me of my friend's younger brother.

"I want to be the one to show you around," he said.

"Johnathon," said Mrs. Sullivan, "don't you have classes you should be attending?"

"Not yet, Mrs. Sullivan," he replied respectfully. "I have a break for the next thirty minutes. Please, can I show Sally around?"

Mrs. Sullivan laughed. "Ok, Johnathon, you can show her where the common rooms are. Bring her to my office before you go to class."

"Yes!" Johnathon jumped up and down. "Come on, Sally. I will show you everything," he said, and then he was gone, jogging down the hallway fast enough that I had to jog too.

"Johnathon, slow down. This isn't a race," I admonished him. He got that sheepish look back on his face.

"I'm sorry. This is so exciting. I get to show the new kid around. Plus, I got to meet you before everyone else. By the way, call me Tider. That's what I like to be called."

"Why?" I asked.

"I'm a water elemental, so Tider like the tides in the ocean that control the water level." He looked at me sideways. "What are you?"

I stopped in the middle of the hallway. I didn't even think about the fact that he had to be an elemental. I don't know how I didn't put it together right away. "It's ok if you don't want to tell me," he said, though I could tell I hurt his feelings.

"It's not that Johna...Tider. I just didn't realize everyone here would have powers too. This is all new for me."

His face lit up. "So, you'll tell me?"

"Of course. Dr. Griffith tested me on fire and water, so I guess I have fire and water magic." I hoped I said that right. I didn't have a clue how to talk about magic stuff.

"Whoa, you have two elements. That's so awesome. You are going to be like me. Can you use both at the same time? Because if you can, that would make you super special."

"What?" I asked him. "Can't most people use two elements?"

"Nah, we only have a few who can do that, but one of them isn't going to be happy to have another person like him. He likes all the attention." I could hear the frustration in his voice.

"You don't like him?" I could tell something was off, and I wanted as much information as possible, so I didn't make myself look like a fool in front of the wrong person.

Tider looked around the hall to make sure no one was nearby and lowered his voice. "No, I don't. He isn't a good guy."

"How do you know that?" I asked him.

He looked at me reluctantly and then looked away. I could tell this was really bothering him, and I wanted to help if I could.

"It's ok, Tider, you can tell me. I won't tell anyone." Now I was worried about Tider. What could make such a happy, excitable person this uncomfortable?

"I can see auras," he replied quickly. "No one but Dr. Griffith and Mrs. Sullivan know, and they told me I should keep it to myself. Most people don't want anyone to be able to tell what they are thinking or feeling."

"You can do that? Do you know what I'm thinking."

"It's not like that. I can tell you aren't sure if you believe me, but you are willing to try, and that you're scared, but nobody else would know that. You hide it well," he said quickly, "and you are a little sad. I'm guessing because you can't see your parents. How did I do?" he asked with a smile.

"Wow. You are good. I didn't know that was a skill."

"There are a lot of different skills, but some of them are more common than others. Anyway, don't tell anyone what I can do," he said and then moved to the next door. "Here, this is the cafeteria."

I looked in the room he opened the door to. It looked like a small cafe. There were stations along the walls for drinks and snacks, and in the center were two different areas that a few ladies were stocking with sandwiches and salads. Along the back wall was another area.

"This is where everyone meets up to eat. All of our meals are served here. You can eat here, or you can go out the side door to a courtyard and garden on nice days. That's where I prefer to eat. You can join me if you want."

"Sounds like a plan," I told him. "I'll look for you at lunchtime." He looked excited that I would sit with him, which made me feel bad. I still couldn't figure out why anyone would mistreat him, and he didn't seem like he wanted to tell me. "What other rooms should I know about?" I asked him.

"Let's go to the library next. It's close by." Tider walked us to the library and opened the double doors. "Not many people hang out in here," he said. "It's usually pretty empty unless exams are coming up."

I barely heard him as I walked inside. It was gorgeous. Couches filled the middle of the room, and a staircase led to an upper level. There was a fireplace in the corner of the room. Facing it was a small couch and a few armchairs where nestled around it. I had a feeling I would be spending a lot of time in this room.

Tider laughed. "So you like books a lot. Your colors went bright purple when you came in here. You must be incredibly happy."

I looked at him. "I am. I love books. You can lose yourself in a story for hours and be anything you want," I said, my eyes shining with delight at all the books I could read.

"I hate to take you away from this, but we need to head back before my class starts. There are a couple of rooms along the way that I'll point out to you as we go." He bounced up on his toes in his impatience as I kept looking around.

"Ok, ok. I'm coming," I said, laughing at him.

As we walked back to Mrs. Sullivan's office, Tider pointed out a door that led to a game room and theatre. "We can look at those later or tomorrow. Oh, yeah. When you come into the school, there are four wings. The east wing is where the girl's rooms are, and the west wing is for the guys. Classes are held mostly in the north wing, and the common areas are in the middle."

"What about the south wing?"

"That has been closed off since I came here. Nobody talks about it, so I'm not sure what happened there, something about a fire." He stopped in front of a door with a nameplate for Mrs. Sullivan. "Have fun in your classes. I'll see you around lunch, right?" Tider seemed unsure now that he was leaving.

"Of course. I'll see you later, Tider," I called as he dashed down the hall.

CHAPTER FOUR

I looked at the door and felt my happiness disappear. Tider had been a great distraction, but now I had no one to keep my mind occupied. I decided to get this part of my day over with and knocked on the door. From inside, I heard Mrs. Sullivan call for me to enter.

"Hi, Sally. Did Johnathon show you around?"

I was confused until I remembered Tider's actual name was Johnathon. "Yes, Mrs. Sullivan."

"I have your schedule set up. Abby will be here in a few minutes to take you to class." I took the schedule and looked it over. My first class was called beginner origins of fantastical myths. My eyebrows rose. I also had beginner magic and beginner mind over matter classes. The other classes were math and english but no science or social studies.

"These classes sound interesting," I said to Mrs. Sullivan. She picked up my incredulous tone of voice and turned away from whatever was on her desk.

"Yes, these classes are different, but so are you. When your teachers feel you have progressed enough, you will be advanced to the next class until you are in your year."

"Wait, you mean I'm going to be taking classes with a bunch of kids?" I asked, concerned.

"Yes. Everyone that comes here goes through the same thing, even though your case is rare. Besides, you will be with your grade level for basic classes."

"What do you mean it's rare?"

"Most powers have awoken by the time a person is ten to twelve years old, so they are usually sent here around that age. Your powers did not awaken until now if I've been told correctly."

"I didn't realize it was rare." I felt like a freak. I was going to be laughed at for having to take classes with ten-year-olds.

"Don't worry," Mrs. Sullivan said. "No one is going to bother you about it." I didn't believe her, but before I could protest, someone knocked on the door.

"Abby, thank you for helping Sally get accustomed to the school. Here is a late pass for your next class."

"Thanks, Mrs. Sullivan," Abby said before grabbing my hand and dragging me into the hall.

"Let me see your schedule." Abby grabbed it out of my hands. "Oh, you have all beginner classes." She smiled at me. "I'll help you practice so you can advance to the higher classes with me. What do you think? Isn't the school awesome?"

I couldn't help but laugh at her cheerfulness. "I'm not sure. I haven't seen a lot of it yet, though Tider took me on a tour of the common areas."

She looked thoughtfully at me. "You met Johnathon?"

"Yes. Why? Don't you like him?"

"I don't know him," she said, laughing nervously. "A lot of people don't. His powers don't freak you out?"

"Why would they? We all have powers." I was starting to feel like maybe Tider didn't tell me everything about his powers.

"I don't know," replied Abby. "Anyway, let's go find your first class. Follow me." She sped down the hallway. Talking about Tider made her uncomfortable. As I followed her through the halls, she pointed out little things so I could find my way again. I was sure the first few days I would be lost a lot.

"Here," Abby said, stopping in front of a door. "This is beginner magic. You already missed your first class. I will show you that one tomorrow. I will be back here after class is over. I'm allowed to leave a few minutes early from my class. Wait for me if I'm not here, so you don't get lost."

"Ok," I replied, but she was already headed down the hall to her own class.

I pushed the door open apprehensively and stepped inside. A booming voice spoke from the other side of the room. "Hello, Sally. I'm Mr. Connor. I will be your teacher for beginner magic. Please come in and sit down." I looked around the room as I walked in. There was an empty seat toward the back of the room, and I headed there quickly.

"Everyone, this is Sally. She will be joining us until she advances to her next class. I want you all to treat her nicely." Mr. Connor started his lecture. I was fascinated and listened intently through the entire thing.

"Remember what we talked about, you can use your magic anywhere as long as your element is nearby. It is rare for a master to not be able to use his or her element. Air is the easiest element since air is everywhere. Earth is also easy to find. Water can be a bit trickier if you aren't a strong elemental, but you can use the water vapor in the air. Even in the desert, if you are strong enough, you can bring water to the surface from below the ground. The stronger you are, the more water you can bring to yourself to use. Fire is the hardest to find in nature, but fire elementals can create a spark of fire with their magic that can then be built into something bigger. Remember this, there will be a test coming up soon on it."

The whole class groaned. The bell rang, and everyone headed toward the door. Mr. Connor called me to his desk to schedule an appointment to test me for air that evening since Dr. Griffith didn't have a chance. I walked out into the hallway to follow Abby to my next class. She was already walking down the hall before she asked me what I thought of Mr. Connor's lesson.

"It was good. I really enjoyed the lecture, even though we didn't do anything practical. Mr. Connor is a good teacher."

She laughed. "He is my favorite teacher too. He makes everything easy to understand and doesn't give us tons of homework. Next, you have Mrs. Shaw. She is a good teacher as long as you work hard in her class. I don't think you'll have any problems and if you need any help she always has time available, or you can ask me. After your class, I will show you the way to the lunchroom. All the students have lunch at the same time. It makes things easier since there aren't many of us. Here is your next class, beginner mind over matter," Abby said. "We'll talk more at lunchtime. Good luck. Listen to everything Mrs. Shaw says, and take lots of notes."

"I'll see you at lunchtime," I said, smiling at her.

"Mrs. Abeneb, hurry to your seat," Mrs. Shaw said as I walked in the door. "Now everyone, let's answer some questions for Sally. Timothy, why must we learn to strengthen our minds?"

"We need to strengthen our minds so that no one else can hear what we are thinking."

"Andrew, why would people be listening to what we are thinking?" Mrs. Shaw called on a boy sitting near the front of the class.

"Some people with power don't make good choices and choose to use dark magic. They would listen to what we think to get us to do what they want."

"Good," Mrs. Shaw said. "Now, Tabitha, tell everyone how we strengthen our minds."

"We start by thinking of a wall. You have to picture every inch of the wall in your mind and keep making it stronger. The stronger your wall, the stronger your mind." Tabitha sounded a little unsure of herself.

"That's correct," Mrs. Shaw said. "This is the first lesson in our class. Everyone has been working on it for a while, Sally. Every day you must picture this wall three to four times, always making it stronger. When you think it is strong enough, we will test it out. On to our next lesson. Jennifer, tell Sally how we use elements with our minds."

"Well," Jennifer said, "you have to have a powerful mind to be able to use magic. If you don't believe you can do something, then you can't do it. So you have to think that water can float even though gravity is trying to pull it down. Once you no longer worry about what can be done scientifically, you can use your element easily."

"Wonderful, Jennifer. Do you understand, Sally?"

"I think so," I said, but I wasn't sure I really did.

"You will have to work on those things on your own time, Sally. Who wants to tell Sally what we are working on now?" I noticed Jennifer's hand went up in the air right away with one or two other people putting theirs up quickly too. "Hannah, go ahead."

"Right now, we are working on how to focus on one object while also trying to do menial tasks at the same time."

"Very good. I will give everyone something to focus on and a task to do. Try your hardest." Mrs. Shaw started walking around the room, telling each child what to focus on and do. Most were told to clap their hands or stand on their tiptoes. A few had to walk up and down the aisle. I wasn't sure what this was supposed to accomplish but figured I would give it a try. Mrs. Shaw came to my desk.

"Sally, you are to focus on that flower pot on the window ledge. Picture every aspect of it in your mind. Once you have that firmly in your mind, begin hopping on one foot, switching feet every ten hops." I looked at her incredulously. This was ridiculous. "You need to be able to do this." Couldn't she have given me something easier? After all, it was my first day, and all the other kids had easy things like walking or lifting their hands up.

I looked at the flower pot and started memorizing the details. It was a clay pot with a blue swirl that began in the center and moved outward. It looked like a typical potting soil mix, with the white beads in it. A thick green stem rose into the air about six inches. At the top was a beautiful purple flower with fragile petals and a bright yellow center. Two large dark green leaves connected to the stem and curved down at the tip.

As soon as I thought I was focused enough, I started to hop on my left foot. The image in my mind wavered, but I concentrated, and it came back to me. I switched legs, realizing I hadn't counted the number of times I hopped. I tried counting while hopping and focusing and almost fell over. Around me, the other kids didn't seem to be having much luck either. My mind started to drift, even though I tried to stay focused.

I thought about my parents and wondered when I would get to say goodbye to them. I was hoping it wouldn't be too late. I could go see Mrs. Sullivan and ask her. Maybe she could reassure me that no one was going to hurt them too. I was worried about Dad getting hurt even more.

By the end of class, I was ready to get something to eat and talk to Abby and Tider, so they could distract me. Abby met me outside Mrs. Shaw's room, and we headed for the cafeteria.

"Hey, Sally," a voice behind me said.

"Tider, how's it going." I smiled at him. "Sit down and join us." He looked at Abby nervously.

"Are you sure?"

"Of course. Why not?" I followed his gaze to Abby. She hadn't stopped staring at him. She looked scared, which didn't make any sense. Tider was a sweet kid. "Abby, are you all right?"

"Sure. I…" Tider and I looked at each other. He shrugged, but I could tell he knew something.

"Out with it, both of you," I said a little sharper than I intended. They both looked at me. "Come on, tell me what the problem is. I'm new here, so I don't know all the ins and outs. You two have a problem with each other. I like you both, so I want to know what happened." I was hoping that Abby would loosen up a bit if she saw that Tider wasn't going to do anything.

"It's fine, Sally." Tider looked down. "I will go find a different place to eat."

"Tider is dangerous," Abby said quickly.

I couldn't help it. I burst out laughing. Tider dangerous? There was no way. He was shy, funny, smart, maybe a bit hyper and reckless, but I was having trouble believing he was dangerous.

"Hey," Tider said. "You don't have to laugh that much."

"I'm sorry." I could barely get the words out. His face reddened in embarrassment, and he looked about twelve years old, standing with his arms crossed over his chest and a big pout on his face. "I just can't… You really believe that, Abby?"

"Please, Sally. You shouldn't make Johnathan upset."

"Johnathon? Oh, you mean Tider. Abby, it's all right. He's my friend. He would never hurt us. Right, Tider?" I leaned over and affectionately ruffled his hair. "Abby, look at him. Does he look terrifying?"

"No," Abby said.

"Tider, are you going to hurt Abby?" I asked him seriously.

"Of course not," he replied.

"See. You are safe from Tider." I smiled at her. "Sit down, Tider. Let's enjoy lunch before it's over. I want to know why Abby is so scared of you."

He looked sheepish. "I come from a long line of dangerous elementals."

"That's it?"

"You don't understand." He ran a hand through his hair. "They are the worst of the worst out there. They practice dark magic and have no respect for anyone else unless they are more powerful. I am supposed to follow in their footsteps when I finish school."

"Do you want to follow them?" He didn't answer right away, and I got a queasy feeling in my stomach.

"No," he finally said, "but I don't know if I'll have a choice. Power corrupts, and I have a lot of power."

"I don't believe that. I think if you don't want to do something, no one can make you. It's always your choice."

"You really believe that?" He looked thoughtfully at me.

"Absolutely. Now, what else happened because I doubt that's the only reason Abby is so quiet."

"When I first came here, I had very little control and a huge temper. That's why my family brought me here in the first place. They couldn't control me. When I would get upset, things would start flying through the air. Tiny jets of water would shoot from everywhere. I didn't know how to stop it. During my first week, one of the boys made fun of me and said I was stupid after I got something wrong in class. He continued bothering me all week, following me around to bully me.

"I finally couldn't control it anymore, and a torrent of water picked him up and held him against the ceiling for what felt like hours, but was probably only a few minutes. Mrs. Sullivan came in and helped me get control over it. The boy was bruised and had a bloody lip and sprained wrist but was otherwise fine. From that day forward, everyone in the school refused to talk to me except the teachers. They were scared I would do the same thing to them. I was too angry to correct the few people who tried to ask me about it."

His story broke my heart. No one deserved to be treated that way. Especially when he was so young and couldn't control himself.

"I never heard it from your side before," Abby said quietly. "The way it is told by everyone else has you doing it for fun. I didn't realize Sean bullied you and forced you to lose control of your powers. I'm sorry."

Tider looked at her for a long time, trying to see if she meant what she said. "It's ok," he said shrugging. "I didn't do anything to help people like me more anyway."

"Who is Sean?"

Abby hesitated before her shoulders slumped. "He's my stepbrother."

"Is he really as bad as Tider thinks?"

"Probably worse. His mom spoils him rotten. She thinks he can't do anything wrong. A few times a year, his father comes and takes him. He is always worse when he gets back from those trips. My dad loves his mom, so I'm stuck with him."

"Doesn't your dad realize what a jerk he is?"

"Sometimes. He has tried to interfere with Sean's behavior, but it always causes a huge fight with his mom, so Dad doesn't get involved now. He mostly ignores it or agrees with whatever she says."

"Abby," Tider said. "I know you are scared of me, but tell me if he bothers you. You don't deserve that kind of treatment. He should know better."

Abby let out a small smile. "You don't have to protect me, Tider, but thank you for offering."

"Sure," grumbled Tider.

"So you have two elements so far," Abby said, trying to change the subject.

"What do you mean so far?" Tider asked.

"She didn't test for air or earth yet. Can you imagine if she has all four powers?"

"What do you mean four powers? I thought there were five."

"There is, but no one has void. I don't know if they can even test for that," Abby said.

"When are they doing your air test?" Tider asked.

"Mr. Connor wants to test me for it after dinner. I doubt I'll have it. I already have two, and that's pretty rare. What are the chances that I would have three?"

"Incredibly small chances. Want to test it out now?" Tider asked. "I can talk you through it. It's one of my powers."

"I don't know if we should. I don't want to get in trouble."

"Like you said, what are the chances you actually have it? You probably won't be able to do anything. Besides, if you do have it, don't you want to know before you make a mistake in class."

He had a point, even though I didn't think it was a good idea. "Fine, but something small. What do you think, Abby?"

"I think you can test it, and if you do have it, keep it hidden except for Mr. Connor. We can always ask him what he thinks you should do if you have it. I actually am starting to think that you need to keep all your powers hidden, so people don't know how strong you are."

"Why?"

"You know about the Pulhu, right?"

"Yes, Dr. Griffith told me about them."

"They are very dangerous. I don't think they can get in the school to get to you, but if you have another element, they might try something."

"I think I need more information on these guys."

"I will tell you all about them. My family is associated with them in one way or another. But right now, we need to test you before the bell rings," Tider said.

"Ok, what do you have in mind?" I put all my other questions away until we had more time to discuss everything.

"Put your plate down and come stand by the stream. There are fewer trees, so you can feel a slight breeze. Hold your hands out, feeling the breeze ripple across your fingertips." I did as he said and felt the breeze moving across my hands.

"Now try to gently wrap the air around your hands. This is a beginner lesson. Once you get the air to wrap around your hands, try to get it to wrap around your whole body like a bubble, that's an intermediate lesson." I closed my eyes to concentrate better and, in my mind, saw the air as silver streams flowing in front of me. I slowly encouraged one of those streams to wrap around my hands and then up my arms. I lost myself in the moment and allowed the air to wrap around my whole body like a cocoon.

"Open your eyes, Sally, but don't stop concentrating," Tider said. As I did, I was shocked to actually see air swirling around me.

"This is amazing."

"Keep concentrating and bring a ball of water from the stream over to you and let it fall on you. It's awesome," he said, smiling. I could tell he wasn't surprised to see me use air. I looked at Abby. She was staring at my air bubble in wonder. I had a great idea and walked over to her and grabbed her hand. The air parted easily for me, and with a thought, I expanded the bubble to fit over her too.

"How cool is this?" I asked her. There was a slight distortion to the outside world, but I thought with practice, I could make it go away. I walked over to Tider, dragging Abby with me and grabbed his hand to pull him into the bubble too.

"This is really good, Sally. You have way more air power than me, but yours is still raw. That's why it's distorted. With practice, it will be completely clear," Tider said.

"Try to grab the water now. I found this out when I was practicing the air bubble in the rain. I can't wait for you to see it." He sounded like a super excited kid waiting for a present.

I tried to focus on the air with part of my brain to make sure I didn't lose it when I reached for the water. Once I was ready, I closed my eyes and thought about a ball of water lifting out of the stream and coming to rest above us. I felt a lot of resistance but continued pulling the ball of water toward me.

I was sweating with exertion by the time I felt like it was above me. I opened my eyes and looked up happy to see that it was right where I wanted it, but it was much bigger than I pictured. I was going for balloon sized, this was at least five times that amount. "Should I let it go?"

"Yes." Tider looked at me slightly concerned. "You are using a lot of energy."

I felt tired, but I wasn't about to tell them that. "I'm letting it go now." We all looked up as the water burst. As it hit the air, it caused a beautiful rainbow of colors to light up all around us. It was like a different world inside our bubble with the most beautiful light show. It only lasted a few seconds before it was over. I felt Tider let his air go, and I tried to do the same. "Tider, how do I let the air go?"

He turned to look at me. His brow creased in surprise, "Picture the air unwinding itself from around you and flowing back in the natural direction it is supposed to go."

I did as he said. "I think I let it go."

"What do you mean you think you did?"

"I did what you said, but I don't feel any different. When I was holding the water, I felt a lot of resistance, but when I let it go, that resistance stopped. Shouldn't it feel like that with air too?"

"Yes, you should feel your energy depleting when using an element, but it should stop once you let go." He looked at me carefully, and I could feel him pulling air from around me. "I don't think you are using any air power right now. You didn't feel any reduction in your energy when you started using air?"

"No," I told him.

"I'm pretty sure you aren't using it, so you should be fine, but if you start getting really tired, we will need to tell a teacher so Dr. Griffith can check on you. I think you have a strong air element, so this didn't really use up any of your energy."

Abby was still looking a bit dazed. "You ok, Abbs?" I asked her.

"That was amazing. I don't know if I've ever seen anything so beautiful. Thank you for sharing it with me."

"I'm glad you liked it. I did too. We have Tider to thank for the light show. I never would have thought of it."

"Thanks, Tider," Abby said.

Tider looked away quickly, but not before I saw his cheeks redden. "No problem. I wanted to see what Sally could do."

"Sally, you have air, and you can use at least two elements at once. This is so cool," she gushed, "but we have to keep this a secret. I think we need to tell Mrs. Sullivan though. She'll know what to do."

The bell rang, and we all looked toward the lunchroom. Anything else we wanted to say would have to wait. We needed to get to class.

CHAPTER FIVE

"Sally, come with me. We have afternoon classes together since they are normal classes," Abby said.

Tider grabbed his stuff and went to leave. "Sally, I'll see you at dinner."

"Thanks for the help today. Don't get in any trouble." I winked at him knowing he was disappointed he couldn't come with us. He finally had some friends, and he didn't want to leave.

We watched him walk away and then grabbed our stuff and hurried through the lunchroom into the hall. We turned into the north wing and ran up the steps. We made it to Mr. Magni's class before the bell rang again. There were tables scattered throughout the room, and I followed Abby over to the one closest to the teacher's desk.

I took the seat next to her and waited for the teacher to come in. Everyone was focused on getting to their desks and getting their work out. So far, I wasn't given any books for my classes, but I noticed the other kids had a math book out.

"Abby, I don't have a book. I didn't need one for my first two classes."

"You got lucky. Normally, you would take notes in all of your classes. Here." She handed me some paper and a pencil. "I'm sure Mr. Magni will have a math book for you."

"Of course I do," came the quiet voice of Mr. Magni. "You must be our new student. Sally, right?"

"Yes, Mr. Magni," I said.

"Good, good." Mr. Magni pushed his glasses up the bridge of his nose to look at me. "I don't think you are going to be any trouble, are you?"

"No, sir."

"Well then, as long as you try your best and ask questions when you don't understand something, like Miss Abigail here, you will do wonderfully in this class," he stated. He turned to go to the whiteboard set up in the front of the class. He started writing a problem down when a commotion from the hallway caused him to look up.

"I don't care about what you want," a boy said angrily.

"My dad will hear about this," another boy's voice shouted.

"So what?" the first boy said. "What can he do to me? Nothing, that's what. You are a spoiled brat who can't stand it when someone doesn't bow to your wants. I've never given you what you want before, and I'm not about to now. No matter how much you threaten me," the first boy said. He sounded as if he was gritting his teeth, and I admired the way he stood up to the other person without yelling back at them.

"Excuse me, boys," Mr. Magni said to the boys as he got to the door. "I don't think now is the appropriate time for you to be arguing about this."

"Whatever old man," the second boy said in a huff as he pushed past the teacher.

"Yes, Mr. Magni," the first boy said.

"Thank you, Richard," Mr. Magni replied to the first boy.

I looked at Abby to see her glowering at the boy who was shouting. I realized that must be her half brother. No wonder she didn't like him. He sounded like an arrogant jerk. I looked toward the other boy, Richard. He sat down and took out his books without glancing at anyone in the class.

"Here, Sally," Mr. Magni said as he handed me the homework from the night before. "Follow along as best you can."

"Thank you, Mr. Magni."

I looked down at my homework paper. I learned all of this last semester in school, so I wasn't lost like in the other classes. It didn't take long to get through all the problems, and then Mr. Magni gave us a quiz.

It was a quick pop quiz with only ten questions, and I finished in less than fifteen minutes. I brought my quiz up to Mr. Magni to grade and waited in line while he was grading Richard's, who had beaten me up there by a minute. I overheard Mr. Magni talking to him.

"Good job, Richard. All correct as usual."

"Thanks, sir. You know I love math," I heard him say.

"Yes," Mr. Magni said. "I know you do, and it shows."

Richard headed back to his seat. He gave me a quick smile as he passed, and I moved forward to hand Mr. Magni my test.

"Sally, you finished quickly. Let's see how you did." He looked over my answers and smiled as he put an A on it. "Wonderful job," he told me. "You know your stuff."

"I like math," I told him. "It was my favorite subject at my other school, along with science."

"Those are my two favorite subjects too," he said in a conspirator's whisper and then laughed. "I think I will enjoy having you in my class, Sally."

I returned to my seat as he started grading the next person's test. Abby was still sitting in her chair. She was biting her bottom lip, and I worried that it would be bloody before she finished. She looked up with a pained expression on her face as she handed in her test.

"All right, everyone, it's time to move on. If you would all look at the board, we will start working on these problems." The rest of the class passed in a blur. I finished all the problems and even answered a few out loud when Mr. Magni called on me. The bell rang sooner than I expected, and we quickly grabbed our things and left Mr. Magni's class.

"I'm never going to get this stuff," Abby complained.

"I will help you," I told her. She looked a little happier after that. We only had a short walk to get to our next class, so we didn't have a lot of time to make any plans. I told Abby that I was supposed to go see my parents in the evening sometime too.

Our last class was incredibly dull. We had english, and the only thing the teacher, Mrs. Newton, did was lecture about a book that we were supposed to be reading. She did give me a copy so I could catch up with everyone else. Nobody seemed very interested in the book or the class, so I figured this must be how it went every day.

"I hope this class gets better," I whispered to Abby when the teacher's back was turned.

"Not much," Abby replied. "This is how Mrs. Newton always teaches, but the tests are pretty hard, so pay attention if you can. Thankfully, she puts notes on each class on the computer so you can check them to study."

"Girls, did you have something to say?" Mrs. Newton asked us.

"I'm sorry, Mrs. Newton. Sally wanted to know what kind of notes she would need to take so she could do her best in your class," Abby lied.

"It's very nice of you to help her, Abby. Anything I say in class has the potential to be on the test, so good note-taking is a must. Ok?"

"Yes, ma'am," I responded. She seemed satisfied with me and continued her lesson.

Abby looked at me and winked. I stifled a laugh and went back to taking notes. I doodled as I listened. After class, Richard walked over to Abby and me. Before he could say anything, Sean appeared in front of us.

"What do we have here?" he asked, sneering at Abby. "You shouldn't be hanging out with filth like this," he told me. "Come on, I will show you around." He smiled charmingly as he grabbed my arm to lead me away from Abby and Richard.

"You're right, I shouldn't be hanging out with filth. What would my parents say?" I ripped my arm from his grasp. "Thankfully, I have friends who wouldn't let me hang out with you." I walked over to Abby and Richard and linked my arms through theirs.

"What? I am the most important person in this school. You would do well to remember that. You are new, so I will forgive you for not knowing any better. When you are ready to apologize, I will be waiting." He stalked off after glaring at Abby and Richard again.

"I won't be apologizing to him," I said.

"Be careful, Sally. You don't want to mess with him. He can be scary when he doesn't get what he wants," Abby said quietly.

"I don't care. I'm not going to let a bully boss me around and tell me who I can and can't hang out with."

"Come on," Richard said. We hurried to catch up with him. His strides made him much faster than us.

"Why is he such a jerk to you?" I asked.

"His family wants the darkness from the prophecy to come. They think they will gain greater power and control the world."

"What is the darkness?"

"No one knows what the darkness is, though there are many theories. They are in league with the darkness, or they hope to be. I'm not exactly sure yet."

"Yet?" I questioned.

"Sean has been trying to get me to join his family in dark magic for years." Richard's voice turned grim. "He has tried every tactic he can think of."

"Why does he want to get you to use dark magic?"

Richard sighed. "Because if I'm on his side, I won't be fighting him."

Abby interrupted. "Richard is the strongest air elemental at school. He is also strong in fire and has a little earth magic."

"That's awesome. If you are that strong, he can't make you do anything."

"At least not for another year," he said sadly.

"Why only for a year?"

"My sister comes next year. She is young and foolish. He might try to use her to get leverage over me. My sister is incredibly willful and won't listen if I tell her to stay away from him. I'm trying to get my parents to send her to a different school, but they don't understand. Most families don't realize how bad things are getting. I wouldn't know either, but Sean wants me on his side, so he brags about all the things they have done to get power. It's disgusting."

"Can't you tell anyone?"

"I have. There is nothing that can be done without proof, which they are too smart to leave out for people like me to find. Sean is their weakest link, and even he is pretty smart. He only talks about it when no one is around to listen and never writes anything down that I could use as proof. For now, we are at a stalemate."

"I'm sorry, Richard. We will do anything we can to help you out. Right, Abby?"

"Of course. I didn't even realize Sean was in that deep. He really does hide it well, but next time I'm home, I will see if I can find anything to use as proof."

"Don't do anything to get hurt though, Abby," Richard cautioned.

"I won't," she said.

We were almost to the common area when Tider came barreling around the corner and knocked me over. I let out a yell as I fell backward. Richard caught me before I went sprawling onto the floor. As Richard's arms came around me, I felt a spark jump between us and flinched away from him. "What was that?" I asked. He looked at me, confused, but shook his head, warning me to keep quiet.

"Johnathon," he barked out. "What are you doing?"

Tider stepped back quickly, looking worried. "I'm sorry," he stammered.

"It's ok." I stepped between Tider and Richard. "He didn't mean it, Richard. He's my friend. I'm sure he has a good reason for trying to run me over." I arched an eyebrow at him. "Right?"

"I do. Mrs. Sullivan sent me to get you," he said hurriedly. "I didn't realize you were around the corner, or I would have slowed down."

Richard calmed down and looked over at me. "Are you sure you're ok?"

"Yes. Why did Mrs. Sullivan want me? Did she say?"

"She didn't say, but I overheard her calling Natasha, so I think she is sending you to see your parents."

"Your parents are here?" asked Richard.

"They are in the hospital, office, whatever you call it. Dad was hurt by some people looking for me, so they are sending them away. I have to say goodbye before they go." I started moving quickly down the hall. "I will see you when I get back. Since I am going earlier than expected, we should have no trouble going to see Mr. Conner tonight after dinner."

I had to keep reminding myself not to run, and within a few minutes, I was outside Mrs. Sullivan's door. She told me to come in before I even raised my hand to knock.

"Natasha should be here any minute. She will take you to the doctor's office, so you can say goodbye to your parents. You must listen to whatever Natasha tells you to do. If she thinks there is any danger, she needs to know that you will obey her so she can protect you. Do you understand?"

"Yes, but why would there be any trouble? I thought the town was protected."

"It is, but there are some Pulhu who can slip in through our protections. We need to know where you are at all times, so don't try to leave and visit the town. Head out front and wait for Natasha to pull up. Behave," she said, giving me one last look.

Natasha was already waiting for me, and I walked down the stairs to meet her. I got into the same car as last time and buckled my seat belt before she took off. I got the feeling she didn't like me, but I didn't know what to do about it, so I sat quietly. Soon we were pulling up to the doctor's office.

"I will be waiting here when you finish," Natasha said as I got out of the car.

I walked into the office and immediately arms wrapped around me. I recognized my mom before she was pulled away from me, so my dad could give me a hug.

"Sally," he said, "we have been so worried about you. Are you ok?"

"Of course I am, Dad. I've been more worried about you. How are you feeling?"

"I'm doing much better, thanks to Dr. Griffith. I swear that man is a miracle worker. I can't believe I'm up and walking today."

I took a minute to look my dad over and noticed he didn't look anywhere near as bad as I expected. "You look great. I'm glad you are feeling better."

"Me too, kiddo." He ruffled my hair and pulled me in for another hug. "You better call us and keep us up to date on everything. I hate that we have to leave you, but Dr. Griffith is sure this is the only way to keep you safe from the Pulhu."

"Are you all right, Mom? You are very quiet."

"I don't want to leave you either. I'm so sorry, Sally. Maybe if I had listened to my aunt, I would have known about this earlier. Then we wouldn't be going through all this now. You would have control, and we could stay together."

"Mom, this isn't your fault. How were you supposed to know? I never had anything happen that could have prepared you for this." I tried to make her feel better about what was happening but couldn't tell if it worked. "I love you, Mom. We will talk as much as possible. You can look at it like a vacation, right?"

She finally smiled at me. "You always put a good spin on everything. Don't worry about me. Your father and I will be fine. We just hate leaving you alone."

"I'm not alone, Mom. I have Abby, Tider, Richard, Dr. Griffith, and Mrs. Sullivan."

"Wow, you met a lot of people in one day, sweetheart. I'm glad you are already making friends. You will have to tell me all about them."

"One day, you will meet them. I think you will really like Tider."

We continued to talk about the school and the people I met so far. Mom and Dad seemed surprised by everything I told them, and they laughed when I spoke about Tider's behavior. I didn't want them to leave and was hoping I could stay here and keep talking to them when Dr. Griffith cleared his throat.

"I'm sorry, but it is time."

I threw myself into my parent's arms. "Please stay safe. I don't want anything to happen to you." I tried not to cry, but I couldn't help myself, and a few tears leaked out of my tightly closed eyes.

Mom wiped them away and gave me a sad smile. "We will be fine. Promise me you will do as you're told and that you will stay safe."

"Of course, Mom. I will be on my best behavior."

I gave both my parents one last hug and walked them to the door. The sun was starting to go down, and I knew this was what Dr. Griffith had been waiting for. This was why he let me talk so long. He wanted it to be darker out, so it would be easier for my mom and dad to slip away unnoticed. I felt like my heart was being ripped from my chest as I watched the car get smaller, but I didn't cry. When the car went around a turn, Dr. Griffith put his arm around me, and I leaned into his chest and let the tears fall.

"Come on, Sally. Let's go inside and get you some tea." I followed him into the office, and slowly my tears subsided. Nana made me a cup of tea and brought out a small plate of cookies.

"Here, dear, eat something. It will make you feel better." I did as Nana said, even though I knew it wouldn't help. I was going to miss my parents.

"The time will go by quickly, Sally. You'll see. You will be so busy learning new things that before you know it, you will be seeing your parents again. We will try to bring them here for Christmas break or send you to them if things have settled down," Dr. Griffith said.

"Do you think my parents will be safe?" I asked.

"Yes. It won't take them long to get to the airport. Then they will be on their way to a safe area. I don't think anyone will be looking for them at the airport. Especially without you."

"I still don't understand why they are after me, Dr. Griffith."

"It's because of the amount of power you used when you broke your ankle. The Pulhu know you are very powerful, though they don't know you have more than one element yet. We will try to keep that a secret, or they will really try to get to you. They only want the most powerful elementals, so they don't go after the kids whose power appears weak when it is first used. And they never try to take kids that are from prominent elemental families. That would start a war, and they aren't ready for that."

"Why can't you stop them. Put them in jail or something?"

"We do when we catch them, but the people who run the Pulhu are cautious, and they never leave any trace back to themselves. For now, we are trying to keep everyone safe and keep people from joining their side." Dr. Griffith finished his tea and stood up. "It's time to head back to the school, Sally. Find Mrs. Sullivan. She will tell you what to do next."

CHAPTER SIX

Before I had a chance to get up, Natasha walked into the room. She went to Dr. Griffith and spoke into his ear. I saw Dr. Griffith's shoulders tense up before he turned to me. "You need to get back to school, Sally."

He pushed me toward the door. "Hurry, Natasha. You should be able to get inside the school protections before they get here."

"What's going on?" I tried to ask Dr. Griffith, but he kept moving me out the door and toward the car. I tried again. "What happened?"

He finally looked down at me as I got into the passenger seat. "There has been a breach in our protection around the town. We don't know why, but we need to get you to the school where it is safer."

"What about my parents?" I cried. "Are they safe?"

"I don't know, but the sooner you get moving, the sooner I can get out there and check on them." I hurriedly buckled my seatbelt, and Natasha got into the driver's side.

"Please let me know as soon as you can," I yelled to him as we started to pull away. Natasha hit the gas as soon as we were on the road and sped as fast as she dared. I didn't try to speak to her. I was consumed with thoughts of my mom and dad.

"Sally," Natasha finally spoke to me. "You are to do exactly what I say, remember."

"I remember. Why?" I felt a lurch in my stomach as I saw how tight her hands were gripping the steering wheel. Something was wrong.

"We have company." I followed her gaze out in front of us and could see something up on the hill. She must have excellent eyesight to see that far away. I could barely make out the shapes.

"What do we need to do?" I tried to keep the fear out of my voice.

"I am going to slow the car down. Not a lot. I don't want them to realize I'm slowing down for you to jump out. It's dark enough that they won't see you if I keep the lights inside the car off."

"I'm sorry, what? Have you lost your mind? I'm not jumping out of a moving car."

"Sally," Natasha said sharply, pulling me out of my rant. "You need to jump and then head west." She pointed to a clump of trees on the side of the road that we were approaching. "On the other side of those trees is the school. You need to run as fast as you can and be quiet, so they don't find you." She looked at me, and I thought I saw compassion, but it was gone so quickly I wondered if I imagined it. Her jaw tensed. "There is no arguing. It is the only chance we have to keep them from getting you. Somehow they knew you would be at the office today."

"But what about you?" I wasn't sure what her plan was, but if she was going to let me jump out of a moving car, our options couldn't be great.

"I will be fine. Once they see it is only me, they will leave me alone. They have no reason to cause me any trouble, and they don't want to mess with my family," she said hurriedly. "I'm going to count to three. On three jump. It will hurt, but you will heal. Don't stop for anyone."

I straightened my shoulders as she slowed the car down. I can do this, I repeated over and over in my head.

"Make sure you roll when you land, it will hurt less." She gave me one last look. "One, two, three. Jump, Sally," she yelled at me.

I took a deep breath and jumped from the car. I tried to roll like she told me, but I had no idea how. I did end up rolling a couple of times, but the landing was so painful that I couldn't get up right away. My arm was throbbing, and it hurt to take a breath. I looked back at the road and saw Natasha driving up the hill. Another car came flying up behind her, and I hunkered down even closer to the ground so they wouldn't see me.

After they passed, I tried to push myself into a standing position but got dizzy and thought I was going to pass out, so I stayed down. I crawled on my hands and knees for a few minutes and made it into the trees before resting again. I could hear shouts coming from up on the hill. They stopped Natasha's car and realized I wasn't in it. Their voices echoed down the hill, and I heard them yelling to find someone. Probably me.

That gave me the push I needed to get to my feet. They would be looking for me. I needed to get to the other side of the trees. I stumbled to my feet and didn't get light headed this time, so I pushed forward, trying to run. The pain had lessened enough for me to take deep breaths.

After a few more minutes, I realized getting through the trees wasn't going to be as easy as I thought. I lost sight of the road, and everything looked the same. I didn't know which way to go. There was nothing up ahead, but I could hear shouts coming from behind me. They must have found where I jumped out of the car. So much for an easy escape.

I started to pick up speed. Soon I was racing through the woods. The pain left me as adrenaline worked its way through my body. I wound my way through tree branches and over rocks, doing my best to be quick but silent. As I went to jump over a log, my foot caught, and I slammed into the ground. Dirt flew up into my face, and I started coughing uncontrollably. I tried to be silent, but I heard my pursuers heading for me and knew I had failed.

I kept moving and thought I saw something up ahead. It looked like a light. At first, I thought the Pulhu had circled me. My heart pumped with fear, and I skidded to a stop looking for a way out. I noticed that the light wasn't moving, and my attackers hadn't used any lights yet either, so it must be the school or a house. Some kind of help had to be there. I took off running with a new burst of speed, and as I rounded another tree, I saw the shape of the school.

I was so excited, I didn't see the attacker on my right before he barreled into me. We went down in a tangle of arms and legs, rolling over each other. He tried to put his hand over my mouth, but I bit down hard. He cursed at me quietly. I tried to scream, but again he put his hand on my mouth. This time I couldn't bite him. He tried to pin me to the ground and grab my arms, but I squirmed so much that he couldn't get a grip.

I brought my leg up into his stomach and kicked him off me. He flew back a good ten feet and hit a tree. I was too stunned to move until I heard crashing in the trees behind me. I sprinted for the open grass in front of the school, hoping I would make it. When I was almost halfway across the lawn, four guys emerged from the trees.

I closed my eyes and tried to remember how I used my powers a few minutes ago when I knocked the man off of me. As I concentrated, I started to feel the Pulhu's power building. They were getting ready to use their power to subdue me. I saw ugly black, red, and green colors swirling around them. I didn't know how since my eyes were closed, but I knew exactly where they each were. Some had a muddier green color, but none of the colors were vibrant.

I tried to get the air to stream around me, and I pulled it over me like a shield. I figured if the bubble of air had kept me from getting wet, maybe it could protect me from their power. When the first hit came, it slammed into me before my shield was up, and pain ripped through my body. My shield almost burst, but I closed my eyes and steadied myself.

Suddenly, I heard a shout and the man who hit me with his power went flying. There was a bright blue flash of power, and another man went flying. I wanted to open my eyes but needed to concentrate or my shield would fail.

I watched the colors flying around and realized whoever was using the pale blue color was on my side. They were fighting my attackers off. I started to back up closer to the school, but as soon as I moved, someone shot power at me. It destroyed my shield, and I fell to my knees, grabbing my head.

"Sally," someone screamed my name. I tried to see who it was, but I couldn't see anything through the haze in my mind. I didn't realize my eyes were still closed until a shimmery yellow color enveloped me. My head immediately started to clear, and I looked up to see Tider and Abby standing at the doors to the school.

"Hurry, Sally," Tider yelled.

Another shot of power flew past me, missing me by inches. "She's not going to make it," Abby yelled.

I turned around and saw three people fighting against one person. I couldn't see who it was, he had so much power flying around him. I realized they were keeping him occupied so two others could come up and grab me. They were only a couple of steps away when Tider yelled, "Sally, get down now."

I fell to the ground and felt Tider's power whip over the top of me and knock one of the men back. Tider came running toward me, and a torrent of water followed his hand. He pushed his hands toward the men, and the water hit them in the chest, causing them to fly backward. They didn't get back up.

A man broke off from the other fight and threw his hands at the ground in front of me. The earth shook, and a dirt wall five feet high rose up in front of me, separating me from Tider. I heard his shout of frustration and a geyser of water shot out from behind the wall with Tider riding it like a wave. As he landed, his wave grew bigger. Small shoots of water were coming out of the ground and joining the giant wave. He yelled in anger as he sent his wave at the attackers near us. They were lifted off their feet and thrown all the way into the trees.

We heard a rushing sound as the wind increased and looked to see the guy with the bright blue power still fighting. He was pulling all the air toward him, and small flames had started to sprout at his feet even though it should have been too windy for the fire to stay lit. The Pulhu were trying to defeat him. The earth groaned as they tried throwing rocks and dirt at him, but the swirling air protected him.

Once he had gathered enough wind, he threw it at our attackers, and the flames went with it, lighting the men's clothes on fire and throwing them into the trees. We heard yells and screams as the men tried to put the flames out. Tider grabbed my hand, and we ran to the school entrance.

Mr. Connor ran out of the door. He threw people-sized tornados at the attackers, keeping them from being able to attack as the person with the bright blue magic ran toward us. I looked at the guy who was trying to protect me. The wind was still whipping around him, but I thought I recognized something about him.

"Come on," I yelled. "We need to get inside."

He turned and looked out at the trees one last time, and then he glided on the wind to us. His power was immense. Once he was closer, I looked up at him, and recognition hit me.

"Richard?" He looked different from during school. He looked older and a little scary.

He took a few deep breaths trying to calm himself, and his face returned to normal. Abby and Tider were staring at him, speechless.

"Wow," said Tider. "I didn't realize how much power you actually have."

Richard laughed. "You aren't too bad yourself."

"They had the weakest on Sally and me. The strongest were trying to keep you occupied."

Mr. Connor ran inside the school and shut the door behind him. "Go get changed, eat, and then meet me in Mrs. Sullivan's office. You are safe now. I need to call Mrs. Sullivan and let her know you are here. We have a lot to discuss," he said before walking down the hall to make a phone call.

"How did you know I needed help?" I asked them.

"When you left, I had a bad feeling. I went and talked to Mrs. Sullivan, and she told me you would be fine, but I couldn't shake the feeling that something was wrong. I grabbed these two and talked to them about it. Abby told me she felt the same way. We have been pacing this hall since then, waiting for you to come back. Mrs. Sullivan came running out a few minutes before you showed up and took off in her car to go to the office for an attack. She said you were on your way back with Natasha, and we should lock up as soon as you got in," Richard said.

"We waited for Natasha, but she never showed up. We were getting ready to take off down the road to look for you two when we saw something in the woods. No one should be out there, so we figured they had to be the Pulhu, and they must be chasing something. We didn't know it was you for sure until you made it out of the trees," Tider said.

"Thank you for helping me. I don't think I would have made it if you hadn't stepped in." I looked at them and realized we were all a mess. We were covered in dirt and leaves, and in my case, blood. I felt my knee where I hurt it jumping out of the car, but it didn't hurt, neither did my arm. There was blood on my clothes, but I couldn't find a single scratch.

"Guys? Why don't I have any scratches or bruises or broken bones? I jumped out of a moving car and then ran through the woods being chased." I looked at Richard and saw a small cut on his right arm, though from the amount of blood on his shirt, it should have been much worse.

"A lot of us heal fast," Richard said. "It's one benefit of having magic, though if you broke your arm and it's already healed, you must have super fast healing abilities."

"But I was hurt pretty bad. I felt like my head was about to explode when that last one hit me. I couldn't even see straight, and then a yellow light wrapped around me, and I felt much better."

"That was probably me," Abby said. We all stared at her. "I don't know what you mean by the color, but I can heal people, sometimes. I sent

43

healing magic to you when I saw how badly hurt you were. I didn't think you were going to make it."

I gave her a big hug. "Thank you for healing me, Abby."

"You're welcome. I'm glad I was able to. It isn't a very reliable power."

"Let's go get cleaned up and eat," Tider said. "Then we can talk about this more."

"I have a lot of questions," I said. "I still don't understand what happened."

"We can talk when we get to Mrs. Sullivan's office but food first, and I have some questions for you too," Richard said.

"Like what?"

"I want to know more about these colors you see."

"Is that not normal?" I questioned.

"Not that I know of," he replied. "Go get dressed. We will meet you in the lunchroom." I looked at Tider and thought about asking him about the colors since he could see auras, but he asked me to keep his secret, and I didn't want to say anything in front of Richard and Abby. I decided I would ask him later when no one else was around.

Abby and I headed to the east wing. "Hey, Abby, can I borrow some clothes? I don't have a clue where my room is or if I even have any of my clothes here."

"I know where your room is. Mrs. Sullivan told me to show you, but I was planning on doing it after dinner. I didn't realize we were going to have such an eventful day."

"Do you think my parents made it to the airport?" I voiced the question that scared me the most.

"I'm sure they did."

"How can you be sure?" I asked her as we finally made it into our wing.

"I just can," she said before she showed me my room and walked into hers across the hall.

When we got to the cafeteria, the guys were already there. They had plates of food for all of us. "They were shutting down for the night, so we grabbed as much as we could for you. Eat up."

"Did you see Mrs. Sullivan?" I asked.

"No, but we will go check her office when we finish here," Tider said.

I sat down in front of one of the plates of food. It smelled amazing. There was ham, potatoes and lots of different veggies. My mouth watered as I unrolled my napkin to take out my silverware. I was suddenly so hungry I couldn't concentrate on anything else but eating.

I quickly devoured all the food on my plate and even looked around for seconds. Tider pulled a few rolls out of a bread basket I missed and handed them to me. "Jeez, Sally, you really are starving." He laughed.

My face colored with embarrassment as I realized I had not even looked at my friends during the meal. "I'm sorry, I didn't know I was so hungry. I don't think I've ever been that hungry before."

"It's a side effect of using a lot of magic," Richard said.

"And of healing," Abby chimed in.

"Why?"

"You are using a lot of energy when you use magic. That energy has to be replenished. Food is the fastest way to do that. Sleep also works, but I doubt you would consider taking a nap right now," Richard explained to me.

"You're right, no naps for me. I have to find out about my parents."

"Let's go see if Mrs. Sullivan is back yet and if she knows anything," said Tider. After picking up our dishes, he led the way back to her office. The door was closed, so we knocked and waited. When no one answered, I pushed the door open.

"Sally, you can't barge into Mrs. Sullivan's office."

"Actually, I can. The door is unlocked. Besides, I'm just going to sit here until she comes back. I'm not going to touch her stuff," I said as I walked inside.

"Sally," Abby hissed at me.

"It's ok, Abby. I promise to be good. You don't have to stay if you don't want to. I understand."

Abby came into the office and plopped onto the little couch. "I'm staying with you." Tider and Richard came in too.

"Well, now what?" Richard asked.

"I guess we wait."

"In that case, let's talk," Richard began. "What were you talking about when you said you saw colors during the fight?"

"When you were fighting, if I had my eyes closed, I could see your power by the color. Yours was a bright blue color, Richard."

"What about mine?" Tider asked.

"You have a very pale blue color, Tider."

"Wow. That's so cool."

"Abby, you have a shimmery yellow color. It's beautiful," I told her. "What do the colors mean?" I asked Richard.

"I have no idea. I've never heard of someone seeing power as colors. So you could see their colors too?"

"Yes, most of them had either a black, red, or a green color. It looked like their colors were tainted by something. They were all very dark-colored."

"That could be the effects of using dark magic. That could be very helpful to know who is on the Pulhu's side."

"I felt you using your power out there, but I wasn't sure what you were trying to do," Richard said.

"I was trying to make a shield out of air so their power couldn't hurt me. It didn't work though."

"I think it did," Tider said. "They didn't hit you until you moved. It didn't make any sense to me at the time. I kept waiting for them to take a shot at you, but they waited until you tried to get to the school. I wonder if it only works when you are still."

"I made it like you taught me to make the bubble of air when we were at lunch. That's the only thing I knew how to do, so I tried it."

"That's quick thinking, but I don't think it worked as a shield," Richard said.

My face fell. I thought maybe I had done something.

"I think it made you invisible to them as long as you didn't move," Richard said. This time my mouth fell open.

"No, we could see her," Abby and Tider said together.

"Yes, but I don't think they could. If they had seen her, they would have continued firing at her, trying to break through if it was a shield. They wouldn't have stopped and waited."

"It makes sense," said Tider. "Except for the fact that I've never heard of it being done before. I didn't think anything like that was possible."

"Really, not possible? You can shoot water out of the ground, but invisibility is impossible," I scoffed at him, and Abby laughed.

"Invisibility is possible, but we haven't heard of it being created without a potion before," Abby said.

"We don't really know what kind of powers are out there. Usually, you get the same ones over and over, but sometimes a strange power will show up in a person. Maybe that is yours."

"I guess it could be worse. Invisibility would be cool."

The door to the office opened, and I flew out of my seat. "Are my parents ok? Did you see them? Did they got on the plane?" I asked before the person even walked in. When I realized it wasn't Mrs. Sullivan, I stopped. Mr. Connor stood in front of us all.

"Tell me what happened from the beginning, when you left Dr. Griffith's office," he said.

I told him exactly what happened all evening. He let me speak, not interrupting, and only inhaled sharply when I said that I jumped out of a moving car.

"Where is Natasha now?" he asked.

"Oh no. I completely forgot about her. She said she would be fine, and I didn't think anything else about it once I got in the woods."

"It's ok, Sally," Mr. Connor said. "I'm sure she is fine."

"I suppose we do not need to test you for air, now do we?" Mr. Connor asked.

"I don't think so."

"What other elements do you have?" I looked at my friends, not sure how much to reveal.

"She has three of them for sure," Richard answered for me.

"Three?" Mr. Connor looked at Richard.

"She hasn't been tested for earth yet."

"You must keep this hidden if you can."

"How am I supposed to do that?"

"I will ask Mrs. Sullivan to put you in a master class with Mr. Jared Merrem. He will be able to work with you on fire and earth if you have it. I can help you with air and water. No one needs to know what you are actually working on. Now, what did the people attacking see you use?"

"I only used air. Why?"

"That is what we will tell people. You are an air elemental."

"Why is it so important to protect me from them? Why are they after me like this and not anyone else?"

"You have a lot of power which they want on their side. They are also after a specific person. They go after anyone who has more than one power in case they are the one the prophecy is talking about. That's why we don't want them knowing how many powers you have."

"What prophecy? I'm not a part of it, am I?"

"We have no idea. Not many people know the full thing. At this point, the prophecy could be talking about any number of people. Let me call Mrs. Sullivan and see what she knows about your parents."

Mr. Connor stepped out of the office to make his phone call, and everyone looked at me. "What?" I asked them.

"You are going to have to be very careful," Richard said. Tider looked worried.

"Don't worry about me, I'm sure I'll be fine. They'll lose interest in me as long as they don't know I have more than one power."

"I don't want you to get hurt. You're the first person in a long time who took the time to talk to me." Richard and Abby looked down as Tider said that. I could tell they were sorry Tider had been treated poorly, but they didn't know what to do or say about it. As I was about to say something, Mr. Connor walked back in.

"Great news, Sally. Your parents made it onto the plane and have already taken off. They didn't run into any trouble at all on the way there. Dr. Griffith thinks the Pulhu were unaware of who was in the car and let them go thinking there would be fewer people around the office, so they could get to you."

I smiled. "Good, I was really worried about them. When will they land? I don't think I will be able to stop worrying until they are in the haven."

"I'm sure Mrs. Sullivan will be able to let you know tomorrow morning. Now you all need to get to your rooms and get ready for lights out. I have some preparations to make for tomorrow's class. Sally, I want you to go to your morning classes. No one needs to know you are going into master classes. We should keep pretenses up as long as possible."

"Ok."

We all headed for the door. I said goodbye to the guys in the common room, and Abby and I headed toward our rooms.

"Goodnight, Sally," Abby told me as I opened my door.

"Goodnight, Abby."

"Knock on my door in the morning, and we'll walk down to breakfast together."

CHAPTER SEVEN

I didn't sleep well because of a bad dream, but I couldn't remember any details. I looked at the clock and rolled out of bed. I wanted to go down to Mrs. Sullivan's office before everyone woke up and ask about my parents. Then I would come back to get Abby.

It was a pretty easy walk to her office, and I found myself in the front hall in no time. Her door opened as I went to knock.

"Have you heard anything? Are they safe?" I asked before she had a chance to talk.

"They made it safely to the haven this morning. They will be safe there until this all dies down."

"When will that be?"

"It might be a while. We need to take extra steps to protect you. You are turning out to be more powerful than we thought." She looked at me for a minute. "Are you ok after last night? I heard about the attack on you. You are lucky you have made such good friends already. We would have lost you if not for them."

"I'm sorry that I'm causing you so much trouble." I felt terrible that all this was happening because of me.

"Don't be sorry. This is what we do. We are here to help and protect you. Sadly, some of the elementals have forgotten that and have become selfish. Don't worry about anything. We need to talk about your classes before everyone wakes up. You are going to have to be very careful."

"I know. Mr. Connor talked to us last night. He wants me to continue my classes, so it looks like I am still learning at a beginner level."

"Mr. Connor will be giving you extra instruction after your afternoon classes on Monday and Wednesday, and Mr. Merrem will work with you on Tuesday and Thursday. If you continue your morning classes, you will be expected to participate and get good grades."

"I understand. I don't want anyone coming after me again, so if this is what I need to do so they don't know anything about me, I'll do it," I told Mrs. Sullivan.

"Good. Make sure you never leave the school grounds. They are protected."

"How will I know if I leave the protected area?"

"You won't be able to tell. Have Tider or Richard show you where the protection lines are. That way you don't accidentally cross them, and don't use your magic outside where others can see you."

"I won't," I told her.

"If you need anything else, please let me know." She handed me a new book bag with a bunch of supplies in it.

"Thank you, Mrs. Sullivan." I left her office and headed to Abby's room, thinking about what I had gotten myself into. I woke Abby up and waited for her to get dressed before we headed down to the cafeteria. Tider and Richard met us as we were getting some eggs and bacon.

"I love breakfast," Tider said happily. I agreed with him. We found a table to eat at, and I looked around, noticing that most of the seats were still empty.

"Where is everyone?" I asked.

"They will be here soon. Most of them don't get down here for a few more minutes. We are pretty early," Richard said.

"I went to see Mrs. Sullivan this morning," I told them. "She said my parents are fine, and we talked about my schedule."

We fell silent as other kids started to trickle in for breakfast. "Do you guys want to go out to the garden until class starts?" I asked, wanting to be away from prying eyes.

"Sure," they agreed. I zipped up my jacket before heading out. There was a chill in the air this early in the morning.

"What master class do you have today?" asked Richard.

"I have Mr. Connor today."

"I will walk down with you after english," Richard said.

"Thanks, Richard."

We headed to our classes, and Abby showed me where my first-period class was. "Have fun, Sally," Abby called as she raced away. "I will see you at lunchtime."

"Bye," I yelled to her. I walked into my class, and right away, I knew I was going to love it. Hanging around the room were constellations and creatures that couldn't possibly be real. One wall was filled with gods and goddesses of ancient times. I couldn't wait to learn if any of this stuff had some truth to it.

"Come inside, Sally. I have a seat for you right here." The teacher pointed to the seat closest to her desk. "I'm Mrs. Maisen. I hope you will be able to jump right into the class, but if you struggle with anything, let me know. We can work something out to help you. I have a folder here going over what we have already discussed in this class."

"Thank you, Mrs. Maisen. I will make sure to look over this and let you know if I don't understand something." Mrs. Maisen smiled at me and walked over to the board to greet the rest of the students as they finished coming in.

"Today, we will learn about Celtic gods and goddesses. At the end of the lecture, you will each pick a god or goddess and write a page explaining why you believe they either did or didn't exist." Mrs. Maisen went on to talk about all the different gods and goddesses and how the Celtic people worshipped them. At one point, she said many of the gods may have come from elementals.

I was enjoying learning something new. I finished my paper as the bell rang and turned it into Mrs. Maisen. I headed down the hall to Mr. Connor's class, eager to learn more about what I was. Mr. Connor didn't disappoint me. The class was really good, and I stayed back for a minute afterward to ask him for notes from the beginning of the semester.

Mrs. Shaw's class was the hardest. She started lecturing about how to control your own mind during a fight with another elemental. It was interesting, but I didn't understand half of what she said. As soon as the bell rang, I walked quickly to the common area to meet up with everyone. Richard was already there, and we headed out to the garden.

"Hi, guys," Abby called as she walked toward us. Tider was a few steps behind her, and he had a huge grin on his face.

"Hi, Abby. Hi, Tider. What are you so happy about?"

"I finally did it. I have been working on it for a few weeks. It's the hardest form of water magic I could think of, and I wasn't sure I would be able to do it." His joy was infectious. He had us laughing as he told us about all his failures while trying to make the magic do what he wanted. My favorite was when he was trying to turn the water into individual flying icicles to hit targets but instead turned the water into snowflakes that gently brushed the targets.

It sounded like Tider had a lot of power and was happy about it. He continued to talk about all the ways his magic failed him in the past until he mastered each new thing.

"Why did it take so long to learn? Is all magic that hard?"

"Some magic is easy," said Tider, "but when you are using a lot of power, it's much harder and takes a lot of skill and practice to learn."

I wanted to ask more questions, but the bell rang. I said goodbye to Tider since he went to different classes and walked with Abby and Richard.

Mr. Magni gave us another lesson that I already knew, so I doodled and tried to go over everything I learned about being an elemental. It wasn't a lot.

Mrs. Newton gave us another lecture on the book we were supposed to be reading, and we took a vocabulary quiz that I hoped I did ok on.

"Come on, we need to get to your class," Richard said when the bell rang.

"Bye, Abby. I'll see you at dinner." He turned into a hallway that led outside. "Where are we going?"

"When you go to your master class, you have to go to different areas. They are strictly off-limits to other students, and each area is surrounded by a dome that no one can see through. That way, people can't watch and try to do the magic themselves. Imagine what would happen if a beginner tried to do magic like Tider did today. They could kill themselves or other people."

"That makes sense," I told him. "Where are the domes?"

"We are going out the back doors. There is a path that leads to them."

"But I can't leave the protection of the school."

"You won't. They are on protected grounds. You will be safe."

I let out a breath. I really didn't want to be attacked again. He led me through the door to go outside, and we walked toward a small hidden path in the trees. It was only a few minutes before we came to a clearing, but I didn't see anything. "I thought you said there was a dome."

He laughed. "There is, but you can't see it."

"I was picturing more of a tinted glass type of dome, not an invisible one."

He grinned. "Technically, it's not invisible. It's reflective. It reflects the clearing so most people wouldn't realize this is a training area."

"What if you walked into it?"

"It's not likely to happen. If you step off of the path, you get a bad feeling, and your brain tells you to get back on the path."

He took my hand and pulled me into the grass. Immediately, I wanted to move back to the path. I felt like if I went any farther, something terrible would happen to me. Richard kept a tight grip on my hand and spoke quietly to me.

"Sally, listen to me. It's a spell. Once you get used to it, you can push it to the back of your mind."

I didn't think I could do this. The spell was getting stronger, warning me to back away. I shut my eyes against the terror I was feeling and took deep breaths. I turned my head and could see colors weaving their way into the air from the ground. It looked like a magical barrier. As I watched the colors, my fear receded, and I could think straight again. "What is this?"

"What do you see?"

"I can see the barrier in my mind. It is made of different colors but mostly greens and browns."

"Can you walk through it now without the spell affecting you?"

"I think so. Let's try."

I walked through the barrier keeping my eyes closed and focusing on the colors. Once we were through, I could see a red-colored dome. I opened my eyes, and the dome disappeared. When I closed them, it came back.

"I can see the dome when I close my eyes," I told Richard.

"You can?" he questioned. "What color is it?"

"It's red. It's beautiful. The red is shimmering across the sky. It sparkles when the light catches it." I opened my eyes and only saw an open field.

Richard moved forward. "You have to look closely, but there is a path to follow."

After he pointed it out to me, it was easy to follow. We came to a stop when the path ended. A large boulder was placed to the side. Richard put his hand on it, and a door appeared in front of us. It looked like the door was sitting in the middle of the field when I looked around it, but when I looked into it, I could see a room that looked like a large gym or training facility.

We stepped through the door and closed it. The dome took shape, and I could see how big it was. We could still see everything outside, but it was like looking through slightly tinted windows.

In the center of the room, Mr. Connor was standing next to a table with various objects on it. I followed Richard toward him.

"Hi, Sally. Do you want to stay, Richard?" Mr. Connor asked him as he turned toward the door.

"Sure," Richard replied and went to stand next to Mr. Connor.

"Today, we will be working with air. I want to get a sense of how strong you are, Sally. The first thing I want you to do is try to lift this ball off the table."

I looked at the ball and saw it was a kickball. I closed my eyes and imagined the silver stream of wind, lifting the ball into the air. With my eyes closed, I could only see the air hovering in front of me, but when I opened them, I noticed that I had not only lifted the ball up, but all the objects on the table were in the air. I tried to gently set them down, but instead, they fell to the table. I looked at Mr. Connor and Richard.

"I tried to be gentle," I told them.

"That's ok, Sally. From what I can tell, you already have a decent amount of power but very little control. Let's work on lifting the ball again. This time, try it with your eyes open. Focus on the ball and see it lifting in your head."

"But then I can't see the colors of the air. How will I direct it?"

"You don't need to see the color, you need to picture the ball hovering in midair, and your magic should do the rest."

I did what Mr. Connor asked and kept my eyes open while I was picturing the ball in the air. Nothing happened. I couldn't seem to make it work no matter how much I tried. The ball just wouldn't lift up. "I don't think this is going to work."

Richard stepped up to me. "Sally, I know you can do this. If you can do it with your eyes closed, you can do it with them open. You have to trust yourself. Remember to think about how the air feels. Think about it being an extension of yourself."

I concentrated and thought about the air gently lifting the ball off the table. I kept my eyes open the whole time, but I thought I saw thin streaks of silver around me. The ball lifted off the table and gently floated up about six inches. Faintly, I could see silver streaks around the ball. I closed my eyes and saw that the whole ball was encased in a silver wind.

"I did it," I yelled to Richard.

"Good job," Mr. Connor said. "Now can you put it back on the table." I didn't even realize I was still holding it. I turned back to the ball and tried lowering it, but again I was unable to control it, and it bounced off the table.

"We will have to work on that," Mr. Connor said. "You will have to practice every day to learn to control your magic in the smallest movements. Once you have better control, we will be able to move on to more intricate things. Now, I want to see how long your magic will last before you get tired. Lift the ball into the air again and hold it there while I give you other tasks to do."

I did as Mr. Connor asked and held the ball in the air. "I want you to try and lift this rock from the other end of the table. Hold them both in the air, and tell me how it makes you feel." It took a few minutes, but I finally lifted the other rock and held both in the air for a few seconds. I didn't see any streaks of silver this time though. After a few minutes, I told Mr. Connor that I didn't feel any difference.

"Try to lift these books too." I lifted the books, and they immediately started to wobble and shift away from each other.

"Don't worry about the books moving, Sally. As long as you keep them in the air, that's all that matters right now. How are you feeling?"

"I'm still feeling perfectly fine. I haven't noticed a drop in my energy at all." I couldn't keep the books in their stack, and I watched as they slowly slid off each other, though they did stay in the air.

"I'm going to give you something much larger to do and see how you feel. Please lift the entire table. If at any time you start to feel tired or dizzy, let it go and tell me," Mr. Connor said.

This time I closed my eyes, knowing I would need to pay more attention. I allowed the air to lift the table and everything on it. It hovered about two feet from the ground, and everything on it hung suspended six inches from the tabletop. "I'm still feeling fine, Mr. Connor."

"Your power is impressive, Sally, but we need to know what your limits are. We will have to try something larger. Why don't you let everything down?" I let the objects down, and they crashed to the ground, bouncing all over the place.

"Sorry, Mr. Connor."

"Don't worry, Sally. All of this can be picked up. We will need Richard for this next test. I want you to try to lift yourself off the ground. This is something that only the most powerful air elementals can do."

I closed my eyes and immediately saw silver air. I wrapped it partly around me and continued pulling it from all over the gym. When I felt like I had enough, I envisioned myself floating in the air. Immediately, I could feel the weightlessness. I felt myself getting higher and higher. I was ecstatic.

It felt amazing. I wasn't even tired and felt like I could do it all day. I opened my eyes, spread my arms out, and allowed myself a minute to enjoy the feeling. I started laughing and called for Richard to join me. He flew up into the air, and we started spinning around and flying back-and-forth until Mr. Connor called for us to come down.

"Ok you two, I think that's enough." I started to lower myself to the ground gently, but I still hit pretty hard. "How do you feel, Sally?"

"I feel amazing. I barely feel tired. I passed out when I used fire, so why is it different with air?"

"I'm not sure. Maybe air comes more naturally to you. We will have to see what happens when you use the other elements. Even though you don't feel tired, your body might be after using that kind of energy. I want you to go get something to eat and relax for the rest of the day."

I looked at the clock and realized we had been practicing for almost two hours. When I looked outside, the sun was beginning to set.

"Ok, Mr. Connor," I told him. "This was a great class. Thank you."

"No problem. It will be interesting to see what you can do. You might even be more powerful than Richard."

Richard scowled. "I don't know about that."

I punched him on the arm and laughed. "I guess we'll find out soon."

Richard and I left and started walking back to the school. It was already getting dark out, and I started feeling like we were being watched. As I looked behind me for the third time, Richard moved closer to me. "Are you ok?"

From the woods to our right, we heard the crack of a branch, and we both jumped.

"Richard," I said, keeping my voice down. "There's someone out there. What do we do?"

"We will run on the count of three. Go as fast as you can. Get to school. We don't want them to see you use power, so let me handle it. One, two." At that moment, we heard running behind us.

"Richard, Sally," Mr. Connor yelled. "I've been trying to catch up to you. You shouldn't be walking alone out here. I didn't think about it until after you left and had to hurry to catch you." I felt the hairs on the back of my neck lay down and no longer felt someone watching us. They must've left when they saw Mr. Connor coming.

"There was someone in the woods," I told Mr. Connor. "We were getting ready to make a run for it and hopefully get back to the school in time before anyone attacked."

"I don't think that it's one of the Pulhu. They wouldn't be able to get on school grounds. One of the students probably followed you out here to try and figure out what you could do," Mr. Connor said as we walked up to the school.

Richard and I headed toward the cafeteria, and Mr. Connor went the other way. Abby and Tider were waiting for us and started asking questions before I even had a chance to eat.

"Hang on, Abbs," I told her. "I need to eat something first, and besides, we need to keep this all quiet, remember."

"Oh yeah, sorry," Abby said. "I can't wait to hear what happened."

I lowered my voice and checked to make sure no one was eavesdropping. "Not much happened. Mr. Connor tested my air magic to see how strong it is."

"And?" Abby questioned. "How did you do?"

"I can lift myself off the ground." I couldn't help but smile. "That was the most exciting part. The rest of the time, he made me lift random objects up. I had no trouble with that. I can't seem to put them down gently though."

"Wow, you are even more powerful than I thought."

"You guys can get Richard to tell you everything else. Now that I've eaten, I'm starting to get tired." I stifled a yawn. "Maybe today's lesson took more out of me than I expected."

CHAPTER EIGHT

A banging on the door woke me, and I staggered to my feet as Abby barged in. "Why are you still in bed?"

I grabbed my clothes and started to pull them on. "Why are we up so early? Classes don't start until eight."

"I guess I forgot to tell you. We have a practical every quarter. I always get up early, so I can enjoy my breakfast and get a good spot in the auditorium. We should hurry up, or we are going to be stuck waiting in line for breakfast." She started to open my door.

"Wait, wait, wait. I need to finish getting dressed. Don't open the door."

"Oops," said Abby. "I guess I didn't realize you were only half ready."

I pulled my jeans on and hurried into the bathroom to brush my teeth and fix my hair. We walked to the cafeteria, and I tried to listen as Abby told me about the different things we would have to do. By the time we finished eating, Tider and Richard had shown up. We waited for them to finish before we headed to the auditorium. I had never been there before, and I was surprised when we headed downstairs.

"I didn't know there was a lower level."

"Yeah, there is a staircase in each wing that leads to the lower level, but it's mostly a few large rooms down here. There is the auditorium, a potions room, and the other rooms are always locked, but I think they are storage," Richard said.

"A potions room?"

"Yep," Tider said. "Mrs. Shaw makes potions from different plants for anyone who needs it." I looked skeptically at them.

"Hey, her stuff works. She even cured me of the flu last year. You'll see, as soon as you get sick, she will make you drink something, and you'll be better in a few hours instead of days. Then you'll believe me," Tider said. We walked into the auditorium, and Abby immediately went for the front row. We whispered to each other as we waited for the rest of the students to find seats.

Mrs. Sullivan stepped forward. "Hello, everyone. Today we will be doing practicals. Everyone knows the rules, and I'm sure no one will be trying to cheat," she said, raising her eyebrow at someone behind me. A few kids snickered.

"After we have completed calling your names and you have met with your teacher, everyone will head to Felan field." She looked back at the students. "Remember which teacher called your name, they will be directing you to your tests."

The teachers stepped forward as they called a name from a piece of paper in their hands. Mr. Magni called my name. Abby was called by Mr. Magni too, and I gave her a small hug, glad that we would be together. As soon as the last name was called, we hurried out of our seats to see Mr. Magni.

"Hi, girls," he said to us as we approached him. "Are you ready?"

"I'm not sure I will be any good at this," I told him.

"Nonsense. I'm sure you will do a wonderful job," he told me. He turned to the rest of our group. I didn't know any of the other kids, but Abby said hi to a few of them.

"We will be heading to Felan field and meeting by the red flag. I need to check off your name, and then you can head over that way. I will meet you there in ten minutes."

Abby led us upstairs and to a door right outside the girl's wing that led to Felan field. When we stepped onto the field, I realized it was in the center of the girl's wing. Each wing was a large u-shape that connected to the common areas. I wondered if the other wings also had a field in the center of them.

I walked with Abby over to the red flag. Mr. Magni directed us into a line when he arrived. I was toward the front, and Abby was in the back. Mrs. Sullivan's voice boomed across the field.

"Students, in front of your line, there are four objects. You will be asked to make one object of your choosing move or change in some way. The more advanced you are, the more the object must move. Good luck."

Mr. Magni moved to the head of the line. Each line faced the center of the field where Mrs. Sullivan and the other teachers were walking around. I guessed they would be doing the judging. Mr. Magni told the student at the front of the line to do her best.

I looked around the kid ahead of me and saw a young girl walk forward. She stopped in front of a bowl of water. She had her hands balled up tightly at her sides, and her shoulders were hunched over. The glass of water at her feet didn't seem to be doing anything, but I heard her gasp and then lean over breathing heavily.

"Good job, Elizabeth. You must be practicing a lot," Mr. Magni said.

"That was the biggest water drop you've done yet, Elizabeth," the boy in front of me said proudly to her.

I didn't even realize she made a water drop. It must have been very small, but she seemed so happy. The kid in front of me stepped forward. He moved in front of a bowl with a candle in it. Mr. Connor walked over to watch. As I looked at him, he caught my eye and shook his head slightly. I got the feeling that he didn't want me to show my powers.

The boy in front of me managed to make the fire grow big enough to leap over the top of the bowl, and he looked at me with relief in his eyes. "You did great," I told him as he passed.

"You'll do great too," he said.

"Sally, it's your turn." Mr. Magni said. "Go to your element and try to get it to move a little."

I stepped forward and looked at the bowls. One had fire, one had water, one had dirt, and the other had feathers. "Mr. Magni?"

"What's wrong, Sally? What is your element?" he asked me as I stared in confusion.

"Air," I told him.

"That's the bowl of feathers. It's hard to see air, so we use the feathers to see what the air is doing. Why don't you try to lift one of them up?"

The two kids before me were barely able to get their powers to do anything, and I wanted to seem like them. I pulled a tiny bit of air, and one feather slowly started to lift up in the bowl. I glanced over to where Mr. Connor was watching from the center, and a quick shake of his head and whispered no made me drop the air immediately, and the feather fell. I quickly turned and walked back toward the line.

"That was excellent, Sally," Mr. Magni said. "You must be a natural."

"Really?" I thought I was keeping a low profile.

"Yes, being able to lift a single feather from the bowl is very tough to do, especially for someone so new to magic."

I groaned inwardly. That's why Mr. Connor seemed upset. I should have moved all the feathers a little bit instead of singling out one. A beginner wouldn't be able to pick one object for the air to go around. I hoped not too many people saw me. I went to the back of the line and waited for the next challenge, hoping I wouldn't reveal myself.

As the last person in our line finished up, I heard a noise from across the field. I could see Tider pulling thin coils of water out of the bowl and letting them hang in the air in an intricate design. Suddenly, another loop of water shot out of the bowl and into the design obscuring it for a moment. When I could see it again, it sparkled in ice.

It looked like a million gems joined together in the sky to create a magical light show. The last coil of water encircled the design in a sphere, and Tider flicked his wrist as if giving the sphere a shake and snow started to fall inside. It took me a minute to realize he made a snow globe out of only water. I began to smile. I couldn't wait to tell Tider how awesome it was.

"Thank you for that dazzling display, Johnathon," Mrs. Sullivan said as Tider's design faded. "Now, your teachers will be splitting you up into partners, and you will be asked to find your element in the maze at the edge of the field. You are supposed to help your partner while at the same time trying to find your own. Your teachers will send the first group up in a minute, and one pair will go into the maze at a time. Once they are finished, the next pair will go, and so on. When you come out of the maze, go back to your teacher, and they will tell you the third challenge."

I turned to Mr. Magni as he began calling out names to partner up. "Sally, Elizabeth, you two will be partners today. You are up first. I'm sure you will do a fantastic job, just remember to work together."

"Hi, Elizabeth," I said, walking up to her. It was the girl who created the tiny water droplet.

"Hi," she said shyly. She was much younger than me and seemed very nervous.

"Is this your first time doing this?"

"Yes, this is my first year at this school. I don't have a lot of power compared to the other kids."

"I think you're doing fine," I told her. "This is my first year too. We'll get through this. I'm sure with practice and time, you will get even stronger."

"I hope so," she replied.

I walked into the maze and turned to watch Elizabeth follow me. Once inside, the entrance closed behind us, and Elizabeth jumped.

I reached over and grabbed her hand. "Come on, Elizabeth, I will help you."

She clung to my hand, and I started to lead her forward. "How do you find your element?"

"I think we are supposed to be able to feel it. At least the teachers here said you should always be able to feel your element," she said.

"Ok, you control water, so let's try to find that one first. Did the teachers tell you how you were supposed to feel your element?"

"Not really, only that we should always be able to feel if it's near."

"Hmmm. I don't think that will work for me, air is all around us."

"But it's very still in here. Maybe they have a big gust of air that you are supposed to feel."

"I guess," I replied. "Let's start with you. Can you feel water anywhere?"

"Not yet. Maybe if we move farther in?" We walked farther into the maze, but Elizabeth didn't have any idea how to feel her element. I decided I would try to feel it too.

"Let me see if I can feel mine," I told her. I let go of her hand, closed my eyes, and concentrated on finding water. I felt a small tug in my midsection. I opened my eyes to see if Elizabeth had touched me, but she was only staring at me. I concentrated and again felt a small tug on my midsection. I turned in that direction and took a few steps. The tug felt stronger, so I figured that was the way to go.

I didn't want Elizabeth knowing I could feel the water element, so I turned and walked back the other way. The tug got weaker with each step. Now I knew how to find water. I concentrated on air this time, and I could feel a tug in a different direction. I went back to focusing on water and then turned to Elizabeth. "I think I felt something. You have to concentrate on your element, and your body should want to go toward it, at least that's what I think it means."

Elizabeth closed her eyes to concentrate but didn't move in any direction.

"Are you feeling anything?"

"I don't think so."

"Here, take my hand, and we can start walking and see if you notice any changes." I took her hand. "Keep your eyes closed and concentrate. I will lead us around the maze."

Elizabeth did what I said and kept her eyes closed as I started walking toward the water. I didn't want her to know I was helping lead her in the right direction, so I stopped at every new path and asked her where she thought we should go. She didn't get it right at all in the beginning, but as we got closer to the water, she seemed to pick up on her element and chose the path with more confidence.

We walked around another turn, and in front of us was a waterfall coming down over the maze. On a table next to it were small bottles. A sign said to fill it up and take it with us to turn in at the end of the maze. Elizabeth got a bottle of water.

"We should go find yours. Do you have any idea where to go?"

"I felt something back when we were at the beginning going the other way." I lied to her. I could feel exactly where we needed to go. "I think we should go this way," I led her back toward the beginning and made sure to make a few wrong turns along the way.

"Do you need me to lead you the way you led me?"

"I don't think so, I think we are getting close." I smiled at her. She was very nice when she wasn't scared. We made a few more turns and ended up staring at a bunch of mini tornados.

"What are we supposed to do?" she asked me.

I looked around and saw the same glass bottles from before. The sign in front of them said bottle a tornado to turn in at the end of the maze. "I guess I have to trap a tornado."

I walked up to the tornado and held my bottle up to it. I used a little air power to push the tornado in and put the lid on.

"Thanks, Sally, I couldn't have done any of this without you."

"I couldn't have either. I didn't even know how to feel for an element until you told me."

"We make great partners."

Behind us came a loud pop, and a door appeared. When it opened, Mrs. Sullivan was standing there. "Come on, girls. This way out of the maze. You both did an excellent job. Go turn your bottles in. Mrs. Chanley is waiting for you." Mrs. Sullivan pointed to a table not far away.

We walked over to the table and met with Mrs. Chanley. I hadn't seen her before, but she smiled at me and called me by name. She didn't look much older than thirty, and she had a t-shirt on that read totally hip teacher. I thought she would be a really cool teacher and hoped I would get her soon.

"How did you do in the maze?"

"We did ok," I answered her, handing over my bottle.

"I did it," Elizabeth said and then blushed. "Sorry. I'm just really excited. I was so scared to go in there, but Sally was a great partner." She turned in her bottle too, and then it was time for lunch.

I went to the cafeteria and saw Abby and Tider.

"Tider, that was amazing when you did the first challenge. I didn't know you could make such cool stuff with magic."

"It takes a lot of practice, but I've been working on it for a while."

"Hey guys," Richard said from behind us. "How's everyone doing so far?" He sat down at the table with us and started eating.

"Good," we told him.

"Sally, how are you handling this? I know you have to keep your power hidden, and I haven't heard anything, so I'm guessing you are pretending to have only a small amount of power."

"I've been trying to be careful, but I already screwed up. I only moved one feather during the first test."

"You have to be careful, Sally or the Pulhu will find out about you," Tider said.

"I wish they would leave me alone. I haven't even been able to talk to my parents yet. Mrs. Sullivan said she was going to have someone magically erase my phone so no one can track it if I call them, but she hasn't done it yet."

"We can go talk to her tomorrow or Saturday," Richard said. "Then you can call your parents and tell them about your first week here."

"That's a good idea."

"Come on," Tider said. "We need to get back outside." We followed him back to Felan field. When we stepped outside, the area looked completely different. Now four large buildings stood at each corner, and in the center was one massive building. The teachers were all standing near the center building. Mr. Magni was waiting and immediately sent Abby to another part of the field.

"Sally, you will be doing an obstacle course where you need to make your way to the end, using your element. The obstacle course changes depending on what level your powers are. The air obstacle course is over by Mr. Connor. You can head there now."

"Thanks, Mr. Magni." I headed over to the corner Mr. Connor was in and waited for him to call me up.

He walked me over to a door and leaned down, whispering, "Only use air inside. No students can see what you are doing, but it is recorded, and all the teachers and the council have access to the recordings. We don't want anyone else to find out about you. The course will get harder each time you use your power. If you feel like you can't complete it, you can step off the course and say I give up. The course will return to normal, and you will be able to leave. Good luck."

He opened the door, and I stepped inside. I looked at the course and was surprised to see that it looked like an ordinary obstacle course, so I wasn't sure why I would need to use my power.

I moved to the first obstacle, a bunch of swinging tires that I would have to cross. As soon as I stepped on the first tire, I realized why this course would be different. The wind began to pick up around me, and the tires started swinging. Trying to get to the next one would require me to use my power, or be very, very lucky.

I used a tiny amount of power to slow the tire and leaped to the next one. Only four more to go. Again, I tried using only a small bit of power to slow the tire as it passed me, and I was able to get to the next one. The wind picked up and moved the tires even faster. Now they were spinning too.

I didn't want to risk using too much magic, so I slowed the tire a bit and jumped. I misjudged and slammed into the spinning tire, but I was able to hold on. I repeated this for the last two tires and finally stepped off of them, breathing hard. The tires immediately stopped spinning and swinging.

I looked at the next obstacle and realized this one was going to be a lot harder. It was a balance beam. I only had to cross it, but I knew it wasn't going to be that easy. I took a few more deep breaths before stepping on it. The first few steps were fine, but then the wind howled through the room. I knew it was going to knock me off if I stayed upright, so I laid on the beam and grabbed on.

The wind tore at my clothes as I inched along the beam. The air continued to try and rip me off. I had to use my magic a few times to keep from falling. It was only a small push against the wind so I could move a little further, but it was like the wind knew I had more power and became more ferocious every time I used my magic.

When I finally got to the other side, I looked like I was in a tornado. My hair was a mess, and my clothes were starting to rip, but I made it without using a lot of magic. I was beginning to feel like I could get through this. The next obstacle changed that.

It was a set of hanging rings. I needed to grab a ring and swing to the next one multiple times to cross. With the wind blowing around me, I didn't think I stood a chance of succeeding without magic. I reached for the first ring and swung myself to the next one.

As I was reaching for the next ring, a burst of wind pushed me off course, and I had nothing to grab. I used magic to push the next ring closer to me and caught it. I tried to use this method again, but the wind pushed the ring back even farther.

My arms were beginning to feel like lead, and I didn't think I would be able to hang on much longer when the wind died down a little. I managed to grab the next ring, and soon I was on the other side. There was only one obstacle left, and it took my breath away.

It was a zip-line, but it only had a place to hold on. There were no safety ropes. I peered out over the edge. It looked like I was at least one hundred feet in the air, even though I didn't climb up anything. Without a safety harness, I was sure the wind would rip me right off.

I was considering quitting when a thought came into my head. I didn't need to use a lot of air magic to do this. I just needed to wrap a little around my hands like a piece of rope so I couldn't let go of the handle. I reached up and grabbed it, and the wind started screaming toward me.

I pulled a small bit of magic from the air and twirled it around my hands so they would be bound to the handle. I tried pulling them off, but the air kept them firmly grasping the handle. I took a deep breath and jumped.

The wind grabbed me and pulled me back and forth. I concentrated on the air surrounding my hands. I looked out and saw the ground coming up way too fast, and was about to use my magic to stop myself when I started to slow down. The wind stopped trying to pull me off the handle and instead pushed against me. I knew I wasn't doing it, and I didn't know who was helping me, but I was grateful.

As I came to a stop, I unwound the air from my hands and fell to my knees, happy to be finished with the course. I started to straighten up when the door in front of me opened, and Mr. Connor and Mrs. Sullivan came in. She took in my appearance and then looked at Mr. Connor angrily.

"She could have been hurt. Why did you tell her not to use her magic?"

"Because they will find out if she shows her power."

"Yes, but she could have been hurt badly if you hadn't stopped her in time."

"I wouldn't have let anything happen. You know these trials are recorded, and the council has every right to request the tapes to see her powers. I wasn't going to take that chance," he said, glaring at her.

"I felt like the wind knew I wasn't using my full power and was trying to make me," I said.

"That's how it's supposed to work. The wind keeps getting stronger until you fail an obstacle, and then it gets weaker again. It is supposed to test you to your limits," she said.

"What am I supposed to do? I can't go out there looking like this."

"Come with me, I can glamor you until you get to your room to change," Mrs. Sullivan said.

"Glamour?"

"Yes, people will see you looking the way you did when you went in."

"Awesome." Maybe I could learn to do it. It sounded like it would be a neat trick.

We walked through the halls and stopped in front of my room without anyone noticing. I went into my room and put on a new pair of clothes. I didn't have a lot of time, so I grabbed my hair and put it up in a ponytail, hoping no one would notice how tangled it was. As I went to walk out of my room, something on the side of my pillowcase caught my eye. I walked over and picked it up. It was a folded piece of paper. I opened it up and started reading when Mrs. Sullivan called out.

"Almost ready, Sally? We need to get back."

"One minute," I called back to her. I looked at the paper. *Find The Water Sprites.* I had no idea what it meant or why it was in my room. It didn't say anything else. I went to put it in my pocket, but it burst into flame. There wasn't a burning smell or ashes to prove the paper ever existed.

I shook my head, wondering if I was going crazy. Paper didn't burn itself up, did it? Maybe I could find some information in the library. I didn't want to tell my friends in case they thought I was crazy too.

Mrs. Sullivan knocked on the door. "Come on, Sally," she said impatiently.

I opened the door and walked out into the hall. Something told me not to tell her what happened, so I started walking down the hallway.

"Your classmates will be performing the last test now. When we get down to the field, Mr. Magni will tell you where you need to go to complete your last challenge. It shouldn't be too hard."

"What is the last challenge?"

"You will be rescuing a water sprite."

"What is a water sprite? And how do I rescue it?" I asked, thinking about the paper I read in my room. Maybe this is what the paper meant.

"It is a creature that looks similar to a small fairy, and the only way to rescue it is to use your magic. Again, I will caution you to use only a small amount of power. You are grouped with the beginners, so it shouldn't be a tough task for you. When you rescue it, don't try to capture it. Sprites do not like to be touched very often, and they will get mad at you if you try and touch them. Ok?"

"So I leave it there?"

"Yes, she has come to help us. She isn't really trapped and can get free at any time."

We walked out onto the field, and I made my way to Mr. Magni, who sent me toward a small tent.

"Wait in line, Sally, and they will call you when it is your turn," he said.

At the tent, I saw Mrs. Newton standing in front of me. "Hi dear, it's almost your turn. Someone's in there right now finishing up, and then you can go in. Do you know what you're supposed to do?"

"I'm supposed to save a water sprite, right?"

"Yes, this task is tough for some people. I hope that it will be easy for you."

A boy came strolling out of the tent with a big smile on his face and headed toward the center of the field.

"It's your turn," Mrs. Newton said. "Good luck."

"Thanks, Mrs. Newton," I replied. I walked into the tent and immediately saw what looked like a little fairy stuck in the middle of a swirling ball of air. I wasn't sure how I was supposed to get it out. I closed my eyes to look at the ball of wind and realized that the ball was not complete, there were gaps and holes in it. I slowly pushed a little air toward one of the holes to widen it. The water sprite's eyes widened. It knew what I was doing.

I continued letting a small amount of magic into the ball of air, making the hole bigger and bigger. After another minute or two, the gap was big enough for the sprite to fly out. It flew over the top of me, and I watched it with awe. It hovered in front of me. I put my hand out, and she landed in it. Her wings stopped moving. They were so sheer that I could see right through them.

"Hi," I said. "How are you?"

She turned her head but didn't respond.

My face fell. Maybe she didn't want to speak to me. I tried again. "I'm Sally. This is only my first week here, and I have no idea what I'm doing, so I'm glad that I was able to rescue you without you getting hurt. It's awfully brave of you to volunteer to do this for the school," I told her. She flew up around me again and touched my cheek before flying away.

I walked out of the tent and told Mrs. Newton what happened.

"You are very fortunate," Mrs. Newton said. "Very rarely will a sprite actually land on a person. She must think you are special."

"Really?" I asked Mrs. Newton.

"Really," she said. "Now run along to Mr. Magni. He will be waiting for you."

I left Mrs. Newton and went to find Mr. Magni. All the students were waiting, and I quickly got in line near the front where Mr. Magni had placed me earlier in the morning. All around us, the other kids were telling their friends how they thought they did. When Elizabeth asked me, I told her I thought I did ok. She thought she did good too. When Mrs. Sullivan came to the center of the field, everyone began to quiet down.

"This completes the end of the challenges for everyone. You are free for the rest of the day."

CHAPTER NINE

As I walked into my room, I remembered the piece of paper someone had left for me. *Find the Water Sprites.* I still had no idea what it meant, and I didn't know who to tell. I didn't even have the paper to prove it.

I walked to the library and started looking at different titles. I wasn't sure what I needed, but I figured the water sprites would probably be around the water elementals. If I could find the water elementals, I would find the sprites.

Richard would be meeting me in thirty minutes. I wanted to look through a couple of books first. I sat at one of the tables and opened the first book, skimming through the pages. I read that there were different waterways the water elementals explored, and the kingdom of the water elementals was the main gathering place for all the sprites. Humans without elemental powers couldn't get there. There was no mention of where the kingdom was besides in the water.

I moved on to the next book. I learned that the water elementals tried to stay out of the fighting between all the elementals, but eventually had to take sides when fire elementals tried to destroy their followers. It said they were banned from having followers by the shadow king. None of the elementals were permitted contact with the humans after the fighting.

"What are you looking at?"

I jumped up, startled, and slammed the book closed. Richard was standing behind me, looking at the book in my hands.

"Don't sneak up on me like that," I told him. "You scared me."

"Sorry, I wasn't trying to sneak up on you. You were very absorbed in the book. I think an elephant could have walked through the library, and you wouldn't have noticed. Why are you reading about elementals?"

"I'm trying to understand more about this world I've been thrust into," I lied.

"If you have any questions, ask. I should be able to answer most of the things you want to know."

I thought about confiding in him about the note but still wasn't sure how he would react. Maybe I could get some information from him without telling him. "The books say that the water elementals weren't punished as harshly as the rest of the elementals. They were allowed to roam the waters as long as they weren't seen, so are they still here?"

"I would assume so. Obviously, no one has seen them for centuries, but elementals live a very long time."

"But wouldn't they have a city or palace, somewhere they could all live together?"

"I'm sure they do."

"Then why hasn't it been found yet? People have been all over the world, researching and mapping our oceans. Wouldn't they have stumbled upon something like that?"

"Not if it was glamoured. They could have towns under the water, and no one would ever know. Think about how you didn't want to walk toward the practice area yesterday. It's the same thing only on a bigger scale. There are plenty of areas that people don't go to because of a feeling they get from it. Most of those places are glamoured. It would make sense that the water elementals also use glamours to hide their cities."

It did make sense, but that didn't help me at all. I needed to know if anyone had an idea where the water spirits lived. "Have you ever come across anything saying where their cities might be?"

"It sounds like you have a reason for learning this and not an intellectual one."

I hesitated, but Richard knew a lot more than I did, and I was going to need help. "When Mrs. Sullivan took me up to my room to change, there was a note on my pillow. It said to find the water sprites. After I read it, the note burst into flame."

"And you have no idea who left it for you?"

"None."

"Why haven't you told anyone about it?"

"I don't know who I can trust, and I was worried people would think I'm losing my mind. Paper doesn't burst into flame."

"Actually," he stated, "it does. That's how some elementals on the council deliver information. That way, it can't be traced back to anyone. I wonder who would be leaving you notes though. You can't trust whoever sent that note to you. It's a spell that takes a lot of energy since the person who cast it wouldn't be close when it was read. You have to be very strong to use that kind of magic."

"But what does it mean? Why would they want me to find the water sprites? And how would I find them? I know they can be around us since they help at the school sometimes."

"I don't know who sent you the note, but I think we should try to find out. For now, we should keep this between us. I will think about who at the school has the power to cast this spell. You need to pay attention to anyone who is watching you too much. And the sprites don't really help at the school. The only time I have ever seen them is at the end of quarter tests, and they never talk to anyone."

"Why not?" I asked.

"I don't know. None of the students know why. We've all asked each other. We need to head to your class. We can talk more about it afterward. You don't want to be late."

I followed Richard, and when we got close, I closed my eyes and saw the magic swirling around the dome. I opened my eyes and looked closely at the ground to spot the hidden path that we needed to step on to get to the door. As soon as I stepped onto it, I could feel the magic beating at me, telling me to turn around. I pushed through the magic and pressed on the boulder. The door came into view. We stepped inside, and I instantly felt better.

"Hi, Sally. I'm Mr. Merrem. I will be helping you with your magic from now on."

"Hi, Mr. Merrem," I said.

"Are you ready to practice?"

"Sure," I replied. "What are we practicing?"

"I want to see how much power you have in fire today and test you for earth. We are going to start right away and see what you can do. Come into the center of the room by this fire, Sally. Richard, I want you to come stand next to me in case I need to shield you from Sally's power."

"What do you mean, shield him?"

"If you hit him with flames, he will get burned if he doesn't deflect it with his own magic fast enough."

"I don't want to hurt anyone," I said.

"You won't," Mr. Merrem assured me. "I put a protective barrier around Richard and myself, so we won't get hurt."

"What do you want me to do?"

"I want you to think about the fire in front of you. Picture it growing, lifting up into the air."

I closed my eyes and thought about the fire. I could see my magic moving around the fire. Bright tendrils of silver snaked from my arms down to the pit. The fire continued to grow, and I felt it pulling at me, begging me to let it rise higher and higher. I opened my eyes and watched the flames. Soon it was blazing so brightly that I could barely look at it. It reached the top of the dome and started growing outward since it couldn't grow up anymore.

I could feel the heat of the fire, but it didn't burn me. I moved closer to it, watching as flames leaped out of the growing fire, trying to get to me. I held my hand out, and the fire jumped to me. It curled up and over my arm, snaking its way up my shoulder and through my hair. All I felt was a slight tingling.

"Sally, stop!" Richard yelled.

I tried to stop the fire, but it was difficult. It didn't want to be contained. I struggled with the fire, forcing it to obey me until I finally got it back into the pit. Then I made it go out.

Richard ran to me. "Are you ok, Sally? The fire grew out of control so fast that we couldn't get to you."

"I'm ok," I replied, "but what happened?"

"That was what happens to powerful fire elementals that don't have control," Mr. Merrem said.

"How do I control it?" I asked.

"It takes a lot of practice. You did well for your first time. I wasn't sure if you would be able to pull it back in with how big you made it. I'm glad you did. Mrs. Sullivan would have been distraught if I lost a student to fire magic," he chuckled. "Let's not do that again until you are more prepared. I wasn't expecting you to be that powerful yet. How are you feeling?"

"I don't feel tired at all, which makes no sense. Last time I used fire, I passed out from using too much energy."

"Your body is still going through the process of getting your powers. Remember, your powers have just emerged."

"What if I hurt someone?"

"That's why I'm here, Sally. Between Mr. Connor and me, you will get control of your powers before anything bad happens. You need to learn how to use them, or the Pulhu will be able to take you."

"How are you going to help me? I don't understand why any of this is happening to me. Why do I have so much power?"

"I don't know why, Sally, though I have my suspicions. Right now, the only thing you need to worry about is controlling your powers. I know you were able to control air when you practiced yesterday. You need to learn to control fire as well." His tone left no room for arguments, and I hung my head. I wasn't sure if I could do this.

Mr. Merrem seemed to sense that I wasn't convinced and said the one thing that would get me to do it. "You need to do this for your parents. They will never be safe, and neither will you as long as the Pulhu are after you. Once you have more control, they will leave you alone. You can pretend not to have strong powers, and they won't be able to tell you are lying. Right now, there is a chance that something will happen to scare you into using magic, and people will find out how powerful you are."

Mr. Merrem looked thoughtfully at us. "I think it's time for you to try earth. I want to see if you have a strong connection to earth magic too. Try raising the ground right here in front of me. Feel the dirt under your feet and connect with the earth. You should be able to pull at the ground, raising it up."

I took a deep breath and tried to use earth magic, but nothing happened. After a few minutes, I looked at Mr. Merrem and Richard. "It's not working."

"What are you thinking about?"

"The earth like you said. But nothing happens when I think about it. I can't even see my own magic."

"This is the first time you are trying to use earth magic, right?"

"Yes."

"That's probably why you are having trouble. Your body doesn't have a connection to the magic yet. The connection is made when you purposely use the magic. Every time you use it, the connection gets stronger. I have an idea." He walked around, looking for something. When he found it, he called me over. "Here, let's start with this." He was looking down at a small white flower growing near the edge of the room. "Focus on this flower, and try to make it get bigger."

I pictured the flower in my mind and allowed it to get bigger and bigger. When I looked at the flower in front of me, it also started getting bigger.

"Ok, put more magic into it. Make it grow more leaves and more flowers. Let the magic flow through you and into the flower."

This time when I pictured the flower, it was growing. Leaves were unfurling from the stem as it continued to get taller, and new buds were forming. The flower in front of me did the same thing as the one I pictured in my mind.

"Good job, Sally. I want you to try to lift the ground up where the plant is now. Only a few feet."

I pictured the ground raising where the plant was, and slowly I could hear the earth shifting and cracking at my feet. When I looked at it, I saw I had formed a hill about six feet around that peaked at about three feet. All of a sudden, a wave of dizziness hit me, and I fell to my knees.

"Sally." Richard ran to me and helped me up. "What happened? Are you ok?"

"I'm fine. I got really dizzy for a minute."

"You hit your limit for earth magic," Mr. Merrem said. "Still impressive for the first time using it."

"Why am I so tired now?"

"You had a similar reaction when you used fire the first time, right?" Mr. Merrem asked.

"Yes."

"I think the first time you use an element and try to form a connection, you use a lot of energy. That's why you are so tired after using earth today, but fire had no effect on you. It makes sense in a way, even though most students always feel their energy drain after using their element."

Richard led me to a chair and helped me sit down. Mr. Merrem handed me a cup of water before striding around the room, muttering to himself.

"Mr. Merrem?"

"Yes, Sally."

"Why am I so different from the other students?"

"I'm not sure yet," he said.

"But you have a theory?" I guessed.

"Yes, but I'm not ready to tell it to you yet. Once I have seen more of your powers and done some more research, we will discuss it again."

He resumed his pacing, and I sat back and sipped my water, waiting to feel some of my energy return. After a couple more minutes, I felt strong enough to get up.

"What are we doing now?" I asked them.

"You are going back to school to eat and rest. Try not to use your powers unless you are with Mr. Connor or me. That way, no one will know what you can do. Agreed?"

"Of course. I'll be super careful."

"I will walk you back to school, so there aren't any problems. I heard from Mr. Connor that you thought someone was watching you yesterday, and they ran away when Mr. Connor showed up."

I felt better knowing that a teacher would be walking back with us. He headed for the door, and I followed with Richard trailing behind me. As we passed through the barrier, I began to get that feeling of being watched again. I walked closer to Mr. Merrem and told him quietly.

"Yes, I feel it too. Can you tell where it is coming from?"

I closed my eyes and tried to pinpoint where the person was, but they weren't using any magic, so I couldn't see them.

"No, they aren't using magic."

"That's ok. I will take it from here. Richard, you and Sally keep walking to the school. Once you are inside, head straight to the cafeteria. I'm going to see if I can find out who is watching you."

"Yes, Mr. Merrem," Richard said and grabbed my arm to hurry me along and keep me steady.

Mr. Merrem let us pass him and then darted into the woods. We didn't see what was happening, but I heard the trees moving in the forest, and a yelp came from somewhere farther in the woods. As Richard opened the door, I looked over my shoulder and saw trees moving on their own, pushing deeper into the woods. I kept staring until Richard pulled me into the school.

"What was that?"

"That was Mr. Merrem using the trees to capture whoever was out there. I doubt they will get away."

"He's not going to hurt them, is he?"

"Of course not, Sally. They will probably get lots of detention for spying on a master class. That's against the rules here. Hopefully, the detention will keep whoever it is busy so they aren't following you around."

We headed to the dining room and saw Abby and Tider already eating. They were talking animatedly and didn't see us come in, so we grabbed some food before going over to them.

I quickly filled them in on the class and how Mr. Merrem was looking for the person following me around. They agreed to keep an eye out to see who had a bunch of detention this week. I listened to my friends talking and laughing about how they accomplished their tasks, but my mind was on other things.

I still felt like I needed to find the water elementals, and I wanted to talk to my parents soon. Everything was happening so fast. I needed a few days to catch up. I was glad it was almost the weekend. One more day of class, and then I could spend the weekend relaxing.

"Hey, Sally, come on, you look exhausted. I'll walk you to your room, so you can get some rest," Abby said.

As soon as I fell asleep, I started dreaming about an awful darkness moving across the sky. I felt like it was searching for me. I tried running away, but it kept coming. Faster and faster I moved, but it still wasn't enough. As it got closer, my body started to freeze. I was shivering uncontrollably, and my teeth wouldn't stop chattering. The dark cloud filled me with terror.

It started to descend onto me, and I screamed in fear, knowing this was the end. I shot up in bed and looked around, bewildered, not knowing where I was for a few seconds. Then it all came back to me, and I realized it was just a dream.

I shook my head, trying to dispel the terror that still lingered, and realized I was actually shivering. My body felt like ice, and I pulled up the covers to warm myself. I glanced at the clock and saw it was still the middle of the night. I laid in bed, trying to calm down for a long time before finally falling back asleep.

CHAPTER TEN

"Can I take extra lessons?" I asked Mrs. Sullivan the next day.

"Of course you can."

"Do you think with the extra lessons I will be able to see my parents sooner?"

"I don't see why not. Once you can protect yourself better and the Pulhu forget about you, seeing your parents will be no problem."

"Are they going to forget about me?"

"They should. As long as you don't ever use your full powers around anyone you can't trust. If you are at school, they can't sense how strong your magic is. The protections around the school prevent it. As long as they don't think you are stronger than them, they will leave you alone."

"How long do you think it will take before I can see my mom and dad?"

"When we get closer to the holiday break, I will come and see how you are doing with your extra lessons. Then I will decide if you are ready to see your parents. Now, I have something for you." She handed me a new phone. "Go call your parents. I will contact Mr. Connor and Mr. Merrem to discuss extra lessons. Make sure you don't say where your parents are out loud in case anyone is listening."

"Thanks, Mrs. Sullivan," I said, walking quickly out of her office. I didn't walk more than a few feet before I was dialing my mom's phone. I walked toward my room while I waited for her to pick up. After the third ring, I hung up and called my dad. He answered right away.

"Sally. How are you doing? We miss you so much. No one is bothering you at the school, right?"

"Hi, Dad. I'm doing good. I've missed you too. No one is bothering me," I told him, not wanting him to worry about me. "I wish you were here. Where is Mom? I tried to call her, but she didn't answer."

"She is working for the haven right now. She doesn't take her phone into the office with her. I'm sure she will be calling you as soon as she gets out."

"Why is she working for them?"

"It's kind of a secret, but they said this is a secure line, so I guess I can tell you a bit. The people here are trying to fight back against the Pulhu, and your mother and I decided we would help them."

"You better be careful, Dad. The Pulhu wouldn't mind hurting you from what I understand. I don't like you guys putting yourselves in a position where you could get hurt. They've already hurt you enough."

"I'm fine, Sally. Completely healed. You don't have to worry. We aren't doing anything more than working on computers, trying to find them. They will never even know that we are working against them. Now tell me all about the last week. Have you made any other friends? How do you like your classes?"

I explained almost everything going on at school except for the attack and the note I found on my bed. I didn't need them worrying. We talked for a few more minutes before my dad said he needed to go and get ready for work.

I hurried to my class and made it just as the bell rang. My classes went by in a blur, and all I could think about was when my mom would call. As I got to the cafeteria for lunch, my phone rang. I looked down and saw it was my mom. I turned away from my friends and answered the call.

"Mom?"

"Hi, honey. Dad told me you finally got your secure phone. I miss you," she said, her voice cracking, and I felt tears spilling down my face.

"I miss you too, Mom."

I felt someone's hand on my back and saw Richard standing there. He directed me toward a door a little bit down from the cafeteria. He opened the door and led me inside to a little office, then walked out and shut the door.

"Sally?" my mom was asking on the phone.

"Sorry, Mom, I was going to a better place to talk."

"Is everything ok there? Your father said you sounded like everything was ok."

"Yes, Mom, everything is good here. I miss you so much. We've never been away from each other for more than a day. I don't like it."

"I know you don't, but we have to keep you safe, and this is the best way to do it."

"I know, Mom. I'm glad I can finally talk to you. Maybe I'll start to feel normal again."

"You are doing awesome. I'm sure we will be able to see each other very soon."

"I hope so. I'm working on controlling my powers, so I can see you as soon as possible."

"I know you will be able to do it. Tell me about your new friends. I want to hear more about this Richard. Your dad said it sounded like you really like him."

"Oh, Mom. Not like that. He's a friend." She laughed, and we talked about my friends until the bell rang.

"I've got to get to class, Mom. Will you call me tonight?"

"Of course."

"I love you."

"I love you too. Be safe. I'll talk to you soon." She hung up, and I walked out of the little office to see Richard waiting for me.

"Come on. Let's go to class. Do you feel better now that you talked to your mom?"

"Yes, I do. Thanks. You didn't have to wait for me."

"I know, but I figured you could probably use a friend after saying bye to your parents. Now let's get to class before we get in trouble."

Classes went by quickly, and the day was over before I knew it. I slept in until almost noon and slowly got ready for the day. I had no idea what the students did here on weekends and was hoping to run into Abby. I looked into the empty library. The halls seemed to be deserted too. I started to walk around the school, hoping to find out where everyone was.

I looked into all the open doors in the common areas but couldn't find more than a couple of kids, so I started walking through the hallways where classes were held. When I checked all the rooms and still couldn't find anyone, I decided to go see Mrs. Sullivan. Maybe something was going on that everyone forgot to tell me about.

"Your extra lessons are going to be on Saturday and Sunday mornings," Mrs. Sullivan told me when I went to her office.

"What time?" I asked, dreading the answer. I guess I wouldn't be sleeping in anymore.

"Eight-thirty," she told me. Yep, I wouldn't be sleeping in, I thought sadly. "You need to make sure that no one finds out what you are doing. Most of the kids are already on their way into town by that time, so it won't be as hard to be secretive, but there are still a few around and some teachers that you need to avoid."

"But what about my friends? They will wonder where I am if I keep disappearing."

"Richard and Tider will know. They each take an early morning class too. I am sending you to the same teacher at the same time as them. That way people will think you are all hanging out."

"What about Abby?"

"Abby usually goes to town, but you can tell her what you are doing, so she doesn't worry about you. Tomorrow you can go to class with Tider. Your teacher will be Mr. Connor. On Saturdays, you will work with Mr. Merrem and Richard."

"Thanks, Mrs. Sullivan,"

I headed down to the library and looked around. I grabbed a few books and headed toward the small couch by the fireplace. I started reading, but something caught my eye. On the top shelf of the bookcase closest to me, I saw a bright light, but it was gone in an instant. I walked over to the bookcase, trying to find what caused the flash of light, but I didn't see anything.

As I turned back toward the couch, I saw the flash of light again. This time I reached my hand up to the very top of the bookshelf and felt the corner of something. I wiggled my fingers around until I could grab it and pull it out. It was a book, but it was different. It was leather and covered in weird symbols and letters. It looked incredibly old and fragile.

I opened the book and saw more symbols on the first page. I flipped through the book seeing page after page of symbols I couldn't read. I wondered why there would be a book in a weird language sitting on the top corner of a bookcase. Maybe other people could read this, and I just hadn't been taught how to yet. I would have to ask my friends.

I started flipping through the pages carefully, trying to spot anything I could read. Toward the end of the book, I finally saw writing in the book margins. There were symbols in the margins with words next to them. It looked like a key to reading it. I looked closer at the margins on all the pages and slowly found even more words.

I got up and looked around the library for paper and a pencil. I spotted some on the other side of the room. I hurried over and grabbed a few sheets before heading back to my spot. I wrote down the letters and their corresponding symbols, making sure I copied the entire alphabet down.

Then I opened the book to the first page. This was going to take me a lot longer than one day. Slowly, I worked my way through the title. All it said was Dark Rising. When I read it, an image of my nightmare flashed through my mind. I moved on to the first paragraph and translated the first sentence. *On this day, we the ageless prophets have prophesied the ending of our world.*

I put down my paper and pencil and stared at the words, feeling a shiver crawl down my spine. I decided to take the book with me so I could work on it in my room. I put the other books away and grabbed my stuff. I finished the rest of the paragraph and the next page and then decided to take a break.

I sat on my bed, thinking about what I learned. The part I had translated talked about the coming of the darkness like it was a living thing. Saying it would take over everything and everyone until there was no life left on the planet. So far, it didn't say anything about how to stop it.

While I waited for Abby to get back to the school, I continued to translate the book. The page I was working on looked different than the first page. It looked more like a poem than a paragraph, and I was hoping it would have more information. By the time I finished translating the poem, it was getting dark out. I sat back on my bed, looking at the poem in a panic. No wonder the Pulhu were after me. They would go after anyone my age who was just getting their powers or showed any sign of their power getting a lot stronger. I read the prophecy to myself again.

On this day we the ageless prophets have prophesied the ending of our world:

One who is wise though their years are few
Will awaken the elements to when they were true
And the worlds in between will awaken soon
After the power is bestowed on you

If they choose dark, the world will be destroyed
But if light is chosen the world won't fall into void
Many will fall to dark's endless ways
But a few will stay strong for the coming days

Under the land on an isle green
The water sprites help if they are seen
Above the clouds where cold winds blow
The sylphs are waiting to help those below

Where fire touches a sky so blue
The drakos are waiting to save a few
But underground bad dryads wait
Except for one who seals alls fate

Friends will help though may be lost
Look around, or you'll pay the cost
All powers together will fight the dark
And seal him away in void's pure mark

I wasn't sure what to make of the whole prophecy, but the first line was easy to understand. It meant a person young enough not to be an adult, but old enough not to be a kid. I was hoping the rest of the book explained the whole prophecy.

I read through the prophecy again. I would need to translate the rest of the book until I could understand everything about it. While I was trying to figure it out, I remembered the paper that had been on my pillow. Find the water sprites. The prophecy talked about finding them too. That couldn't be a coincidence, could it?

I hid the papers I was writing on under my bed, and then headed down to the common room to see what everyone was doing.

When I got closer, I could hear a lot of talking and laughing. As I walked into the room, I was confronted with a group of kids led by Sean and a girl named Sasha, circling two younger kids. They were pushing them around and laughing.

"You don't even know how to use what little power you have," Sasha said, laughing at the girl. "How do you think you could ever help the magical community?"

"They can't," Sean sneered. "They will never be useful. You should run back home to your mommies. You will never be accepted into our community. Go home and live like a non-magical person until you are old enough to serve us."

"Why would we serve you?" The boy whimpered as someone else pushed him.

"You will serve us one day. That's what non-magical people are for. Their place is to do as we say." He stepped up to the kid and pushed him in the chest. The boy fell, and the girl rushed to his side.

"Leave us alone," she cried.

I couldn't stand the sight of these kids picking on the two smallest. There were at least eight kids in the crowd cheering on Sean and Sasha. I walked over to the table and stood on a chair.

"Leave them alone," I yelled, getting everyone's attention.

"What if we don't want to?" asked Sasha. "Will you make us? You haven't shown any true potential for magic yet, so I doubt you can stop us."

"I can stop you without magic, Sasha," I told her angrily.

She laughed and threw her hands out with a blast of fire magic. A small ball of fire sailed toward my head, and I ducked to the side to avoid it. Sasha threw another fireball. I jumped behind a couch to dodge it and heard Sasha swear when she failed to hit me. I saw the two kids they were picking on slip away while no one was watching. Now it was just them and me.

Sean stepped in, and a small tornado formed in front of him. He sent it hurtling my way as Sasha threw more fireballs at me. I scrambled over the couch, trying to reach the hall, when a wall of kids formed in front of me, blocking my escape. I ran directly toward the tornado, falling to my stomach and sliding under it before it hit me. I used a small amount of air to keep from being ripped off the floor as I went under it, but I didn't think anyone noticed.

Most of these kids only knew how to use brute force with their magic. Sean didn't strike me as the kind of person who would ever be subtle. Neither did Sasha. I kept running straight toward Sean now that I was past the tornado. When I was close enough, I punched him directly in the gut. His tornado failed as the wind left his lungs. He leaned over, gasping for breath, and I turned to Sasha. She created a wall of fire in front of her that I couldn't cross. I walked around her wall, searching for a weak spot.

As I was about to use air to create one, I heard Sean trying to sneak up on me. When I sensed him directly behind me, I whirled and punched him in the gut again, but he was ready and put his arm out to defend himself. He backed me up until the flames were almost touching me and then brought his hands out in front of him to blast me with his power.

I was going to have to use my powers on him and hope no one noticed what powers I used. I raised my hands to counter Sean when all of a sudden, the flames went out, and a whirlwind of air flew around us, holding everyone in place. I saw Richard on the far side of the room near the hall. He did something, and the air bands around me loosened.

I ran to Richard's side and waited to see what he was going to do. After a minute, when he still hadn't moved, I placed my hand on his arm and got the same shock as the day Tider knocked me over into him. I kept my hand on his arm, and he turned to look at me. I could feel a tingling in my hand, and I closed my eyes to see if something was going on that I couldn't see.

With my eyes closed, I could see the amount of magic Richard was using. The whole room was filled with his bright blue powers and blue coils wrapped around everyone, keeping them from moving or speaking. I couldn't imagine the amount of energy he was using to sustain the magic.

Where my hand laid on his arm, silver tendrils of magic floated from me and twirled around his arm, slowly snaking their way around him. As my magic flowed around him, parts of it moved up to his hands, where it entwined with the magic he was sending out into the room.

Silver streaks started to fly through the room and into the blue coils that held everyone in place. As soon as I could see silver colors in each person's air bindings, I opened my eyes and looked back at Richard. He seemed more relaxed than a few moments ago.

"What in the world is going on here," came a yell from behind Richard.

"Sorry, Mrs. Sullivan," Richard said. "I came into this room to find Sean and Sasha trying to hurt Sally. They were using magic against her, even though she didn't use any, and everyone knows she doesn't know how to defend herself yet. Their friends were blocking her from escaping, so I figured I better step in before someone got hurt. I'm glad you are here. I'm exhausted."

Richard didn't look exhausted, but I guessed that he didn't want the other kids to know he was able to use that much magic without being worn out.

Mrs. Sullivan looked around the room and then back at me. "I'm not sure what happened here, but because you used magic for fighting, Sasha and Sean, you will get detention. I'm very disappointed in you two, and I hope this will be the last time that there are any issues."

"What about Richard? He used his powers?" Sasha said.

"Richard was trying to stop all of you from doing something that would get you in more trouble. You should be thanking him for interfering. Now, I want everyone to go about their business, and if I hear of any more problems from you, there will be no trips to town over the holidays." Mrs.

Sullivan turned on her heel and marched back down the hallway.

Richard walked over and put his arm around me. I leaned my head against his shoulder. "Why does it shock us when we touch while using magic?"

"I'm not sure what's going on," Richard said. "I do know that I was getting tired when I was using the bands of magic to hold everyone in place. Then you came up and put your hand on my arm, and I could feel your magic mixing with mine. Suddenly it wasn't hard to hold on to that amount of power. I think your magic stabilized mine, making it easier for me to use."

"I wonder if that only happens to us or if it would happen to anyone I touch."

"We will have to ask Abby to use her powers and see what happens when you touch her. That would be a power I've never heard of before and could come in handy during a fight. Before you use it too much, we need to test it out and see what exactly it does and what the limits of it are."

He asked about the rest of my day, and I told him about the prophecy and that I was translating it.

"Everyone knows there is a prophecy, but only a few people have seen the full thing. I don't think anyone knew there was another book on it in the library."

CHAPTER ELEVEN

"Richard, is there any way to make a safe place for us to talk?" I asked him at dinner that night.

"Yes, I have been working on something specifically for that purpose but haven't tried it out yet. We can try it tomorrow," he suggested.

"What's going on tomorrow?" Abby asked.

"Sally is going to watch me practice in the morning. It might help her get the hang of her magic faster," he lied in case someone was spying on us.

"I think we should call it a night," Tider said. "It's been a long day, and we have an early morning." We all agreed and headed to our rooms. I continued working on the translation and finished a few more pages before going to bed.

The person in the prophecy would have to find the elementals. I wasn't sure how they would do that since the elementals were not allowed to have contact with humans. I fell asleep thinking about how to find them and had the strangest dream.

The water sprite I rescued during the test was hovering in front of me saying something. I tried listening to what she was saying, but I couldn't understand. She pointed at my hands, and I looked down to see the prophecy book in them. She pointed at the book again, and I held it out to her.

She flipped it open and pointed at different symbols. I recognized a few of the letters she pointed to and tried to put them together in my head. Eventually, I got a word. Study.

"Study what?" I asked her.

She tilted her head at me and then pointed to the book I found in the library.

"You want me to study the prophecy?" I asked.

She shook her head and pointed at a bunch of the letters and symbols.

"You want me to study this language?"

She nodded.

"Why?" I asked her.

She put her hands on her hips and started talking again and pointing at me.

"Ok, ok. I'm sorry. I will study it. Then you can tell me what you need from me."

The water sprite nodded again and flew around my head for a second before taking off into the sky. As she disappeared, I woke up. I quickly got up to check and make sure the prophecy book was still under my bed and felt better once I saw it. I looked at the clock. Only five in the morning.

I wasn't sure I would be able to go back to sleep, so I started translating more of the book. I'm not sure why I felt the need to listen to my dream, but it couldn't hurt to know the language that the water sprite was speaking. Maybe one day, I would actually use it.

I kept at it for a while and then left to find Richard so we could go to my extra class.

"Did you bring the translation?"

I pulled the sheets of paper I wrote everything down on out of my pocket. "This is everything I have translated so far." Richard stopped and read them.

I went to say something, but Tider stepped out of the dome. He waved his arms and ran toward us. "I can't believe you're taking a class with me. This is going to be awesome."

"I don't know about awesome, Tider, but it is going to help me learn. Hopefully, I'll learn everything I need to know by Christmas, so I can go see my family."

"Don't worry, Sally. I'll help you. I'm sure you'll be able to get it. We better get inside, Mr. Connor is waiting."

We walked in and said hi to Mr. Connor before he turned to Richard. "Are you staying today to watch or to participate?"

"I'm only here to watch. That way, Tider and I can walk her back at the end of the lesson. There is one thing I was hoping you could work on with Sally today."

"What is that?" Mr. Connor asked.

"We think someone is trying to spy on her. I researched the best way to make a privacy bubble and was hoping we could teach her that first."

"Of course," Mr. Connor said. "Since you already learned how to make it, why don't you show her first, and then I can make sure both of you are doing it correctly. Tider, why don't you do it too. This will be a good thing for you to learn."

Richard made an intricate symbol with his hands. I could feel the power flowing around him. He took his ring off, put it on the table in front of him, and channeled all the magic into his ring.

"Sally, do you have anything like a ring or necklace that you can use to channel the spell?"

"I have the necklace that my mother gave me," I said, grabbing the necklace hidden in my shirt and pulling it out to show them. It was a heart-shaped locket, and in the center was a picture of me, my mom, and my dad. It was one of my favorite necklaces, and I always wore it.

"That will work perfectly," Richard said.

"You need to focus on using all of your magic to create the spell. Picture your magic creating the barrier, and force your magic into the necklace."

"I don't use only one element?"

"No, you need to use all of your elements together," Richard said.

"Try to pull them all together now." Mr. Connor said.

I tried using all of my elements together but couldn't make it work.

"I'm not sure how to do it. It isn't working."

"Tider, you try and see if it works for you," Mr. Connor said. Tider completed the spell without any issues.

"What am I doing wrong?" I asked.

"I think I know," Tider said quietly.

"Well, tell me."

"I don't think you are going to like this."

"Come on, Tider. I can take a little criticism."

"It's not criticism, Sally," he said slowly. "I don't think you are using all the elements that you have."

"What do you mean? I'm sure I am using them all," I said, exasperated.

"No, you don't understand. I don't think you are using all of your elements."

Richard shook his head. "No, that can't be, can it?" He turned to Mr. Connor.

"It's possible, but I don't know how to teach that."

"Can someone please tell me what is going on?"

"We think you have void. It would make sense that the spell won't work if you do. You have to use all your powers for this spell."

"I thought void was extremely rare."

"It is. But you may have it. You already have four elements, which is rare. Why not one more?"

"How do I know if I have it?"

Mr. Connor shook his head. "I think you have to call on it like your other elements."

"What is void? The other elements are easy to picture. I don't know what to picture for void. Is it like a black abyss?"

"No. Void is everything that holds the universes together. I'm not really sure how to explain it."

"I think I can help," Richard said. "I read this in a book a few months ago, and it stuck with me. Give me a minute to find it. I took a picture of it to use as a reference for a paper in class."

He pulled out his phone, looking for the description of void that he read about. Once he found it, he started reading it out loud.

"Void is like the blackness of space, it is all around us, but we can't see it. There are no shadows to hide in and no light to bathe your spirit. There can only ever be emptiness, but even the emptiness can't be bothered with you. To this part of the void you are a mere speck of life, nothing more than a grain of sand it has no desire to be around. But there is another side. A perfect opposite to the emptiness. It is where peace reigns, and there is only the feeling of love. Both are parts of the void though they are eternally separated. The void hears every whisper, every thought, every feeling of all things, and decides what will be done with them. It is the master of all creation and destruction. It holds every object in the position it has chosen for them until they have served their purpose, and then it destroys them. To void, there is no time. Everything is happening here and now, and it won't stop for anything. The void is the most beautiful of your scariest dreams, for even in fear, there is beauty."

I looked at Richard as he spoke, and a chill crawled down my spine. This was an actual element that I was supposed to call on. A power that could destroy everything.

"It doesn't say who wrote it, but it goes on to talk about void as if the person had seen it. It did say that there were a few people who could use void, but they had to choose to use either the light or the dark only. Once chosen, they couldn't change their minds. Supposedly both paths are filled with peril."

"How could using the light be filled with peril?"

"It said something about when you use the light, you can't do any magic that would cause harm."

"What about defending myself?"

"I don't know," Richard said.

"Don't worry," Mr. Connor said. "We will figure this out together. There are plenty of people who are willing to help you."

"Yeah, Sally. You know I will help," Tider said.

I looked at my friends and Mr. Connor and realized that I wasn't alone. They would help me. I knew I was going to have to use void, especially if I wanted to be able to do any spells.

"Why don't you try to feel void. See if you can even access the magic. If you can, we will know that you have it, and you can use it for the privacy spell. That way, we can all research void and try to come up with appropriate spells to practice," Mr. Connor said.

They all stepped back as I closed my eyes and tried to see void. I tried picturing it the way Richard described, but the more I thought about it, the more the picture changed. In my head, it looked similar to a galaxy, but on one side, it was as dark, and on the other side, golden light burst from the center. I started to pull from it, encouraging strands of the golden light to flow into me and down my arms.

At first, some tendrils of black tried to come too, but I turned them back and only allowed in the light. As the magic filled me, I could sense perfect peace and love. Everything in my world felt right. I no longer had any fears or doubts. I knew exactly what my purpose was and how it could be done. I was content to stay that way forever until a voice broke in.

"Sally," Richard said.

I slowly let the golden light go and opened my eyes. I saw them all standing around me with smiles on their faces. "That was amazing," I said.

"We could feel it too," Tider said happily.

"I don't think I've ever felt so," Richard struggled to find the word, "peaceful."

"That was wonderful, Sally. I can now say with as much certainty as I'm able, that you have void." He smiled at me. "If the whole world could feel that, they wouldn't do anywhere near as much fighting." He kept smiling, and I realized I was still smiling too. We all were.

I started to giggle. "We are going to have to stop grinning like idiots before we go back to the school, or people are going to know something is up. None of you smile this much normally."

Mr. Connor laughed. "I suppose you could all try practicing. The frustration might cause you to start acting more like yourselves. Though I must say, I think I like the happier version of you two more," he said, laughing at Richard and Tider.

"Hey, we are always pretty happy, Mr. Connor," Tider said, trying not to smile.

"Yeah, I think we are very happy considering everything going on," Richard chimed in smirking at Mr. Connor.

"Ok, ok," Mr. Connor said. "Let's start practicing. Tider, I want you to go to that side of the room and try to recreate the spell you used during your practical but on a much smaller scale. It will help with your control. Richard, practice working on making your own air currents that another air elemental won't be able to tell are not natural."

"Sally, I want you to try to create the privacy bubble again, this time pulling on void too."

I did everything the same as before, but this time I included void. A silver ball surrounded me, and I opened my eyes to look at Mr. Connor.

"Any luck, Sally?" he asked me.

"I think I got it," I told him, but he shook his head at me and pointed to his ear. I quickly pushed the magic into the necklace and repeated what I said.

"I think you do too. Now that the spell is complete, you only need to say the correct words, and the privacy bubble will appear. You seem to be a natural at learning magic. Everything we ask you to do, you do with little effort once you understood what we want."

He called Richard and Tider over and had them show me different ways to manipulate the elements. Richard taught me how to use air to slice through targets, and Tider taught me to use only a handful of water to create a barrage of thin, needle-like pieces of ice to throw at someone attacking me.

"Hey guys," I said after learning what they taught me. "If Richard is right, I'm going to need defensive techniques not offensive. Remember, I won't be able to use void to harm anyone."

"We don't know if that's true," said Tider.

"No, we don't, but I think it's smart to learn more defensive magic. We can work on some offensive stuff, but I want ways to protect myself."

"Ok, we can start working on that. Remember, you can do anything you want with your powers as long as you can imagine it, and you have enough energy."

This was the part I was having trouble with. I couldn't imagine doing anything with my powers because I still had trouble believing in them most of the time. I knew I needed to wrap my head around all of this and soon, or I wouldn't be able to see my parents for Christmas. I tried to think of something I could do with air since it was the easiest for me to use, but my mind was utterly blank.

"What you really need to have is imagination," Mr. Connor said.

"I don't think I can imagine anything. This is too new for me."

"Once you get used to believing in all things magical, this will be a lot easier," Mr. Connor said gently.

"I know. I will try."

"That's all we can ask of you. Let's work on a few more things before we head back to the school."

By the time we finished, I was exhausted. They had me try a dozen different things with air and water, but I wasn't used to using so much magic in different ways. Mr. Connor thought I had a lot more magic in me, but because I was not fully embracing it, I was getting tired and using up more energy than I needed to.

"I'm going to spend the rest of the afternoon at the library if anyone wants to join me. I have a lot of stuff to research and not a lot of extra time to do it," I said when we were sitting in the cafeteria after class.

"What are you researching?" Abby asked.

I looked at the guys, and they both nodded. "Can you do it, Richard?" I asked. I didn't want to use the spell in case someone could tell I was using more than air.

Richard put the privacy spell in place, and I walked over to Abby and gave her a hug. "Richard put up a privacy shield so we can talk without anyone being able to hear us."

"I've heard about those. How did you do that?"

"I will show you when we have more privacy," Richard said.

"Abby, I'm going to research more about magic, specifically void," I said. She looked at me in surprise. "Do you think you have it?"

"We know I do. We found out this morning, but I don't want to use it until we learn everything that we can on it."

"I can come with you to help."

"So can I," Tider said.

"I can't. I have another class to get too," Richard told us.

"You take another class? What for?" I asked.

"I have a class with Mrs. Shaw this afternoon to practice earth magic. It's pretty weak, so I've been trying to use it more often."

"I don't think we should keep the privacy shield up too long, or someone might get suspicious when they can't hear us talking," Tider interrupted, looking around.

"I need to get to class anyway. We can talk later," Richard said.

CHAPTER TWELVE

As I walked into the library, I walked over to a bookcase and pulled out a book on fire elementals. I also grabbed a book about the other elementals, the books about void, and even one about mythical places before heading over to Abby and Tider.

"What else are you looking for?" she asked me.

"I'm looking for the place where the water sprites live."

She looked at me, surprised. "Why?"

"I didn't get a chance to tell you. I got a note telling me to," I whispered. "I will tell you more when Richard is with us."

"Ok, I will try to figure it out too, though no one has seen them in centuries."

"Thanks, Abby," I told her before opening the book on water elementals. I read through some of it, but I couldn't stop thinking about the book on void.

I picked up the book on void and paged through it. I learned almost nothing. There was a lot of speculation about what a person with void magic could do, but most of it was so ridiculous that I took it lightly. At one point, the author said void magic could be used to turn rain into flower petals that fell through the air. The whole book went on like that until the last chapter.

He wrote that anyone using void for a selfish or harmful cause would be bound to the dark magic of void forever. On the last page, the author wrote that if anyone was stronger than the darkness and could use both sides of void, they would be the strongest elemental the world had ever seen, possibly even stronger than the first elementals that came here thousands of years ago.

I shut the book and took a minute to collect my thoughts. Things were not looking better. In fact, they were worse than before I read the book. I was hoping that the next book would have better information. I looked at Abby and saw her reading with her brow furrowed.

"You ok, Abbs?"

"Yeah, I think I may have something, but I'm not sure yet. I need to check a couple more books first."

I took the first book on void back to the bookcase and returned to my seat. As I sat down, Sasha walked into the library.

"Look who I found," she said over her shoulder gleefully.

"Who did you find?" Sean asked, walking into the library behind her. "Oh, look what we have here. It's my step-sister and her dork friends. What are you doing in the library on the weekend?" He grabbed one of the books on Abby's pile and read the title. "Fire elementals: A beginning. Why are you reading this? You don't even have fire magic."

"She is helping me with my studies since I am so far behind." I stood up and glared. "What are you doing in the library on the weekend?" I shot back at him. "I thought only dorks hung out here."

He turned an unusual shade of red and started to stammer. "You…how dare you." He stomped toward me. "My dad will…"

"Do what Sean?" Tider interrupted, striding forward.

Sean took a step back as Tider kept moving closer. "What will he do, Sean?" Tider asked again.

Sean took a deep breath. "I don't know, but I'm sure it will be awful," he said, sneering as he walked quickly out of the library with Sasha following behind him. She gave us one last glare before the door closed.

Abby and I looked at Tider, and we both started laughing. "What?" he asked.

"He is so scared of you. Whatever you did to him really scared him. He is such a jerk. Thanks for keeping him from bothering us."

I reached out and tousled his hair until he pulled away and glared at me. "I'm not a kid."

I couldn't help it, I started laughing again. "I know, but you remind me of my friend's younger brother back home." I tossed my arm over his shoulders. "If I could have a brother, I would pick you."

Tider blushed and shook his head. Quietly he said, "I wish I had you as a sister too."

I smiled, and then Tider cleared his throat. "I think we need to get back to reading, or we won't ever be able to help you," he said.

We sat back down, and I looked at the book in front of me. My last chance to learn something about void and how to use it. I opened the book and started reading. Immediately, I was swept up into it. The author had void magic and detailed everything about it when she first started using it. The book was like a diary.

She described how the light magic felt perfectly. I read through the first few chapters quickly. She explained how to start practicing with it and the different things it could do. I was jotting down notes as fast as I could, so I would be able to practice this stuff later.

The author started talking about wanting to try to reach out to the dark tendrils of power that were always trying to be used, but she was still too scared to try. For the next few chapters, she talked about the battle between using or not using the dark. It seemed to always be calling to her.

Toward the middle of the diary, she wrote that when she was practicing in the beginning, she didn't know not to use the dark tendrils. She thought she may have used the dark magic, and that's how it was able to get a hold on her. As the book continued, her writings started to get more frantic, and she talked of ending her life before the darkness could compel her to do anything terrible.

She didn't end her life, though. She used dark magic to kill the family of a boy that scorned her for another girl. She gave the girl awful nightmares so she wouldn't be able to live in peace. The diary ended right after she wrote that down. I wasn't sure if she ended her life or not after that.

I closed the book and clasped my hands together to keep them from shaking. There was no way I was going to be able to use void magic after reading the two books. Void was incredibly dangerous magic that no one should have access to, not if it could corrupt someone so easily.

I needed to go talk to Mr. Connor and see if he found out anything else about the prophecy. I didn't want to be the one it spoke of. I was completely ok with never using magic again. Maybe there was a way to bind my magic so I couldn't use it. One of the teachers would know a way to help me.

"I think I found something," Abby yelled.

"Shhh," I told her. I didn't see anyone else, but I couldn't see the upper level very well.

"Sorry," she whispered. "Look at this." She held out the book on water elementals that she was reading. "It says that the water sprites once ruled with the water elementals in Hibernia in a majestic underwater castle."

"Where is Hibernia?" I asked.

"No idea," she replied. "There's more. It says to get to their castle, you have to find your way to the western shores and then to the largest isle. Once on the isle, you can cross on foot through mountains and forests, or boat around to the northwest side. You would know you were in the correct place when you saw a small lake separated from the ocean by a stretch of land with steep rocky sides. At that point, you would need to go into the ocean and find the cave below it. That's the entrance to the castle."

"That doesn't sound hard to find at all," Tider said sarcastically.

"I'm just telling you what I found. There has to be a way to find out where this is."

"I need a little break from all of this," I said.

"Ok," Abby said and started to put her books away.

I followed her and put mine away too. When I put the book on void away, a chill fell over me. I turned away from it and hoped that it wouldn't cause me to go crazy like the other girl. I said bye to my friends and left the library.

I started to consider where the water sprites could be. I typed the name Hibernia into my phone, and a bunch of articles came up for Ireland. It was supposedly called that by the Romans. Now I knew where I needed to start my search. Hopefully, they had the same castle now that they did back then.

I pulled up a map of Ireland and searched for the largest isle. It was called Achill, and it looked to be fairly rugged terrain in spots. I would have to study the map closer to see if I could find the exact area where I needed to look.

I wasn't sure how I was going to get to Ireland if that's where I needed to go, but I thought maybe if I could go see my parents, I could look around then. I was sure I could get them to take me to Achill as long as they thought it was for sightseeing. I hated lying to them, but they definitely wouldn't let me check it out if they thought it could be dangerous. I had a lot to do if my plan was going to work.

It was already the second week of November, and I needed to prove to Mrs. Sullivan that I could control my magic by the beginning of December. That's the only way she would let me visit my parents for Christmas, or I wouldn't be able to see if the water sprites were there.

The next couple of weeks passed by in a blur. I was so busy with my regular classes and the extra classes that I barely had time to think. I kept working on controlling my magic. I was getting pretty good at it, but I still wasn't using void. I wasn't comfortable with it and didn't want to make a mistake and use dark magic. Mr. Connor and Mr. Merrem never pushed me to use it either.

All of my powers were growing stronger, though I still couldn't do delicate tasks easily. During the last week of November, I asked Mr. Connor if we could tell Mrs. Sullivan about my progress and see if I could spend Christmas with my family. He said he would invite her to the dome, so I could show her at my next class.

I could barely wait to show her how much better I was. I knew she would say yes once she saw me use my magic. I knew how to keep it hidden most of the time when I used it. The Pulhu hadn't bothered me, and even Sean and Sasha didn't give me much trouble. I thought all of the trouble at the beginning of the year was over.

When my next class with Mr. Connor came, I was ready to impress her and did everything Mr. Connor asked me to do. Mrs. Sullivan stopped us at one point and asked me to lift all the feathers that were in the room up and space them evenly apart in the air. Once I had them in the air, I had to take water from the bowl in the center of the room and make each feather damp. Then I had to use fire under each feather to carefully dry them.

That was the hardest one to do, and I was sweating from the effort by the time the last feather was dry. For earth, Mrs. Sullivan asked me to make the plant that was sitting on a table grow and unfurl many new leaves to catch all the feathers. When I finally finished and returned everything to normal, Mrs. Sullivan was looking at me speculatively.

"Well?" I asked. "How did I do? Can I go see them?"

She sighed and then nodded. "Yes. I can see how hard you've been practicing. If you keep this pace up, by the end of the year, we won't have much left to teach you. I'm still not sure that the Pulhu have forgotten you. The more I watch you grow into your powers, the more I wonder if the prophecy is about you. You can go, but you need to be careful." I thanked Mrs. Sullivan again, and she told me she would get me the details of the trip by the end of the following week.

When I got back to school and found my friends, I told them I would be going to Ireland. They were excited for me but also concerned.

"I will text you guys every day," I laughed. "That way, you know I'm being careful."

"You better," Abby smiled. "We aren't going to be there to keep you out of trouble."

"I'm not planning on getting in any trouble. I am going to see my parents."

"And look for the water sprites," Tider whispered with a frown.

"Maybe, if I have time."

They all looked at me. "Ok, ok. I'm going to look for them."

"What happens if you find the true elementals and they aren't friendly. They are not allowed to be seen by us, remember. They might be furious that you came to find them."

I shook my head. "I'm supposed to find the water sprites, remember. That's what the paper said."

"Who knows where that paper came from. Besides, we don't know anything about the water sprites or the elementals. They could be in another war for all we know."

"I doubt they are in a war. The water sprites help us during our practicals. They shouldn't be upset. Plus, I only want to see if I can find the place. I won't go into the castle. I will see if it's there and that's it. That way, we know if we are in the right spot. Like you said, they could have moved to a different spot a long time ago, and we would never know. I might be going to look at ancient ruins."

Tider shook his head, and Richard looked even more upset.

"It will be ok, guys," Abby told them.

"I have some things to take care of. I will see you guys later. Make sure you start studying too. End of quarter tests start soon," Richard said and headed down the hallway.

"Tider, are you coming with us to start studying?"

"I need to go take care of some stuff for the holidays," Tider said.

Tider left, and we went to the library to study. I was surprised to see a couple of kids sitting around the tables and asked Abby about it. Usually, no one was in the library.

"The tests in December and June are the biggest tests of the year besides practicals. Everyone studies for them."

"Why don't we go back to my room, it will be less crowded," I said. "I am hoping to move up to intermediate studies. That way, I'm with kids closer to my age."

"That would be great. By summer, you could be in advanced studies with me."

"That's my goal," I smiled. "It will be nice to catch up to everyone else."

After a while, Abby said goodnight and left for her room. It was still too early for me to sleep, so I took out the prophecy book and translated another page. I wasn't working on it as much as I should, and I didn't know if I was going to need to be able to read and speak the language, so I resolved to work on it every night.

I didn't get a lot of time to hang out with my friends during the week. We were all busy studying, and I spent even more time translating the book. So far, it didn't mention anything specific. Only theories on what each line meant, but I was learning the language. I could almost read everything without having to translate it first.

Mrs. Sullivan called me to her office at the end of the week and gave me the information about the flight. Natasha was going to pick me up and take me to the airport. After Mrs. Sullivan dismissed me, I went up to my room to start packing. I was leaving in two weeks to go to Ireland. I couldn't wait.

We started finals, and I had no trouble getting through them. We wouldn't get our grades for a few days, but I felt good about the tests and was pretty sure I passed. Abby wasn't so sure about her math test, but I persuaded her not to worry about it until the test scores came back. When the results came back, I was surprised. I managed to get an A in every class. Mrs. Sullivan sent me a note telling me I would be moved to intermediate classes at the beginning of the next term.

I went to Abby's room, and she threw the door open and hugged me.

"I passed all my classes, even math."

"Good job, Abbs," I told her. "I knew you could do it."

"How did you do? Are you moving up in your classes?"

"Yes. I'm switching to all intermediate classes next term."

"We had a great semester."

We headed down to the common area to see how everyone else did. All the students were celebrating when we got there. It must've been a great semester for a lot of people. Even Sasha and Sean seemed happy.

"When are you leaving?" I asked her.

"Tonight. My dad is coming to pick me up. You can meet him."

"I would love to meet your dad," I told her. "I hope you have lots of fun, but it stinks that you'll be gone so early. I'm going to be here a week without you."

"I'm sure Tider or Richard will be here too."

"Hopefully, or else I'm going to be super bored."

"We will ask once we see them," Abby said. We stayed in the common area for most of the afternoon celebrating with the other kids while we waited for Tider and Richard to show up.

"Are either of you staying at the school over Christmas break?" I asked them when they finally came to the common room.

"No," Tider said. "I have to go home for the holidays. I don't have any choice." He looked upset, and I wondered again how bad his family really was.

"What about you, Richard?"

"I'll be going home for a few days, and then I have other things that I need to do before I come back."

"What other things do you have to do?" I asked Richard curiously.

"Just some stuff," he replied. He gave me a long look and then looked at Tider. Something was going on with those two, but I wasn't sure what. I thought it might have something to do with me.

"When are you guys leaving? I don't leave until the twenty-third."

"I'm leaving Sunday morning," said Tider.

"I'll be staying until then too, Sally," Richard said.

"Good, I won't be by myself the whole time."

"What time are you leaving?" I asked Richard. "Natasha is picking me up at five in the morning."

"She will be picking me up at the same time. We can ride together to the airport."

"I didn't realize you needed to go to the airport. How far away do you live?"

"I'm not going nearly as far as you," Richard laughed. "My family has a place in New York that I'm going to."

CHAPTER THIRTEEN

Before I could respond, Abby looked over my shoulder and then sprinted around me. I turned and saw a man giving her a big hug. She looked back and waved us forward.

"Sally, Tider, Richard, this is my dad. Dad, these are my friends."

Her dad shook hands with each of us and smiled at me. "I've heard so much about you, Sally. I'm glad I got a chance to meet you. How do you like school?"

"So far, I'm enjoying it. Abby is helping me get the hang of everything," I told him.

"That's great." He smiled again. Abby stilled and then closed her eyes and took a deep breath as a tall, gorgeous lady walked toward us.

"Abby, how lovely to see you again," the lady said in a high voice. "I see you finally made some friends." Abby's dad turned toward the lady with a small frown. She put a hand on his arm and smiled at him. "You know how much I worry about her. It makes me happy to see her hanging out with other kids."

Abby's dad smiled. "It is good to see her happy."

I immediately didn't like the lady. What she said wasn't meant nicely, and I looked at my friends to see if they caught it. Richard was frowning, but Tider looked pissed.

"Of course she has friends. Abby is one of the nicest kids at the school. Most of the students like her. She is very busy studying, so she doesn't always have time to hang out," Tider said angrily.

"And who might you be?" the lady asked him.

"My name is Johnathon." She looked at him disdainfully. I was surprised that he used his actual name since he always wanted to go by Tider.

"Well, Johnathon, I'm Laura Ravenis." She seemed to expect us to be impressed by the name, but I had no idea who she was. Richard had a grimace on his face, and Abby was looking down.

Tider pulled his shoulders back and looked her in the eye. "Your name means nothing to me. Let me give you my full name. I'm Johnathon Murdell."

Mrs. Ravenis gasped and took a small step back. "I didn't realize. I mean, I knew you were at the school, but I didn't expect you to be friends with my stepdaughter."

"Maybe you should see who you are talking to before you open your mouth. My family will hear of this." Tider's voice sounded strange. It was a mixture of pure fury and coldness. It was awful coming from one of my best friends. I looked at Tider from a different perspective. I didn't know him long, but I thought I knew him well. I had never seen this side of him.

"I'm sorry, Mr. Murdell," Mrs. Ravenis apologized. "It won't happen again. I don't think your family needs to hear of this." There was fear in her eyes, and her hands were slightly shaking.

"You should be on your way," Tider told her.

She reached for Abby's dad, but Tider stepped between them. "No, just you."

Mrs. Ravenis turned and walked away quickly. As soon as she was gone, Abby's dad perked up. "Hey, where did Laura go, she was right here?" I looked sideways at Abby. Why wasn't her dad saying anything about what happened?

"We should really get going. Laura wanted to pick you kids up quickly so we can get our vacation started."

"Ok, Dad. I'll be right there."

Abby walked over and gave me a hug. "I'll see you soon," she said.

"Wait, Abby. What just happened? Why didn't your dad say anything?"

"That's pretty normal for him. Whenever she gets near him, he forgets everything around him and can only focus on making her happy. Even when she is mean, he has trouble realizing it. I used to think it was a spell, but I never found anything to prove it."

"Can't you talk to him when she isn't around?"

"I've tried." She sighed. "It doesn't work. It's like he doesn't hear anything bad against her. I've even snooped around looking for the spell, but there isn't anything. Maybe he really does love her, and love is blind, right?"

"I don't think that's what that means. I will help you figure it out if you want."

She looked hopeful, but then her face fell. "Not right now. You have more important things to do."

"Nothing is more important than my friends, and besides, your dad seems like a good guy. He doesn't deserve this if he is under a spell."

Abby hugged me again. "I better get going, or she will be more difficult. Have a safe trip."

"You too." I watched as Abby and her dad walked away. I turned to the guys. "What did you think about that?"

"About what?" Richard said.

"Abby's dad acting so weird," I said slowly.

"I didn't notice anything different, did you?" He turned to Tider.

"Yes, I did. She has control of him somehow. I've seen it before. It's something the Pulhu do to people they need to control."

"How do we fix it?"

"I have no idea. I'm not even sure if it's a spell, or if it's an enchanted item."

"Why doesn't Richard see what happened to Abby's dad?" Richard was looking at us, confused.

"His family isn't part of the Pulhu, so he's not immune. All the families associated with the Pulhu are immune and can see what is being done. Those who aren't Pulhu don't even realize something is wrong. They just see a pleasant conversation taking place."

"Is that what you saw, Richard?"

"In the beginning, Mrs. Ravenis seemed very rude, but the more I listened to her, the more I realized I was wrong for judging her right away. She was trying to be nice to Abby and give her a compliment. It just came out the wrong way."

"Ok, Richard. Thanks." I stepped away from him and moved toward Tider. "So how do we fix Richard? And why doesn't it affect me?"

"He's fine. It doesn't affect him any other way. And now that she's gone, he will be himself, except he will remember this conversation differently than we do. He's pretty strong though. He remembers her being rude in the beginning. That's a lot more than everyone else would remember. And I don't know why it doesn't affect you."

"Why doesn't Abby do whatever Mrs. Ravenis asks, like her dad?"

"Mrs. Ravenis must have given her something to make her immune to it. She probably enjoys harassing her and knowing that her dad won't stop it."

"We need to find a way to end it. It's not right for people to be used that way. He doesn't deserve this. And Abby has to watch her dad being controlled. He won't even defend her when Mrs. Ravenis is mean."

"I know. It's bad. We can try to find a way. When I go home, I will see what I can find."

"Good," I said but then remembered who his family was. "Don't get caught. I don't want you to get in trouble."

"I won't."

"Your family must be pretty scary. It ran off Mrs. Ravenis pretty fast."

"Yeah, we are one of the most powerful and not in a good way. I'm pretty sure everyone knows they use dark magic, but no one has the power to stand up to them. As you saw, even the Ravenis family are scared of my family name."

"If your family is that bad, how did you manage to not be corrupted like them?"

"It was actually their own fault. My mom sucks at the whole mothering thing, so she brought in a nanny. What they didn't know was that the nanny would take me to all the typical places a kid would want to go, including the park and to get ice cream. I learned kindness from her, and I started making friends when we would go out places. I got to see how ordinary families acted, and I spent a lot of time around nonmagical people.

"They always seemed so happy, and the parents always seemed to care about the kids. When I asked my nanny about it, she told me I can choose to live in a world where people act that way, or where they act like my family. It was up to me. I've been choosing to act like the other people instead of my family ever since. When I go home, I have to act more like them, so I don't get into trouble, but I only have a few years left before I can leave. I'm hoping they don't manage to corrupt me before then."

"What do you mean?" Richard asked as he walked up to us. He looked more like himself.

"Every time I go home, my family tries to get me to do dark magic, but I've managed to wiggle my way out of it so far. I don't know how long that will last."

"Why do you go home?"

"I don't have a choice. They won't let me stay away forever. I am supposed to be taking an interest in the family business after all. I'm glad they sent me to this school instead of one of the others. Mrs. Sullivan tries to protect me from them as much as possible. So far it's been working, and I only spend a few weeks out of the year at home."

"I didn't realize things were so bad at your house," Richard said to Tider.

"It's not a big deal," Tider said.

"You know," Richard said, "you could come stay with me for the holidays. Tell your family that you are trying to get me to agree to be on the side of the Pulhu. That might get them off your back, and then you don't have to go home. They want me bad enough that it might work."

"That will definitely work. They have been trying to get to you and your family for years. If they think I'm close, they might pull Sean off of you too. I know you are worried about your sister, but if her powers aren't strong and we say that I'm working on you, they might not threaten you with her either."

Richard and Tider both looked excited. "This could work," they said.

"I still need to go home for a few days to make an appearance and tell them I'm working on getting you to join the Pulhu though. Then I can head to your place. Are you sure your parents will be ok with it?"

"Yeah, they'll be fine with it."

They talked a few more minutes about exactly what they needed to do. Then Tider said his goodbyes and took off to get the rest of his stuff packed before he was picked up in the morning. I stayed with Richard for a while and then went to my room to do some more packing.

Most of the kids already left or were packing to leave today, so no one bothered me during breakfast. I wrote down notes about how I was going to deal with my trip to Ireland while I ate. I narrowed the area I needed to search down to a few beaches. Hopefully, it would be one of those, or else I didn't know what I was going to do.

One beach, in particular, looked promising. It even said people shouldn't swim there because the water was so dangerous. It sounded exactly like where I needed to go. I plotted out a few different routes to get to each beach. I would need at least a full day to search each one. Maybe more if the cave was really well hidden.

As I was finishing breakfast, Mrs. Sullivan walked in and headed straight for me.

"Good morning, Sally. Why don't you walk with me in the garden?"

"Good morning, Mrs. Sullivan," I said, standing up to follow her.

"Mr. Merrem wants you to meet him at the dome after you finish up here. He will be teaching you every day until you leave to make sure you are ready in case something happens," she said quietly once we were out of earshot.

"Ok," I said.

Mrs. Sullivan talked to me about my studies for a few more minutes. She gave me another warning about staying in the haven once I got to Ireland before she left. I went up to my room to put my notebook away and grab a sweatshirt before heading to the dome. Mr. Merrem was waiting for me and immediately wanted to get to work.

"You are going to be using your magic to defend yourself. When you were attacked your first day here, Richard said he thought you became invisible. Do you remember how you did that?"

"Yes, but I wasn't trying to be invisible. I was trying to create a shield."

"That's ok, I want you to try to do that again. If it works, we can try to change it a bit so you can move and remain invisible. This magic isn't completely uncommon, so I have a pretty good idea how to help you with this. Go ahead when you are ready."

I walked away from Mr. Merrem and closed my eyes, imaging air wrapping around me like a shield. I opened my eyes and looked at Mr. Merrem from inside my shield.

"Can you see me?" I asked.

"Yes, I can."

"I'm not sure why it didn't work."

"I want you to think back to the attack. What did you think when you created the shield? That may have influenced your magic."

I thought back to that day. "I wanted to get away from them and make it to the school. I remember being scared and trying to create the shield. I was hoping they wouldn't be able to hit me with their magic."

"Try thinking about it like that again. Think about not wanting someone to be able to hit you," Mr. Merrem said.

I did what he told me and could feel my magic changing subtly. I closed my eyes and noticed the silver color was much brighter than before but also almost opaque. It looked different than the first shield.

"Good job, Sally," Mr. Merrem said. "It worked. I'm not able to see you at all. Now try moving toward me."

He talking to me, but he was looking slightly to my right. I stifled a giggle and took a step forward. Immediately, I felt my magic change again.

"It didn't work when I moved, did it?" I asked.

"No, it didn't, but that's ok. We have something to work with, and I'm sure it can be improved. Stay focused on not being seen. Start with slowly lifting a hand to see what happens."

When I tried, I could see and feel the difference as soon as I started to lift my hand. I stopped.

"How did it go, Sally?" asked Mr. Merrem. "I could see a small shift in the air but didn't see you."

"Not well," I said honestly. "As soon as I started to move, my magic started to change too."

"Explain how your magic felt," he said. I told him, and he thought about it for a few minutes while I kept trying.

"I think the best way to overcome this is to listen to your magic. Close your eyes, and watch how it changes. You might be able to see where the change is starting, or figure out how to stop it once you know exactly what it looks like."

I agreed and watched my magic as I lifted my hand again. As I lifted it, I saw a spark of gold flow through the silver right where my hand was. I kept moving my hand, and the gold spread out. It was very faint but still there. I put my hand down and moved even slower, trying to keep the gold magic from forming. I wondered if it was void magic, which I didn't want to use. At least it didn't look like the dark side of void.

After a few more attempts, I was able to lift up my hand very slowly. I was sweating by the time I finished. Keeping the gold magic out was very hard.

"Ok, Sally. I think we have that figured out. The bad news is that it is going to take a lot of work to be able to move while you are invisible. The good news is that you can become invisible."

I shook my head in frustration. "Why am I having so much trouble with this?"

He laughed. "Magic takes a lot of control. You were born with a lot of power, but you still need to practice your control. Remember this is your first year, some kids your age still don't have full control of their powers, and they have been going here for years. You should be proud you are doing so well."

"I know I should be." I hung my head. "I guess I'm impatient."

"It's ok, I understand why," Mr. Merrem said. "I know you are worried about the Pulhu, and you can't do as much as the other kids until Mrs. Sullivan is sure they aren't after you. So far, you are doing great at hiding your powers from everyone else. I'm sure if you continue working on your control, by the end of the year, you can go out with the other kids to town or to the beach."

"Thanks, Mr. Merrem. It is hard being cooped up here. I can't wait until I don't have to worry anymore."

I spent the next couple of hours working with Mr. Merrem on how to use my magic defensively. He would pretend to attack me with his magic, and I would defend myself. I practiced all of my magic except void and learned that I could protect myself from almost everything he sent at me.

"I think I'm getting the hang of this," I told him.

"You are doing great, but so far, I have only used a small amount of magic on you."

My magic faltered as I stared at him, and my windstorm died as he threw a firebolt at me.

"Duck," he shouted.

I threw myself to the side as the firebolt soared past. It grazed my thigh, and I yelped in shock. I looked down at my leg and saw his magic had burned right through my clothes and left a one-inch streak across my thigh.

Mr. Merrem ran up to me and kneeled, checking my leg to see the damage.

"We need to put something on that right away. Here, Sally. This will help the burn heal. It may hurt for a second."

He poured a small amount of liquid onto my burn, and I tensed up as a sharp pain hit me. It was gone in a second, and I stared in wonder as the burn healed before my eyes. Within seconds it was completely gone, and the skin looked as good as before. The only evidence that something happened was the burn hole in my jeans. Mr. Merrem helped me stand up and walked back to put the vial away.

"What happened, Sally? You were doing great. All of a sudden, your magic was gone."

"It was my fault, I got distracted when you said you weren't using a lot of magic on me. It made me completely lose my focus, and my shield collapsed."

"It's ok, Sally. I'm glad it wasn't any worse. I can only heal small burns." He smiled in relief.

"Is what you said true? You aren't using a lot of magic on me?"

"Of course I'm not using a lot of magic on you. This is your first time fighting with magic. I don't want you to get hurt."

"So if I'm attacked, I probably won't be able to help myself," I said.

"Why would you think that?"

"Because it was hard to defend against you, and you weren't using a lot of magic. What happens when someone uses their full magic on me."

"Don't worry. That is why we are going to be practicing every day until you leave. You will be more comfortable using your magic and stronger the more you practice it."

I still wasn't sure if I would be able to defend myself, but I was going to do my best. "Ok, let's keep practicing."

"I think that's enough for today," Mr. Merrem said, laughing. "You need to eat something after practicing all morning. I will see you tomorrow at the same time."

I found Richard and was surprised when he said we would be looking for the water sprites together.

"What do you mean, we? I'm going to be in Ireland looking, not here."

"I know. I will be there too. At least for part of it. Mrs. Sullivan asked me if I would go with you."

"Why?"

"In case there is trouble."

"So you are one of the people assigned to watch me? Do you know who else?"

"Technically, I am not assigned to watch you. It will look like I am there visiting. You will still have a few adults watching you. I'm there to help you if you need it."

"But what about Tider? He is supposed to be coming to stay at your house."

"He is going to be coming too. He will come to my house for a couple of days, and then we will fly over there. Wait for us before you go searching," he said, giving me a stern look.

"I will wait for you," I told him. "It's only a couple of days, and I want to spend some time with my parents first anyway."

"Thanks, Sally. I don't want anything bad to happen to you."

"I know, Richard. When you guys get there, we can start exploring. I already know exactly where I want to start. It's an area called Annagh Bay. It's the perfect spot for water elementals to hide."

"Sounds good. We need to make sure we are prepared when we go. We don't know what we will find there."

"I know. We will be," I told him. I headed down to the library to do a little more research on the first elementals. After looking through the books for a couple of hours, I still hadn't learned anything new. No one really knew what the elementals were like in the beginning. A lot of the books repeated the same tales over and over with different people trying to decipher them. I put the books away, grabbed dinner, and headed to my room.

CHAPTER FOURTEEN

I knew I was dreaming right away. The field of daisies I was standing in was too bright, the whites and greens standing out sharply against the browns of the ground. Even the blue of the sky was too blue against the white puffy clouds. I started walking along the path, trying to figure out where I was.

I felt a peacefulness in the air around me, and everywhere I looked, animals were running around. I saw a mama rabbit with her babies and sat and watched as they scampered in the tall grass, playing with each other like they didn't have a care in the world. Their mama looked up, startled, and quickly nudged the babies into her den.

I looked around too but didn't see anything. I continued along the path and came to the edge of a lake. I looked out across it in wonder. It was so huge I couldn't see the other side. A splash caused me to look out at the water. A few feet into the lake, a dolphin poked his head out of the water. He made squeaking and chirping noises at me, but I didn't know what he wanted.

He kept making noises until I walked toward him. He dipped under the water and came even closer to me. When I was close enough to touch him, he pushed his nose at my hand. A barrage of images flew into my head.

He was swimming near the center of the lake. When he came up for air, I saw an island covered in black sand. There were ruins on the island. I could feel waves of misery coming from the shore. As the dolphin watched, black clouds began to gather above the island, and the wind started to kick up the sand and waves.

The island soon became obscured, and the dolphin dived under the waves, swimming away. He popped his head up one more time and looked back. I saw that the dark clouds were at least twice as big as before, and I could hear the wind.

I opened my eyes and looked down at the dolphin. "What was that?" I asked him, not really expecting an answer.

He shook his head and then touched his nose to me again. I saw a picture of myself in a boat rowing out there with Richard, Tider, Abby, and another guy I didn't know.

"Wait. Are you saying I'm supposed to go there?"

The dolphin nodded.

"Why?"

As he touched my hand again, I saw the darkness taking over the earth. I stood with my friends on the island, and a circle of light glowed around us.

"That's the prophecy?" I asked.

He nodded again.

"Why are you showing me this?" I needed to know more. He looked back out at the lake, and this time I could see dark clouds. They kept getting bigger, and I could hear the wind getting closer. He nudged me with his nose urgently. I saw a picture of a large white wolf standing on a cliff with his head thrown back. I heard the words, "Find him," before the picture changed, and I saw myself running back to where I started the dream.

As the image faded, I heard the howling of the wind as it tore at my clothes and hair. The dark clouds were getting closer. The dolphin looked at me one last time and then dived under the water.

"Run," I heard in my head. I turned and ran. The wind whipped past me, dragging long strands of hair into my eyes, making it almost impossible to see. The sand flew all around and stung everywhere my clothes didn't protect. I ran faster. I knew if I let the dark clouds get to me, I wouldn't be able to wake up.

The world would be covered in darkness, and evil would rule. I couldn't let that happen. I pushed myself even harder, sprinting past the rabbit's den, hoping they would be safe in the storm. I made it back to the spot I started in and closed my eyes, hoping to wake up.

When I opened them I was back in my bedroom at school. I was covered in sweat and could feel the grittiness of sand all over my body. It hadn't been a dream. Somehow I was really there at the lake even though I was still in my bed.

Shakily, I got to my feet and headed toward the shower. I wanted to get the sand off of me, and I needed a few minutes to pull myself together. I wasn't sure what happened, but I knew it was a warning. The darkness was growing closer, and somehow I had to stop it. At this point, I was starting to believe I was the one in the prophecy.

I felt a little steadier as I headed down to the common area. I knew the cafeteria wasn't going to have breakfast ready yet, but I didn't want to stay in my room. Maybe I would hang out in the library for a while. I glanced at my phone, only a few minutes after five. I grabbed a book and started reading.

I finished reading and grabbed some breakfast before meeting Mr. Merrem. He had me practice everything I learned since I came to the elemental school.

I met up with Richard that afternoon, and we walked down to see Mr. Connor. He wanted to go over a few last-minute things before I left, and I was glad I would get a chance to say bye to him. He was still one of my favorite teachers. When we got to his room, he stood up from his desk with a big grin.

"I hope you have a good time seeing your parents," he said. "I have something for you to take on your journey." He pulled out a small black bag, opened it, and took out the contents. There were a bunch of small vials filled with different liquids. "I made a bunch of potions for you to take just in case. Don't worry about getting through security at the airport with it. It's enchanted to look like a regular bag of toiletries," he said, laughing. "It's a great disguise. No one wants to go through someone else's personal bathroom products."

I laughed as well. "That is a great disguise. What are they for?"

"There are a couple of healing potions in the red vials, a potion that enhances your sight in a blue vial, another one that enhances hearing in a green vial, and a few that explode like bombs. You need to be careful with those last ones. They are in the black vials. They only blow up a small area, about a five-foot diameter, but it might come in useful. Don't blow yourself up."

"I will be extra careful," I told him.

"Good. Only use them if you really need to. It's incredibly hard to get all the ingredients for some of these, but I want to make sure you can defend yourself if anything happens. With the Pulhu, you can never be too safe."

"Thank you, Mr. Connor. I won't use them if I don't have to. Hopefully, I won't need them. I'm hoping to have a nice holiday with my parents." We chatted with him for a few more minutes before leaving.

"That went well," Richard said as we walked out. "I definitely think these might come in useful on your trip."

I spent the rest of the evening in the library but didn't find anything new. After a few hours and lots of yawning, I finally gave up and went to sleep. I didn't have any more weird dreams and felt fully rested when I woke up. When I got to my class, Mr. Merrem made me practice everything he could think of to prepare me for any problems on my trip the next day.

I was up early and waiting for Natasha to pick me up twenty minutes before Richard even showed up. I couldn't help it. I was super excited to see my family. It felt like I had been away from them forever, even though I talked to them almost every night. As soon as Natasha pulled up, I hurried down the stairs, put my stuff in the trunk, and hopped into the car, ready to go. Richard took longer, and I started tapping my fingers impatiently.

"You need to relax," he whispered to me. "The plane is leaving at the same time, whether you get there in ten minutes or in forty-five minutes. You are still going to have to sit at the airport and wait," he said, laughing.

I shot an irritated look at him. "I know. I just want to get there. I will feel better once I'm at my gate. Right now, anything could happen. What if we get stuck in traffic, or get a flat tire?"

He laughed again. "I'm sure Mrs. Sullivan thought of everything. That's probably why we are leaving so early. Your flight doesn't leave until ten. You are going to be stuck in the airport for a few hours."

"What time does your flight leave?"

"Not until eleven. I'm going to stay with you until you board, then I will head to my gate."

"You don't have to stay with me. I will be fine."

"I'm sure you will, but there's no reason either of us needs to sit at the airport alone." He glanced toward Natasha quickly and then looked at me.

He didn't want me saying anything in front of her. I closed my mouth. I didn't even think about the fact that I needed to be careful about what I said around everyone else. I didn't want anyone knowing that Richard was really here to protect me, even if I didn't want him to be. I looked up to the front of the car and saw Natasha watching us from the rearview mirror. Richard was right, we couldn't trust anyone.

"Fine," I huffed, "but you get to buy me breakfast."

He laughed and sat back in his seat. We were both quiet the rest of the way, and I was glad when it was over. I kept looking around, making sure no other cars were following us, but I didn't see anything. When we got out at the airport, Natasha pulled me aside.

"You need to be careful," she hissed at me. I looked at her in surprise, she barely ever spoke to me.

"The Pulhu are still watching you," she said quietly. I could barely hear her. She turned and walked away so fast that I almost stumbled forward since I had been leaning in to hear her.

I looked at Richard, but he didn't appear to notice what happened. I knew Natasha didn't like me, so I wasn't sure why she was warning me. Besides, I didn't see anyone follow us. I didn't think they could possibly know I was leaving school. I looked one last time at Natasha getting in the car. She didn't even look up at me as she drove away.

I debated if I should tell Richard, but I decided against it. We made our way closer to my gate before stopping and grabbing breakfast. While we waited for our food, I saw Richard looking around.

"What's wrong?" I asked him.

"Nothing. I want to make sure no one followed us or recognizes you. This is one of the worst parts of your trip."

"We are at the airport. I can't imagine someone would try to take me from here. Did you see all the security?"

"Yes, and I'm sure Mrs. Sullivan has people here keeping an eye on you too."

"See, we don't have anything to worry about."

Richard still looked skeptical. Once we finished, we sat down at my gate to wait. We only had another hour until boarding, and other people were starting to fill up the seats. I looked at all the people waiting but didn't see anyone watching me.

Suddenly, Richard reached out for me and hissed, "Put your head down."

I did as he said and pretended to be reading something on my phone so I could keep my head down for a while. I let my hair fall slightly over my face, trying to hide it. "What's wrong?"

"One of the Weetwoods is here. I think it's Sasha's mom or her aunt. I'm not sure, but I don't want her recognizing you."

"Is she getting on this plane?"

"I don't think so. It looks like she is waiting at the gate across from us, but she doesn't have any luggage."

"Maybe she is meeting someone here."

"Who would she be meeting?"

"No idea. I would assume a kid since she is at the gate. I didn't think you could get past security unless you had a ticket or were getting a child off of a plane."

"It's the Weetwoods. If she wants to be in here, she will be, with or without a ticket."

We fell silent as we watched her out of the corner of our eyes. She wasn't paying any attention to us, and I started to relax. Right before my plane boarded, another plane pulled in to the gate where Mrs. Weetwood was. I hung toward the back of the line so I could see who she was waiting for. Richard stayed near me and walked up in line with me.

As we crept closer to the flight attendant, I finally saw Mrs. Weetwood greeting somebody. I didn't have a clue who it was. It was a tall man dressed in a suit with a tie and briefcase. When I looked at him, alarms rang in my head. This man was scary. He started to turn toward me, and Richard grabbed my arm.

"Calm down, Sally. I can almost feel how scared you are. What's wrong?"

"I don't know. That man with her, do you know him? Something about him terrifies me."

"I think I recognize him from somewhere, but I can't remember where."

I turned away from them, holding my phone up as if I was taking a selfie, but instead took a picture of the man. As I snapped the photo, he looked up at me. He couldn't see my face since I was facing away from him, but I was sure he knew it was me.

"Sally, you have to go. There's barely anyone left here. You need to get on the plane before they notice you."

"Ok," I said shakily.

Richard put his arm around me and gave me a hug. "Don't worry, I don't think they saw us."

I hugged him back and turned to hand the flight attendant my ticket. When I looked back, Mrs. Weetwood and the man were gone.

"Ms. Abeneb, you need to board the flight now," the flight attendant said, bringing my attention back to her.

"Bye, Sally, see you soon," Richard called as I boarded.

I hoped he was right. I put my luggage in the overhead bin and took my seat, trying not to think of everything that could go wrong. I pulled out my phone to look at the picture and try to figure out who the man was. As soon as I pulled it up, a gasp escaped me. The man was looking at the camera and winking. He definitely knew who I was.

He had a thin, gaunt face, and his eyes were such a dark brown they looked black. His lips were set in a cruel smile, and I hoped I never had to see him in person again. What could Mrs. Weetwood be doing with this man, and how did they disappear so fast?

"Are you ok, miss?" asked the old man sitting next to me.

"I'm fine," I told him. "I'm not used to flying."

The man smiled at me before putting out his hand. "I'm Chet. I've been on this flight a dozen times. I've never had a problem before. Why are you headed to Ireland?"

I looked at him closely, remembering Richard telling me to be more careful. This man seemed like a good person. He had blue eyes that seemed to sparkle when he laughed and a great big smile. He looked like the perfect grandpa.

"I'm Sally. I'm heading to see my family for the holiday."

"That sounds like it will be fun. Do you have any plans while you are visiting?"

"Not that I know of." I didn't want to give him too much information about me to be safe.

"You're going to love it. There's so much to do and see." We spent the next couple of hours talking about all the different sights in Ireland before my eyes started drooping.

"I can see I've talked your ear off, and you're about to fall asleep," he said.

I assured him I was enjoying our conversation, but he insisted on letting me rest for a while. He said he could use the rest too, so I put in my headphones and started watching the movies I downloaded on my phone. Eventually, I fell asleep, and when I woke up, we were descending. I looked over and saw that Chet was still sleeping. I reached over to gently shake him awake.

"We're here," I told him when he finally opened his eyes.

"Time for me to get to work then."

"What do you do?" I asked him. I forgot to ask earlier.

"I study ancient cultures."

"You're an archaeologist?"

"Yes, but I don't go out to sites that often anymore. It gets too tiring."

"Why are you headed to Ireland?" I was excited to find out. I loved learning about ancient history.

"That's where I work. I have a place in Castlebar that I work from most of the year."

"Oh," I said, disappointed. I was hoping there was a site he was going to.

"Don't be disappointed. Why don't you come to my shop? I will show you what I have been working on in the area."

"Really?"

"Of course. I can tell you like history, and I love to encourage young adults to learn. Here's my card. It has the address of the shop on it. I'm usually there until three every day, but if not, ask for Tad. He'll know where I am and can send a message to me. I'll tell him to keep an eye out for you."

"That's awesome, Chet. Thank you," I said, excited. I hoped I would have time to go visit his shop.

The plane pulled up to our gate, and we both stood up to grab our things and get off. I turned around as we got off the plane, shook hands with Chet, and thanked him one more time before saying goodbye. He headed toward the baggage claim while I headed straight toward the pickup area. Someone was supposed to be meeting me there.

As I stepped outside into the darkness, I realized I forgot about the time change. I checked my phone to see what the time was in Ireland and was shocked to see it was the middle of the night. I turned and saw my mom and dad standing in front of a black car waiting for me. As soon as they saw me, they ran forward, throwing their arms around me and giving me lots of kisses.

"Ok, ok," I said, laughing. "I missed you guys too."

"We haven't seen you in forever," my mom said. "I think you've gotten taller."

"I don't know, Mom," I said, standing next to her. "We were about the same height last time I saw you."

She laughed. "I keep picturing you as my little girl. I forget how old you are. You are almost an adult now."

"I've still got a while before I'm eighteen, Mom. I haven't been away from you for that long." We laughed, and she gave me another hug.

"Let's get in the car, and we can talk more," my dad said, smiling. "We have lots to catch up on." When we got in the car, I saw that someone else was driving. He turned around to shake my hand.

"Sally, this is Gary. He's going to be hanging out with us while you're here," my dad said.

"It's nice to meet you," I said to him.

"You too. Let me know when you want to go somewhere, and I will take you."

"Thanks." I turned back to my parents. "Is this normal for you? Do you have someone keeping an eye on you all the time?"

"No, I think they are upping the protection since you are here."

"I wish we didn't have to worry. I'm sorry, Mom and Dad."

"There's no reason to be sorry. None of this is your fault. There are some bad people that want you. I'm glad we have people like Gary to help protect you."

I looked at my parents and smiled. "I'm so glad I'm here," I told them.

"We are too, honey," my mom said. "Now, let's get back to the haven."

We spent the ride talking about what was going on in my life and some of the new stuff I was learning. It would only put my parents in more danger if they knew too much about me, so I skipped past a lot of stuff. I asked them about their new jobs, and they both seemed delighted to be living and working in Ireland.

When we pulled up to the haven, my eyes widened in surprise. It was a beautiful castle. It even had three towers. I couldn't wait to go explore it when the sun came up. As soon as we got out of the car, an older gentleman walked down the stairs to greet us. "Mr. and Mrs. Abeneb, how wonderful to see that you made it back safely. And Sally, we have heard so much about you. How are you?"

"I'm good." I wasn't sure what to say.

Dad stepped in. "Sally, this is Mr. Ruter. He's the head of the haven."

"Nice to meet you, Mr. Ruter," I said to him.

"It's nice to meet you too. Come in, come in, don't let me get in your way. I'm sure you would love to do some exploring with your parents. Everyone wants to see the castle the first time they come here. Be careful, and please stay on haven grounds unless you let me or one of the staff know first."

"Yes, Mr. Ruter. I will," I called to him as we walked inside. I was surprised that he was still up, considering the time here.

The inside was as impressive as I expected it to be. It definitely still looked like a castle inside but with a lot of modern touches.

"You get to live here?" I asked my mom.

"Yes. There's plenty of space. The adults and guests are on the south side, and the kids are on the north side. We don't go over to that side very often. There's no reason, so I'm not sure if there's anything over there you would want to see. Most of the adults stay over here or in the towers."

"This place is awesome." My parents continued showing me around until we went to the second floor, and they stopped in front of a room.

"This is your room," Mom said.

"Where is yours?" I asked, not wanting to be far from them.

"We are on the third floor," Mom said, "but don't worry, it's a quick walk to get there. This is the key to your room, it will also give you access to other parts of the castle."

I looked around the room before going to the couch and sitting down.

"These are big rooms," I told my parents.

"I know, but you get used to them pretty fast," Mom laughed.

It made me so happy to see her and Dad laughing and relaxed. I was worried they were miserable here. It made me feel better knowing they weren't. I started putting my stuff into the dresser while I talked to my parents. Once I was done, they showed me how to get to their room, and then walked me back to my room.

"Get some sleep. We have a big day tomorrow," Dad said.

"What are we doing?"

"It's a surprise. You need to get some rest now. We do too."

"Ok," I said. "Thanks for staying up with me."

"I wouldn't have been able to sleep until we talked for a while anyway," Mom said as she gave me a hug goodnight. Dad gave me a hug too, and they both left.

I wasn't sure I could sleep yet, so I walked around the room. Doors led out onto a balcony, and I pushed them open and stepped outside. It was a bit chilly but beautiful. I could see more stars than I ever had before. I wished on the first one I saw. I wanted my mom and dad to stay safe. After a few minutes, I walked back inside and shut the doors. I grabbed a blanket and my phone and curled up in the chair to read a book. When I started to get sleepy, I crawled into the bed.

I woke up and took a shower before heading to my parent's room. I couldn't wait to find out what surprise they had set up for the day. I knocked on their door and waited for them to open it. When they did, I gave them big hugs.

"What are we doing today?"

"It's a surprise," Dad said.

"But I want to know. Maybe a little hint?"

"No hints. You'll see soon. First, we need to let Gary know we are ready." Dad grabbed his phone and sent a text to Gary.

"He should be here in a few minutes. Let's head down to the entrance."

As we walked down, I saw a lot of people coming out of their rooms and hurrying through the halls. No one gave me a second look, which I was grateful for. I still hadn't gotten the creepy man from the airport out of my head. I was worried he would send people here to try and take me.

Gary pulled up in another black car, and we got inside.

"Hi, everyone," Gary greeted us.

"Hi, Gary," we all replied.

"Where should we start?"

"Let's start with breakfast at Annie's. She has the best waffles, and Sally loves waffles."

"Sounds good. We should be there in about twenty minutes if traffic isn't too bad."

Breakfast at Annie's was spectacular, and she really did have the best waffles. My dad knew me well. I was stuffed when we got back in the car.

"Where now?" I asked.

"Gary knows where we are going, but it's going to be a long trip."

"That's ok, we will have plenty of time to catch up."

We spent the entire drive talking about all the different things they were learning and how much fun they were having discovering new things. They were happy when I told them about my friends and how glad I was to have met them. I didn't tell them any of the bad things. I didn't want them to worry about me. Gary pulled the car over, and we got out.

"We have a short walk, and then we are there," Dad said.

We walked down a small path, and I saw where they had taken me. We were at the Cliffs of Moher.

"I remember how much you always wanted to go see them," Mom said. "I figured this was the perfect time."

"Thanks, Mom." I threw my arms around her and then ran up the path to stand as close to the edge as I dared. I could barely breathe, looking out at the beauty surrounding me. I always wanted to come here. I was glad I got to see this with my family. I smiled as they walked up and put their arms around me. This was the best surprise ever. We spent the rest of the afternoon walking along the cliffs and relaxing like a normal family. Eventually, my parents dragged me back to the car to go get dinner and head back to the haven.

CHAPTER FIFTEEN

Christmas morning came quickly, and I wasn't surprised when my mom and dad dragged me over to their tree to give me presents. Since I couldn't leave the school, I didn't have anything to give them.

"I want to try to make you something," I told them. "Do you want to watch?"

"Of course we do, but you don't have to give us anything," Mom said.

"I want to," I told them. "As soon as I have the right stuff, I will try it."

"Whatever makes you happy," Dad said.

It ended up being a fantastic day. We spent the whole day relaxing and filling ourselves with delicious food that my mom made. I hadn't felt so relaxed since before I learned I was an elemental.

We didn't get to see any other cool sites the next day, but I loved walking through the gardens around the haven. Sometimes I would catch my mom or dad looking at me strangely, trying to figure out the new me, but then they would smile, and I knew everything was ok between us. I didn't realize what a stress it was not seeing them while I was learning about magic.

A few days later, I was walking around the haven, waiting for my parents to come down when someone grabbed me from behind. As I reached up to try to hit them, a familiar voice spoke. "Hey, Sally, did you miss me? I know you must have." Tider laughed before releasing me.

"Really, Tider?" I scowled at him. "I could have hurt you."

"Nah, you would never hurt me," he said, dancing away as I took another halfhearted swing at him. Finally, I burst out laughing. "You know it's only been a few days since I saw you, right?"

"It's been forever. You should be missing me terribly."

I laughed again. "I did miss you, Tider." He smiled triumphantly at me. "I missed you like a big sister misses her little brother, so really not that much."

I laughed as his triumphant look fell. "Honestly, though, you know I missed you," I said, throwing my arm around him and ruffling his hair.

He pulled away from me, but not before I saw his big goofy grin. I couldn't wait for him to meet my mom and dad. They would love him too. I heard a quiet laugh behind us. I spun around and saw Richard leaning against the wall. When I looked at him, he straightened up and walked over to give me a hug.

"Hi, Sally," he said. "What have you been up to?"

"Hi, Richard. I have been hanging out with my parents. I waited for you to get here like I promised."

"So, what's the plan?" Richard asked.

"Yeah, when are we sneaking out of here to look around?"

"Not yet," I said. "I figure we can get a ride to the bay where I think we need to look and check things out before we go sneaking around. It will be faster if we have someone from the haven drive us than if we try to sneak through the woods by ourselves."

"I think that's a great plan," said Tider. "When can we leave?"

"I don't know. I have to ask my parents first. I wasn't sure when you were coming, so I have plans with them. Maybe we can change them a little, and you two can come with us."

We talked about their trip for a few more minutes before my parents walked in.

I gave them a big hug and turned to introduce them to my friends. "Mom and Dad, this is Tider and Richard. I've told you about them."

"Hi, Tider," Dad shook his hand. "How are you doing?"

"I'm doing good," Tider said.

"How are you, Richard?" Mom asked. "We've heard a lot about you too."

"I'm good, Mrs. Abeneb," he said politely. Dad walked up and gave him a firm handshake.

"Thanks for helping Sally out with everything she's learning." He looked at Tider and Richard. "Both of you. It's good to know that she has good friends who are there for her. If you boys ever need anything, just ask. If we can do it, we will."

Dad stepped away from them as he cleared his throat and walked over to me. "Since your friends are here, we can reschedule our plans for today. I'm sure you would love to show them around."

"We were going to see if we could go to Annagh bay. We learned about it in school."

"Of course. Let me call Gary for you."

"Don't you want to come too, Dad?"

"Oh no, honey, you guys go ahead. Your mother and I will spend a nice day relaxing until you get back. Then we can all grab dinner."

"If you're sure," I said. I wanted to spend more time with them, but if they came, they might get suspicious and not let me leave the haven.

"Of course we are," Mom told me. "Go have fun with your friends. There will be plenty of time to talk later."

"Thanks, Mom and Dad."

"It was good to meet you, boys. We will see you all for dinner," Mom said.

"Gary will be here in a few minutes. I let him know where you wanted to go. Don't be too late and listen to Gary," Dad told us.

"Ok, Dad, I love you guys," I said as they headed down a different hallway.

Gary got there a few minutes later, and we all piled into the car. We were pretty silent the whole way there since no one wanted to say anything in front of Gary.

"When someone goes out of the haven, do they always get protection?" I asked Gary when I couldn't take the silence anymore.

"No. Very few people need protection. The key members of the haven have security, and your parents have protection to a lesser degree, but that's about it. Occasionally, we will be called for security for someone else at the haven, but it's usually only for a day or two."

Gary took us as close as possible to the bay before pulling to the side and parking. "We will have to go on foot from here."

Gary walked to a small path that led up into the hills. "Make sure you stay on the path," he warned. "I don't want anyone slipping and falling."

We followed him single file along the overgrown path. I was so distracted by the sights that I didn't see the loose rock until it was too late. I tripped and fell into Tider's back. Richard reached out and grabbed my pack to keep me from falling over, but Tider ended up sprawled on the ground.

"Sally," he said, turning toward me. "What happened?" Both Richard and Gary looked at me too.

"I tripped on a rock," I said, my face turning red. "I'm sorry I knocked you over."

He laughed. "It's ok. Try to pay attention to what's around you this time."

"I will." Gary and Tider turned back around and headed up the path.

"Are you sure you're ok?" Richard asked.

"Yeah, I wasn't paying attention. It's so beautiful here."

"It is, but remember what we are doing. We have to be careful, Sally. Especially if that guy at the airport knew you. The Pulhu could easily know where you are."

I swallowed dryly. "I know, I'm paying attention now." Every time I thought of that man, my skin crawled.

I watched the area around me, making sure no one followed us. I didn't see anything and began to relax as we stepped to the top of a hill. When I looked out, I couldn't believe my eyes. We made it. Sitting below us was a small lake that was separated from the ocean by a narrow stretch of land.

We still had a small hike to get down to the beach, but I didn't care. We walked down to the lake with no more falls and stopped to have a small snack. As I walked around the lake, I could feel magic thrumming in the air. I knew we were in the right place. Everything I read said we would need to find a cave underwater to get in. I turned and headed for the beach, the guys following me. As I walked the shoreline, I kicked a few pebbles into the bay. I reached down and filled a small plastic container I brought with sand.

I came prepared and started to take my shirt off. I had a bathing suit underneath so I could go into the ocean and start searching.

"Sally, what are you doing?" asked Gary running up to me.

"Going for a swim," I told him calmly.

"You can't go for a swim now. It's too cold, and this area can be dangerous for swimming."

"It's ok, Gary. That's why we have magic, right?"

"I'm sure we can make a fire when we get done, so we don't freeze. Look how beautiful it is. The sun is shining, there aren't any clouds, and the waters are calm. Come on, we just want to go swimming for a little while. I promise we will be careful, and we'll stay close to each other."

"Fine, but you have to stay where I can see you. Understood?" Gary didn't look happy, but he didn't fight us either.

"Thanks, Gary."

I quickly walked into the ocean before he could change his mind. The temperature stole my breath away. Now that I was in the water, I could feel magic swirling around me. It was part of the waves, and it confirmed that this area was magically protected in some way.

I wasn't sure where to begin, so I dived in the rest of the way and opened my eyes. Everything looked a bit distorted underwater, and my eyes stung from the salt. I swam farther. I needed to be able to get far enough out that there could be a cave beneath us. After searching for twenty minutes, I realized this could take a lot longer than I thought. I looked at the beach and saw Gary waving at us.

"Richard, can you head in, see what Gary wants and keep him occupied? I'm going to use my water magic to move faster in the water so I can check a bigger area. Tider can do the same in the opposite direction."

"No problem, but be careful out here. The Pulhu might not be around, but this current is pretty strong."

"We will."

Richard headed toward shore, and I nodded at Tider. We both took a deep breath and went under. I called my magic to me and forced it to create a small wave around my feet to push me forward. I also made sure it flowed easily away from me, so it wouldn't blur my vision. I moved farther up the coast looking for any signs of a cave but found nothing. The water was starting to get more powerful the farther I went, but I didn't want to stop.

I used a little bit of air magic to make a bubble of air for me to breath and continued forward. Soon the water was pulling at me from all directions, but I still didn't find anything. After a few more minutes, I finally came to the surface. I swam farther than I intended. I could barely see Richard and Gary waving at me. I headed in, and Gary told us it was time to head back if we wanted to be at the haven in time for dinner. I was so focused on finding the cave, I didn't realize how much time passed.

When we got back, we each went to our rooms to change and met back at my parent's room.

"We made a big dinner since we figured your friends would be with you," Mom said. I looked around their room again. It was easily twice as big as mine, and theirs had a little kitchen and dining area. It was more like an apartment than a room.

We sat at the table and waited for Mom to bring the food in. I tried to help her, but she wouldn't let me, so I sat down and listened to Dad, Richard, and Tider talk. I was surprised to hear them talking about some sort of sport that was played in the magical community. I had no idea what it was, but they all seemed excited by it.

The more I listened, the more it sounded similar to the practicals we had to do at school. I wasn't sure that would be much fun, but I didn't interrupt them to say anything. I enjoyed watching my dad talk to them about magic. Even if he didn't have any, he was still learning a lot about it.

After dinner, I pulled the jar of sand out of my backpack and put it next to the fireplace.

"I'm going to try to make your gift now," I told my parents. "Make sure I don't light the whole place on fire," I told Tider and Richard. I was a little nervous about using magic in front of my parents, but I really wanted to see their reactions.

I sat down and started a fire in the fireplace, willing it to get hotter and hotter but not too big. Once it was hot enough, I emptied the sand out and used air to scoop it up and hold it over the fire. It immediately started to melt, and I continued using air to form the shape of a glass ball with the melted sand. Once it was as good as I could get it, I let the fire die but kept the glass ball in the air so it would cool. I grabbed it and turned to my parents once it was cool.

"Here, this is for you, for Christmas. Now you have something that I made for you with my new powers," I said, smiling at them.

At first, they just stared at me. Then my mom rushed forward to give me a giant hug. My dad was right behind her.

"We are so proud of you, Sally. Instead of being upset about all the changes in your life, you are embracing them and trying to do your very best. This is the most beautiful thing I have ever seen. We will put it right here on the mantle so we can see it every day," my mom said.

"Thanks, Mom," I said, "but you can't tell anyone I made it. No one knows I have this magic."

"We won't, Sally," my dad assured me.

I was exhausted after making their gift, and Tider and Richard could tell. They told my parents we were all tired from the hike, and we quickly said our goodbyes. I made plans to meet Richard and Tider the next morning, and my parents said they would see us at dinner again. Dad would let Gary know to pick us up around nine, so we could go sightseeing.

In the morning, we got in Gary's car and headed back toward the bay, looking for signs of anyone following us. We didn't see anything, and soon Gary was parking. I was still tired from yesterday, but I grabbed my bag and started the hike right away. I wanted as much time as possible at the bay.

We knew the way, so the hike went much faster and easier. I stopped at the lake again and couldn't help but be stunned by its beauty. I could almost feel the magic of the bay here at the lake. I went to dip my hand in, but a noise pulled my attention away. Richard was staring out at the ocean, and I turned to see what was bothering him. At the shore, a group of friends were playing soccer and running up and down the beach. Two golden retrievers ran with them.

"Shoot," I said. It would be hard to search for the entrance with them watching. I wouldn't be able to use my magic, and I didn't think I could get deep enough without it.

"What do we do?" whispered Tider, making sure Gary didn't hear.

"I'm not sure. I guess we will have to try to search without magic and hope they leave soon."

"Ok." He didn't look convinced.

Richard walked back to us. "We can try to get them to leave. I can use my magic to make it a little windy, maybe that will work."

Richard raised his hands slightly, and a breeze slid past me. Slowly Richard's power built up, and the breeze turned into light gusts of wind. I watched as one of the boys on the beach chased after his hat that the wind had stolen.

Quickly they packed up their things and headed up the hill toward us.

We watched until they were out of sight, and Richard let the wind die down.

"Why are you trying to get them to leave?" Gary questioned us.

"We want a little peace and quiet. I would rather not have a bunch of other people around either, in case the Pulhu do find me here. Those other kids shouldn't be caught up in it. They could get hurt."

"I hope the Pulhu don't come after you here," Gary said. He looked out at the bay and then started walking toward the ruins.

"We are going swimming again," I told Gary.

He frowned. "I thought you might want to go look at the ruins this time since we didn't have a chance yesterday."

"I do, but I don't get much of a chance to swim anymore, so I want to swim first."

"Tomorrow, if you want to go swimming, there is a beach much closer, or you can use the pool. It's heated. The water in the bay at this time of year is freezing."

"I know, but it's invigorating. You should try it sometime."

"I think I'll pass. I think the three of you are a little crazy."

We laughed and jumped into the water. I swam quickly toward the area I was searching yesterday and dived down, using my magic to look for the entrance. Tider explored the other side, but after an hour we still hadn't found anything. Richard searched the center but gave up and headed toward shore. Tider and I followed shortly after. Richard grabbed a towel for me to dry off and started a fire again, but I was so disappointed I barely even noticed the cold. We searched everywhere and still hadn't found it. I looked at my friends and shook my head.

"I think it's time to head back."

"I thought you wanted to see the ruins?" Gary said.

"Oh yeah, as soon as we dry off," I told him. I didn't want him getting suspicious, and I really did want to see the ruins.

Gary pointed toward the ruins. "These settlements have been here a long time. They are from regular nonmagical people, but long before them, this area was filled with elementals. We don't know why they left, but you can feel their magic. Many people have searched the area for any sign of them, but there is nothing left standing. There isn't a single building left that they made. Not even any ruins. It's one of the greatest mysteries of this place."

As we got closer, I could feel the magic. It was a small tingling across my skin. After we looked through the ruins, we walked back to the car and drove toward the haven. When we got back, we each went to our separate rooms to relax before dinner. I hadn't made it more than a step into my room before I heard my name being called from across the hall. I turned and couldn't stop my grin. "Abby, what are you doing here? I thought you were spending the holiday with your dad."

Abby looked down. "Change of plans," she said.

She didn't raise her head right away, which worried me. I grabbed her hand and dragged her toward the chair in my room.

"What's wrong?" I asked her. "What happened?"

"The Pulhu. They wanted information about you," she whispered, "I'm sorry. I had to tell them, or they would have hurt me." She started to cry.

"It's ok, Abby. As long as you didn't get hurt. We can deal with whatever they know."

"I didn't tell them everything. Just where you are, which they already knew, but they wanted confirmation. And that your control over air is very good. They didn't ask about anything else, so I didn't say anything," she said, sniffling.

"Don't worry, Abby. We'll get the jerks that did this to you. Do you know who they were?"

"Yeah, Mr. Damon was the one who had me questioned. I don't know much about him except he's near the top of the Pulhu, and he's terrifying."

"How did they get you? I thought you were with your dad."

"I was. Sean and his mother helped. You know how Dad is around her. This time I think they went too far. Dad seems to know something is wrong. That's why we are here. He doesn't really remember them taking me, but he said he has some blurry images. He's worried, so he brought me here, and he came too. He's not seeing her anymore until he figures out what is wrong. The council is going to try to help him. They said it's a spell, but they don't know how to fix it."

"It's going to be all right, Abby. We will find a way for them to fix your dad. As long as he is here, you will be safe."

"That's just it, Sally. We won't be safe. I told them you are here, so they will come for you, and me and Dad too." She started sobbing. I felt my heart clench and knew that I needed to help her. All of this was because the Pulhu wanted me, and I didn't know how to fix it.

"I'm sorry, Abby. This is my fault," I started to say.

Abby cut in. "This isn't your fault. This is because of the Pulhu and their power-hungry leaders. You did nothing wrong, and you certainly don't deserve everything you've been through. You can't take the blame for this, Sally."

I knew she was right, but I still shook my head. I didn't like that they were willing to hurt my friends.

"We need Tider and Richard here. They need to know what's going on."

"They're here?" she asked.

"Yes. They came to keep an eye on me and to help out."

Her eyes suddenly got brighter. "Did you find it? Can we go there? Does anyone still live there?"

"Slow down, Abbs. We haven't found it yet. I'm positive it's at the beach where we have been looking, but we can't find the entrance. We have searched everywhere." My shoulders slumped.

"We'll figure it out. We still have a week until we need to head back to school."

"You're right," I said. "Let's go find the guys and head to my parents. We are meeting them for dinner if you want to join us."

"Of course I do. I'm not sure I want to spend much time around my dad right now," she said, a shadow crossing her eyes. I wished I could take that look away. Maybe a day out tomorrow would be good. I would have to talk to Gary.

Tider and Richard were surprised to see Abby at dinner and asked a ton of questions about why she was here, but she was reluctant to tell them.

Eventually, they stopped asking, but they knew something was wrong. Tider pulled me aside at one point to ask what happened, but I told him she would tell him when she was ready. After that, we enjoyed the rest of the evening and decided to call it a night after dinner. We agreed to meet up first thing in the morning to go out again.

CHAPTER SIXTEEN

"Can we go to town today?" I asked Gary the next morning. "There's someone I want to see."

I told them about the man I met on the plane and how he knew a lot about archaeological sights. "It's something I'm really interested in if you guys don't mind going."

I was also hoping that he might have an old book or document that could help us out. Archaeologists always had old stuff, and he might have a lot of old stuff from this area. There had to be something. I was sure it was at that beach.

"I'm ok with it," Richard said.

"Me too. I wouldn't mind going into town for a little bit," said Tider.

"Same here," said Abby.

"That's not a problem. I know exactly where that is," said Gary, "but you have to do what I tell you. If anything bad happens, we can't use a lot of magic. There are regular people in town, and we don't want them knowing about us."

"Ok," we all agreed.

As we were driving, I noticed Gary looking at his mirror a lot and questioned him. "What's going on? You seem a little jumpy."

"I want to be extra careful. I thought I saw someone following us, but they turned off, and I haven't seen anything else for a while now."

Gary pulled into town and parked right outside of a shop called Ancient Beginnings. We all walked inside the shop. It was crammed with boxes and shelves pushed up against every wall. There wasn't an inch of unused space in the place. In the center were scrolls, pots, cloth, and even little fragments of bone. I gave a quick shudder.

"I'll be right up to help you," called a voice from the back of the shop.

I looked around at everything while we waited for him to come up front.

I was looking for maps or books when he finally came out to greet us.

"Hi," he said. "Sally, you came, and you brought friends." He smiled at me. "I hope they are as interested as you are in ancient things."

"Maybe not as much," I said, smiling back at him. "It's great to see you again."

"You too. Why don't I make a pot of tea for everyone, and you can tell me what you are looking for?"

"I'm going to wait out front and keep an eye on things," Gary said, moving toward the door after checking around the shop to make sure we were alone.

"Ok," I told him.

Chet ushered us into the back room where a couch and a few comfy chairs sat around a coffee table. He put out cups for everyone to use and poured steaming water in them. Once everyone was seated with a cup of tea in their hands, he looked at me. "What are you looking for? I can tell that you aren't here to talk about what I'm researching."

I squirmed in my chair. I didn't know how to ask for information on the entrance to the water elementals palace without sounding like an idiot. "I'm not really sure, I'm looking for information on a myth."

"Sounds like an interesting story goes with this request."

"Not really," I said, trying to sound like this was a normal everyday thing for me.

He laughed and then raised his hand, fire encircling his whole arm. He met my eyes before letting the fire die. "I know what you are, and I'm here to help you if you let me. I have a feeling I know who you are and what you want already, but I need to be sure first."

I jumped up and started looking around panicked. Why had this man invited me here, was he part of the Pulhu? Were they coming to get me right now? My friends jumped up too, and each had their hands out, ready to do battle with whatever came at us.

"Calm down, children. I can see that you have had some troubles along the way and are scared of me. It's ok. I'm not planning on hurting you, though I do have a favor to ask if you are the ones I'm thinking of."

When nothing else happened after a minute, I started to relax and lower my hands. "How do you know who I am?"

"I know only your first name from the plane, Sally. I think I know what you are because a few months ago I went to a seer and she told me that this day would come. She said a young lady would come to my door in Ireland with a group of friends asking for help in finding a lost palace. If I could help her, I would find my grandson again. I have spent every extra minute of my time learning about every lost city, especially in this area, waiting for this moment."

We all looked on in stunned silence.

"I really am sorry I scared you. I just want to find my grandson, and I was so excited that you were here."

I took a deep breath and then released it. Everything this man said seemed genuine. I looked at Tider, and he nodded his head. Chet wasn't lying. We needed his help, and he thought we could help him too. I didn't know how, but we would do our best.

"I am looking for a lost palace," I told him. "I'm pretty sure I know where it is, but I can't get in."

"Are you talking about the water elementals?"

"Yes," I responded, excited that he knew what I needed.

"It's at Annagh bay," he told me. My heart dropped. I already knew that.

"Yes, but where? I can't find the entrance anywhere, and we have looked. There is no cave or door, or even a ledge to swim onto to check."

"Have you looked in the lake?"

"The lake?" I repeated.

"Yes, in the lake." He got up and pulled a book down from a shelf. "Here," he said, rifling through the pages. "This is an ancient book that someone wrote about the city. The information was passed down from father to son after the shadow king forbid the elementals from communicating with humans. The humans hoped that they would one day go back to the palace, and they didn't want to forget where it was, so they made up stories about it."

"Why isn't this in any of the books I read?" I asked.

"Only a few books were written about this, and they were kept secret. They feared the shadow king would find out and destroy them. The book says you have to go through the lake next to the bay to access the door. A special key was worn by any who wanted to enter."

"A key? Where would I get a key? I don't even know what it looks like?"

"I think I can help you there," Chet said, grinning at me. "Try this. I found two of them when I was up there last time." He handed me a bracelet with a small Celtic knot on it. "My grandson took the other one. Hopefully, you can save him."

That brought me back to reality quickly. "What do you mean, I can save your grandson? Where is he?"

"He is in the water elemental palace. At least I think he is."

"Why do you think that? They aren't allowed to have contact with any humans. Why would they have your grandson?"

"I sent him out there to investigate that area about six months ago. I heard some rumors about the ancient site, and he was helping me with my work. He went out there many times, always bringing back a small trinket that made me believe there was more. One day he didn't come back. I went up to look for him, but every trace of him was gone. Even his clothes and pack had disappeared. I searched for him and even told the council, hoping they could help. They put some of their best trackers on it but found nothing. Finally, they said he may have run away."

"Did he run away?"

"No. He wouldn't leave me without a word. He was planning on taking over the business." Chet had tears in his eyes. "I know something happened to him. They must have found him and done something. He's a fire elemental after all, and fire and water don't mix well. They were always fighting back then, so they may not like one sneaking into their palace."

"Wouldn't he have told you before going in?"

"No. Whenever he brought up doing something dangerous, I would tell him to leave it. It's not worth it if it risked his life, but he is a teenager. He didn't always listen to me. He may have done it thinking he could ask for forgiveness later. Please, if you're going in, can you look for him. Find out what happened?"

"Of course we will look for him. If he is in there, we will find him."

"Thank you so much," said Chet. "Here's a picture of what he looks like. I can't imagine they have many people locked up down there, but just in case." I looked at the photo and put it in my pocket.

"I will do my best."

Chet got tears in his eyes again, but blinked them away and shook his head. "Back to business. There is so much you don't know about the elementals. Their palaces and castles move on a different time than ours. When you go into one, time changes. I'm not sure how. It is something I read a long time ago. I don't know if it goes faster there or slower. I guess you will have to figure that part out."

The door crashed open, and Gary ran inside. "We need to leave. The Pulhu have found you. One of my people, Macie, is trying to stop them, but without being able to use much magic, she isn't going to be able to hold them off for long."

"Come quickly," Chet said. "There is a tunnel that runs all the way to the edge of town. You can use it. I have magical shields that will keep them from getting into this tunnel for a long time. You should be able to make it through the tunnel safely, but then you are on your own. I don't have anything else that will help you."

Someone barged in and yelled, "Hurry, they are almost here. I used a freeze spell on them in the alleyway. Hopefully, no one will notice, but they are already starting to move. We only have a few minutes."

Chet pulled a bookcase away from the wall, and we all stared inside. It was almost pitch black. He handed me a flashlight. "Try not to use your magic, so they can't find you if they have a tracker." We all walked into the tunnel, but Chet grabbed my hand and pushed it onto a flat rock. As soon as he let go of my hand, I grabbed the bookcase to stop it from closing.

"Aren't you coming?" I asked him.

"No, I'm too old to run from them. I'll wait for them and tell them you hightailed it out of here when that girl came in yelling about you being attacked."

"But."

"No buts. I'll be fine. I won't tell them anything about what you were doing here. Now, get on your way."

"Thanks again, Chet," I said quietly as he shut the bookcase the rest of the way. Everyone was waiting for me, so I turned the flashlight on and started walking. "I guess we should follow the tunnel," I said as we walked. It was too dark to run, so a quick walk was the best we could manage.

"What happened, Macie?" Gary asked.

"The Pulhu showed up," she huffed. "They really want you."

"How did they know where I was?" I asked. "We didn't tell anyone where we were going."

"What about you, Macie? Did you tell anyone?" Tider aimed the flashlight toward her.

"No, I didn't call the Pulhu on you," she sneered, but something in her voice made me pause.

"That's not what he asked. Did you tell anyone where we would be today?"

When she didn't answer right away, Gary grabbed her. "Macie? What did you do?"

"I didn't do anything. I'm sure they followed you."

"They may have, but tell me what you're hiding," Gary growled. I didn't ever want to get on his bad side.

"I told my boyfriend we would be in town."

"What boyfriend?" he asked. "I've known you forever and thought you would have told me if you had a boyfriend."

"We haven't been together long, and we are keeping it a secret," she said, glaring at him.

My stomach sank even more. "Which one of you wanted to keep it a secret?" I asked.

"We both did," she said.

"Really, Macie? You wanted a secret relationship that you couldn't share with your friends?" Gary asked.

"It wasn't like that. He needed to get his parents to understand. They are very old-fashioned and want him to date a girl that will help bind another family to his."

"And that sounded ok to you?"

"He's a good guy," she said, defending her boyfriend.

"Really?" Gary turned from her. He started walking in the tunnel again. "Let's go, everyone. We have to hurry. What did you tell him, Macie?"

"Only that we were going to be at Ancient Beginnings sometime today. He likes to know where I am. He said it makes him feel better since I work a dangerous job."

"When did you meet him?"

"I don't know, probably about a month ago. We met while I was in town, getting some coffee. He was in line behind me. We started to talk, and things felt right. We even like the same things."

"Oh, Macie, you idiot, he played you. He knew exactly where you would be and when because you always do the same thing. And he could have watched you for weeks beforehand trying to figure you out so he could make sure you would like him back."

"But Sally wasn't here, so why would he do that?"

"That's around the time when she planned her trip over here. It all makes sense, Macie. You were being played."

Macie still looked skeptical.

"How would he know that Macie would be assigned to watch me?" I asked.

"If he knows anything about this haven, he would know Macie is always assigned to the most important cases with me. She has been my partner for a few years now. And I always get the most important case."

"Why did you take me then? Isn't it like babysitting?"

"Any time the Pulhu are involved, it becomes important. I'm trying to get enough evidence so the council can do something with them, but they never leave any trace behind."

"That's a good idea," I said.

"Yeah, but like I said, I can never find a trace of evidence."

We continued down the tunnel silently, each lost in their own thoughts when we finally hit a dead end.

"Where do we go from here? Did we miss a turn?"

"I think we go up. See," I said, pointing the light upward. "There is a ladder. Can one of you give me a boost up?"

"Let me go first," Gary said. "I can make sure the coast is clear."

Gary jumped up and grabbed the ladder, making his way to the top. "There's a small landing up here. Start climbing up while I try to open the door. Richard, come up last since you are the tallest. The others are going to need a boost to reach the ladder."

Richard tried to help me up, but I pushed Abby in front of me. I wanted her as far away from the Pulhu as possible. I followed Abby up the ladder and heard Gary swearing.

"I can't get the door open. It's jammed."

"Let me see," I said, taking the light from him and shining it around. I tried pushing on the door, but nothing happened. It really was stuck.

"What do we do now?" Abby asked.

"I don't know," said Gary, "but we can't go back the way we came."

"Hold on. Maybe we can use our magic to move the door."

"Let's make a hole next to the door, so we can see what is blocking it."

"Ok," Gary said. He raised his hands and pointed them to the right of the door. We watched as the earth started to fall away from a small spot in the tunnel. After a few minutes, we could see through it.

Richard looked through the hole. "I think we can get out this way. There's a boulder in front of the door, but now that we can see it, we should be able to move it."

Gary looked through the hole. "Give me a few minutes, and I will try to break it up. I need a quick rest first. I've been using a lot of energy." I looked closely at him and realized he did look a bit tired.

"You really used up all your energy?" I questioned him. "I didn't realize making the hole would be so hard."

"It wasn't that. I've been using a lot of energy since I met you and haven't had a chance to recover. Plus, I used a lot when we were at the shop. While you were inside, I caused a water line to burst at the corner of the street. I figured if the cops came to deal with traffic, it would slow the Pulhu down since Macie said they were getting close."

"Wow, I didn't realize you were using your powers so much. So you have water too?"

"No, I used earth to break the pipe. It will look like the ground shifted over time, causing the break."

"Gary," Richard interrupted. "I'm going to move the boulder. We don't have time to wait. We don't know if they are coming down the tunnel. We need to get out of here as fast as possible."

"Go ahead and try," Gary sighed, "but don't use too much energy. It will be hard to carry you out of here if you pass out."

I looked at Richard. Gary had no idea who he was dealing with. Richard was the strongest magic-user in our school, and from what I had overheard, he was one of the strongest out there. At least in air magic.

I closed my eyes and watched as Richard's magic surrounded the boulder. I felt him push the boulder away from the door with a stiff breeze. He reached out and carefully opened the door. Thankfully, there was a rock ledge above us, so the light didn't penetrate into the tunnel, but I could see some light up ahead.

"Let's go. Follow the light, it should lead us out of here. We are going to close the door back up." Quickly, everyone passed us, and once I was sure everyone was out, Richard closed the door. Right before we turned around to leave, I put my hand over the hole and used earth to close it.

We followed our friends out of the tunnel, and I blinked uncontrollably when I stepped into the light. It was so dark in the tunnel that my eyes couldn't focus now that I was outside. When I could see, I looked around, trying to figure out where we were. It looked like the tunnel led us right to the edge of a cliff. Somehow as we walked through the tunnel, it went downhill and took us deeper into the earth. We were standing at least fifty feet below the top of the cliff, and the only thing in front of us was a drop-off and water.

"There must be a way to get either up or down," I said. "I doubt Chet would have left us stranded. There must be stairs or handholds."

We started to look around, trying to find anything that looked like it would help. Finally, Abby called me over.

"I think it's here," she said.

"What is?"

"The way up, or down. I'm not really sure, but it looks like there is a palm print right here."

I remembered Chet putting my hand against a rock and quickly placed my hand on the palm print. Immediately, stairs appeared where before there was only a rock face. "How is this possible?"

"This is expensive magic. Chet must have some really good friends. Only the most powerful can do spells like these, and they charge a lot of money," Gary said.

"I'm glad he does," I said. "Otherwise, we would be stuck."

We headed up the stairs and peeked our heads over the top. As soon as I saw that the coast was clear, I walked up the last few stairs. Once we were all up, the stairs disappeared. It looked like they had never been there. "I wonder if there is a way down?" I asked, looking for another palm print.

"I don't think we have time to worry about that," Gary said.

CHAPTER SEVENTEEN

Gary was right. I could wonder about the stairs at a different time. Preferably when the Pulhu weren't chasing us.

"We need to figure out how to get back to the haven," Richard said.

"Let's walk," I said. "Or you can send Macie to town to get a car for us," I told Gary.

"Do you really trust her?" Tider asked, glaring at Macie.

"She may have made bad choices, but I don't think she tried to give me up to the Pulhu. She should be able to get a car with no problem, and this time if anyone asks, she can lie and say we are going to one of the beaches we haven't been to. Right, Macie?"

She shrugged. "I can do that."

"Call us once you have the car," Gary told her. "We'll let you know where we are."

"Ok," she said and took off toward the town.

It would take her at least an hour to get the car and get back, so we started walking.

"Do you know how far the haven is from here?" I asked Gary

"Yes. It's going to be a long walk if Macie can't get the car."

"We need to make sure she doesn't bring the Pulhu back with her," Tider said.

"Don't worry. We can leave Gary behind when she calls, and when she gets to the pickup point, he can check everything out before coming to pick us up at the real spot."

"How will you know if something's wrong?" Gary asked.

"Right before she gets there, you can call us, and we will stay on the phone with you. If things sound bad, we will run and find cover, but if everything is good, you can tell us. Or we could all go together and go on the other side of these hills when Macie is coming. You could go check it out and wave to us if everything is good."

"That could work. I would rather stay close to you in case something happens. Let's keep walking this way, and we'll see how it goes," he said. We walked down the street, but as soon as I was sure Macie couldn't see us, I darted up the hill on one side of the road and walked along the top of it.

"What are you doing?" Abby asked, racing up to me.

"We can still follow the road from up here, but if someone else comes along, we can get down on the other side of the hill so they don't see us. Plus, we can see a lot more of the road from up here," I said.

Abby waved her hands for everyone else to come up. We walked along the ridge in silence before Tider told us all to get down, someone was driving toward the town. We peeked over the hill and watched as the car drove slowly down the road.

I closed my eyes to check their magic and make sure they weren't getting ready to use it.

"I think we're good," I told everyone. "They aren't using magic."

"How can you tell?" asked Gary.

"It's an extra gift I have."

"I think there's an awful lot you aren't telling me."

"Maybe, but it's for your protection as much as mine," I told him truthfully. I hated lying, especially to people who helped me.

"One day, you are going to need to tell me the whole story." He held up a hand before I could protest. "Not now, but once all of this is over, and you don't have to worry about it."

"I can do that."

I smiled, thinking about how nice it would be not to have to hide my power.

"The Pulhu are acting differently with you. Maybe it will throw them off enough that they will screw up and leave evidence behind. Evidence that I can take to the council." I looked at him worriedly.

"If you ever take anything to the council, they will know who did it, and your life will be over. They are more powerful than you are aware of," Tider said.

"How would you know?" Gary asked.

"My family is a big part of the Pulhu. I know way more about it than you do."

"That's right. When I researched you, your family name came up. I can't believe I forgot. You are nothing like them, so it's hard to remember you are related."

"I'm a lot more like them than you realize," Tider said.

Gary looked at him silently for a minute and nodded. "Why aren't you worried about being around him?" he asked me.

"Like you said, he isn't anything like them. Tider is like a brother to me, regardless of what family he is from."

Richard walked up on my other side. "I think we have company."

We all quickly got down on the other side of the hill and peeked over. We saw a car speeding down the road, this time away from town. With how fast it was going, it was either Macie or the Pulhu looking for us. As the car sped past, I looked for a magical signature. This time I got it and wasn't surprised to see three more signatures in the vehicle.

"That's not Macie. At least not only Macie."

"We better keep moving," Gary said once the car was far enough away that they wouldn't see us, "but keep an eye out. When they don't find us, they will head back this way."

"Yeah, they know I'm not in town anymore. We better get going quickly." We walked as fast as we could, making sure not to trip on any rocks. We didn't need to be tumbling down the hill right now. Within a few minutes, another car made its way down the road away from town. This time it was going slowly, and when I closed my eyes to check, there was only one signature.

"It might be Macie. There's only one magical signature in the car, though I suppose I wouldn't be able to tell how many people are in there if they aren't using magic."

"What are you doing?" I hissed at Gary as he stood up. The car was far enough away that the driver probably wouldn't see him, but in another minute, he would be visible if they looked this way.

"We need to see if it's Macie so we can get out of here before the Pulhu come back. I'm going to check it out."

"Fine, but you better be careful," I told him. He jogged down the hill toward the car. It stopped as he came into the driver's view.

I watched carefully as he approached. When the driver got out, I started to stand up, but Richard grabbed me. "Stay down, something's wrong," he whispered.

I watched as the driver pointed at the hill and then back at Gary. Gary pointed back toward the town and across the road. Gary watched as the driver got back in the car and turned it around, heading back the way he pointed.

He waited until the car was out of sight before sprinting back to us.

"What was that about?" I asked him impatiently.

"It was Macie."

"What do you mean it was Macie? Why didn't we go down there then? She could have brought us back to the haven," Tider said.

"Something was wrong. She pretended not to know me and then asked about some very dangerous travelers who she was looking for. I told her I had seen a few people head across the land the opposite way from us and the haven."

"Good thinking," I said. "I hope Macie is ok."

"She looked fine. I think someone is keeping a very close eye on her right now though. I bet she called her boyfriend and asked him about some of this, and he didn't like it."

"Once we get back, I will call Macie and tell her you guys are back at the haven. Hopefully, they will send her back, and we can figure out if she's all right."

"But what do we do now? We can't walk the whole way. Can we?"

"We could, but it would take a long time, and it would be dangerous. I'm going to call someone to help us," said Gary.

"You can't. What if they are on the side of the Pulhu? We can't trust anyone," I said.

"I'm calling an old buddy of mine. He's a regular human, so he's no threat to you. He has no idea about the Pulhu, though he does know about the haven, and he can take us there."

"How can we trust him?"

"He was a marine for a long time. He came over here to get away from everything and relax. His training saved my life when I got into some trouble a few years back. I've trusted him completely since then, and he's never let me down. Plus, he won't ask any questions. He always says everyone has secrets, and unless you can tell someone yours don't expect them to tell you theirs."

"Sounds like a smart guy," I said. "Call him, we don't have a lot of options here."

Gary dialed the number and waited for him to answer. When he did, Gary told him a little bit about our situation, without telling him about the Pulhu and hung up. "He'll be here in twenty minutes."

"Do we need to wait here or keep walking?"

"Keep walking. I told him we would keep moving until we saw him. It's better than staying in one spot."

When we spotted the next car, it had only been about fifteen minutes. Gary decided he would go down to meet the vehicle alone in case it wasn't his friend. When the car got close to him, he started waving his hands at us to head down. We ran down the slope, trying to be as careful as we could while going as fast as possible. Gary opened the door, and we hopped in. Gary got into the front seat, and his friend sped down the street.

"So you have a bunch of people after you, and you needed a quick getaway," the man said.

"Seems that way," Gary responded. The man laughed.

"You're the one who's supposed to be helping people get away from whoever is chasing them, not me."

"Yeah, this one didn't go as planned, and I didn't have any other options."

"You know I'll always help you if I can. How far in over your head are you? Do you need a hand?"

"Not that far yet," Gary said. "I think after this, they will be staying in the haven until it's time to leave."

I made a small noise in the back of my throat. The stranger heard it. "You disagree with what Gary's saying? You want to go into town again so whoever is looking for you can find you?"

I didn't say anything until Gary turned around. "You aren't seriously thinking about leaving the haven again, are you? I am recommending to the council that you not be allowed to leave until your flight."

"You can't do that," I said.

"Yes, I can. They obviously want you bad enough to send a lot of their good people here. I don't want to be responsible for them kidnapping you when we can't protect you. If not for Chet, you would have been caught today."

"But they didn't get me, and they won't next time either. We don't even need to go into town."

"Where is it you want to go?" Gary asked.

I looked at the stranger. I didn't want to say anything in front of him.

"Fine, you can tell me when we get back, but the answer is probably still going to be no."

"Why?"

"Because someone is going to get hurt. I don't know why you want to keep running off when they are after you. It's a bad idea."

"There's something I have to do. Then I'll stay in the haven for the rest of the time. Please, Gary. It's important, or I wouldn't ask. You know I don't want anything happening to my friends. Do you think I would risk them for something stupid?"

Gary sighed. "I will think about it. Let's get back to the haven first."

"Everyone down," the stranger said. "A car is coming."

I looked out the front window and saw a car driving in the other lane. It was the same one that passed us earlier with three magical signatures. I ducked down and used my magic to create a shield around everyone but the stranger. I didn't know if it would work, but since we weren't moving, I figured I would be able to keep an invisibility shield around all of us.

"No one move. They can't see us if you stay still," I said.

Once the car passed, the stranger looked at me. "Handy skill to have. Even I couldn't see you all."

"I suppose it did come in handy." I smiled a little. At least we were past them. Hopefully, there wouldn't be any more problems.

We came to the haven gates and got out. "Thanks for helping us," I said to the stranger. "I still don't know your name."

"It's better if you don't," he said. "I'm glad you are all back safe. Now stay inside and listen to Gary." He got in his car and took off.

"Interesting friend," Richard said.

"Yeah. He can be a bit abrupt, but he's a good guy, and he got us home."

"Now, before I go to the council to report today's problems, how about you tell me what you want to do tomorrow."

"We need to go back to the beach."

"For what? I knew you weren't there to swim. You were looking for something."

"We are," I told him, "and Chet gave us the location of it, so we need to go back one more time."

"And this is really that important?"

"Yes."

"And you can't tell me?"

"No."

"Why?"

"Because they may have some mind readers, and I don't want them hurting you if they find out you know."

He laughed. "Is that why you won't tell me? Because of some mind readers possibly breaking into my mind?"

"Yes," I told him, confused that he was laughing.

"I wish I had known that sooner. I know all the mind readers. At least the strong ones. And yes, they do have a few, but they can't read my mind."

"Why not?"

"No one can read my mind."

I looked at him, still confused.

"Let me explain it this way. I'm like a black hole. If anyone tries to read my mind, all they get is empty space, and if they keep trying, they start to lose their secrets to me. It's like my mind tries to destroy theirs. That's why I'm the head of security at such a young age. Nobody can get any information from me about the council without my permission."

"That's so cool. There are so many different powers that people have. It's awesome."

"I guess I never looked at it like that. There are your basic powers, but most of us have something different that very few people have. It's actually pretty neat now that I'm thinking about it."

"Yeah, it is."

"So about this beach trip. Are you planning on it being dangerous?"

"Not really, but it could be."

"Are you going to tell me what's really going on now?"

I explained to him a little bit about having to find the water elementals but didn't tell him why.

"You're sure that's where they are?"

"Nope, but I think it is. If I'm wrong, I'll have to keep looking."

"And if you're right?"

"Then I can find out what they want from me," I said.

"That's all?"

"Yes," I said, "and Chet wants me to see if his grandson is there. He's been missing for a couple of months."

"And he thinks they took him?" He lifted an eyebrow. "This sounds more dangerous than you're letting on."

"They asked me to come, so I don't think it will be dangerous. It will be more dangerous getting there without the Pulhu finding out, but that's what you're here for, right? You can find a way to get us there without them knowing."

"Macie isn't going to be with us, so they shouldn't be able to find out," he started to say.

"Don't trust anyone else either. Who knows how many others have been influenced by them?"

"I won't," he said. "I'm assuming you want to go tomorrow."

"Yes, the sooner, the better."

"Ok, I'll figure it out, and we'll go tomorrow, but that's it. I don't want to keep putting your lives, or mine and the other security guys lives in danger if I don't have to."

"Deal," I said, heading toward my room. "Hey," I said, stopping to turn around. "Let me know how Macie is when you hear from her."

"I will," he replied.

It was surprisingly early in the afternoon, but it felt like I had been out for much longer. I said bye to my friends and went to my room to rest for a bit. I wasn't surprised when Abby knocked on my door.

"How are you doing?" I asked her as she came in.

"I'm better," she said.

"What if we don't find it?" Abby asked.

"We will. I'm sure of it. Otherwise, we will have to sneak out."

We were ready to go first thing in the morning. We made quick work of the hike, each of us lost in our own thoughts. When we finally got to the bay, I took off my clothes, so I was in my bathing suit. I shoved them in a plastic bag and zipped it up. I didn't want my clothes to be soaking wet the whole time we were in the palace, so I came prepared.

At first, I couldn't find anything in the lake, but eventually, Tider swam up to me and grabbed my arm, pulling me with him. He pointed to an area in the rock that looked a lot like an arch. I started running my hands over it, looking for any sign of a keyhole or handle we could use. The rock was covered in algae, making it even harder to see. I swam back a few feet and looked at the arch again. I could make out an area that looked like it had less algae on it than the rest of the door.

I swam over and saw a small indentation in the rock. It was shaped like the Celtic knot on the bracelet. I knew this was the spot. I wasn't sure how the magic would work, so I got everyone's attention. I didn't want anyone to be left behind. I reached out and grabbed Richard's hand. He grabbed Abby's, and she grabbed Tider's. Tider swam up and put his arm on my shoulder. I pushed the Celtic knot onto the indentation.

Immediately, I felt magic pushing out from the arch. It swirled around us, and the inside of the arch turned transparent. I could see a hallway leading away from it, and I pushed my hand against the translucent stone. It went right through. I swam through the arch, and my friends came with me. As soon as we were through, we fell to the ground in a tangle of arms and legs.

"What happened?" Abby asked.

I looked back at the arch. I could still see the water on the other side, but there wasn't any in the hallway. "We fell out of the water. Next time let's swim toward the bottom of the arch. That way, we don't fall as far." I smiled at everyone. "We made it."

"Yeah, but now what do we do?" Tider asked, looking around. There was only one hallway, but it was massive.

"I think we should stay quiet. I would like to find out where Chet's grandson is. He would have come back if he could. He must be stuck here somehow."

"No splitting up," Richard whispered.

We came to another hallway that split off from the main one. There wasn't anyone in either hall, and I didn't know which way to go.

"I think we should stay in the main hall. We can look down the other ones later, but until we know more, we could get lost or be going in circles if we start splitting away from the main hall. Besides, this should lead us somewhere good. It's almost twice as big as the other hallway," Abby said.

We continued down the hallway, looking for any signs of water elementals, sprites, or Chet's grandson. The hall went on forever. It split up a few more times before finally opening into a large room.

At the other end of the room, I saw two intricately carved thrones. Thankfully, they were empty. I wasn't sure I was ready to meet whoever sat in those thrones. I wanted to find the water sprites since that's what the note said to do.

"Let's head back and check out the other halls," I said.

"Yeah, I don't really want to get caught in this room," said Abby.

We turned around to head back but were met with a wall of water coming down the hall. There was nowhere to go but forward, and we ran into the throne room, trying to get to the other side. I raised my hand and saw Tider and Richard do the same. As I was about to use my magic to stop the water, a hand gripped me from behind. I was lifted up and thrown over someone's shoulder. I began thrashing around, trying to break the grip of my captor.

"Enough, or I'll make sure you can't do anything," a male voice threatened me.

I looked over to see my friends had also been picked up. Richard hung limply in his captor's arms, but Tider was still fighting. The man holding him reached up and hit him over the head. Tider went as limp as Richard.

"No," I yelled. "Don't hurt them." I could see Abby on my other side. She wasn't struggling, so they hadn't knocked her out. "Please don't hurt them. We aren't here to cause any trouble."

"Yeah, right," the man holding me said.

"We really aren't. I was told to come here."

"Whatever," he replied. "Humans aren't allowed here, and yet lately, we seem to have an infestation of them." He had to be talking about Chet's grandson. I didn't say anything.

"Let's go," he said to the others.

"I can walk," I told him. "I won't try anything."

He laughed. "Even if you did try something, we would stop you." He put me down and grabbed my shoulder.

He pushed me toward a door on the other side of the room. Once I started walking, he loosened his grip. Not much but enough that I could look around. I hadn't noticed at the time because of my struggling, but these guys were glowing. All around them was a pale blue light. I turned further to look at the one gripping me. His glow was stronger than the others. It was a darker blue too.

"What are you?" I gasped.

"What?" he asked incredulously. "You don't know what we are, and you're in our palace."

"Wait, you're elementals? Really?" I asked excitedly. "Then you can tell me why I'm here."

He looked even more confused. "We don't know why you are here. You shouldn't be."

"I was told to come, so you have to know why I'm here." I could hear the pleading in my voice. What if everything we had done was for nothing. There had to be a reason I was here.

"You are trying to confuse me, witch," he said and pushed me forward again.

"I'm not," I said. "I want answers."

"We never told you to come. We don't allow humans here."

"But."

"No buts. I'm not sure what you are doing, but I've had enough."

He marched straight through the door and down a long set of stairs. There were a lot of different hallways, but he kept going down the stairs. It took a long time before we came to a door at the end. The dungeon. It had to be.

"Please. There must be someone that knows why I'm here. Please ask. I was sent a note telling me to find the water sprites. Ask them."

"Lies. Sprites don't bother with humans. Humans can't even talk to them."

"I can. They showed me a book to help me learn their language. I've been translating it and learning the language for months. I'm not great at it, but I'm getting better. Please listen to me."

He pushed me into the first room, and the other men put my friends inside. They didn't throw them, but they weren't gentle either. The door slammed behind us, and I heard the men leave.

CHAPTER EIGHTEEN

I rushed to the door and pulled on it, but it was locked. I tried using my magic to break the door or the wall, but something was blocking it. I pulled on all of the elements, but my magic wouldn't work. I closed my eyes and concentrated. I saw light grey magic snaking up and down the walls.

When I tried using my magic again, the light grey color glowed. That's what was keeping it from working. I searched the walls. The grey magic seemed to be strongest at the door, so I moved to the opposite side of the room. This time when I pulled on my magic, I could see a small trickle of magic circling my hands. I tried to pull more, but it took a lot of energy. I didn't want the magic to go to waste, so I called Abby over.

"Grab my hand and try to heal Richard and Tider."

"I can't," she said. "My magic isn't working." She looked panicked. I only had my magic for a few months, and I hated not being able to use it. She had magic for most of her life. It would be like losing a big part of yourself.

"I can share my magic with you. I have a small amount that I can use right now. I will pass it to you." She looked at the door. "It's not enough for us to get out," I told her.

"Ok." She grabbed my hand and knelt next to Richard and Tider. "I don't know how much I'm going to be able to do. Hold on to my shoulder, so I can work on both of them at the same time."

I put my hand on her shoulder and watched as she put a hand over each of their foreheads.

"Now," she said.

I closed my eyes and channeled all the magic I collected into her. I watched as her hands filled with healing magic and poured into the guys. After all of her magic was used, she slumped forward. The guys began to stir as I knelt down.

"Were those real elementals? I didn't think there would be any living ones here. I thought we would be looking for something in a dead palace," Tider said.

"Definitely not dead. They are strong, and they don't seem to like people."

"Did you tell them who you are?"

"I don't even know who I am yet. I did tell them that the water sprites told me to come here. They laughed at me. The guy in charge said no one can talk to water sprites."

"That's not true. There are more than a few people who can talk to them."

"I am going to have to use more than air magic here," I said. "We are going to need everything we have if this comes down to a fight."

"Thankfully, the Pulhu can't get in here, so you should be safe from them finding out."

"Hey, whoever you are over there," someone yelled from outside the room. "What are you talking about? Do you have a way out of here?"

We all turned toward the door, startled.

"Who's there?" I asked.

I saw a boy about my age looking through the bars on the door across from us.

"I'm Adam. Who are you? And how did you end up in here?"

"Adam, you wouldn't happen to know Chet, would you?"

"I sure do. That's my grandpa. How do you know him?"

"He asked us if we could look for you while we were in here. I guess we found you."

"I've only been gone a few days, and he sends in the rescuers. He could have given me a little more time."

I stared at my friends, worried, before responding. "Adam, you've been missing for four months."

"What?" He stared at me. "That's not possible."

"We may have a problem," I said, turning to my friends. "Chet mentioned time moved differently in the elemental realms, but I didn't really understand what he meant. I think this is what he was talking about. Time must move slower in here."

"I'm more worried about the elementals that put us in here, and what they want with us," Richard said.

"What's going on over there?" Adam yelled.

"We are trying to figure things out. We aren't sure what's going on. When you were looking around, did you see anything strange?"

"I saw elementals using their powers, which was strange. Something is wrong with the king's face too. It's only his eye and forehead on the one side, but somehow it makes him look off. I don't think he was born that way. I overheard him talking to one of the guards. He said without his staff, it will eventually take him over. I think he meant a curse, and that's what is going on with part of his face. They think I took the staff since I was caught in their palace sneaking around."

"Wow. You've seen a lot since you got here," I said.

"You didn't take the staff, did you?" Abby asked.

"No, I didn't take it. I might know who did. They wouldn't listen to me though."

"I'm not surprised. They don't seem big on listening to anyone. Especially humans. The guards seemed really unhappy that we are here."

"Well, they are banned from having anything to do with humans. The shadow king could come down and destroy them for even being near us."

"For now, we need to get out of here." Richard raised his hands and tried to use his magic. When his face fell, I spoke up.

"Don't waste your energy. We already tried using magic. It's not working. There's a spell on the room that prevents us from using it. At least most of it."

"Most of it?"

"Yes, I can use a little bit. That's how Abby healed you both."

"Thanks, Abby. I didn't realize you needed to heal us."

"Hey, Adam," I called out. "What do the elementals want with us?"

"No idea what they want with you, but they want me to tell them where the staff went."

"How do we get an audience with their king or queen? Maybe they will listen to us."

"Don't worry. Since they caught me, they have taken me up to see the king in the evening before they give me dinner so he can yell at me to tell him where the staff is. He will probably want you up there too."

"Once we can use our magic, we might be able to get away," I told them. Don't try to use your magic until we are out of this cell."

We sat down and started whispering, trying to come up with a plan. Occasionally, Adam would yell across the hall to see if we had any ideas. It was hard to make a plan when we didn't know anything about the palace. We heard footsteps coming down the stairs. The guards slammed our door open and started yelling at us to get up.

"Let's go, you have an audience with the king. Now!" he yelled when I didn't get up fast enough.

We stumbled to our feet and quickly walked through the open door. We were each paired up with our own security guard. Mine was the same one from earlier.

"What does he want with us?" I asked.

"Probably to find out what you are doing here, and who sent you," he growled.

"I already told you all of this. Why didn't you tell him?"

"Trust me, I did tell him. He doesn't believe you, and neither do I."

"Why else would I come here?" I demanded as we walked back up the stairs.

"Who knows? Probably for power, or maybe you are working for the fire elementals. They always wanted to end us. Maybe they think they can by sending humans in to do their dirty work. Well, I'm telling you now, it won't work."

"I already told you. I'm not here to hurt you. I was told to find you."

"Let's see what the king thinks of you." He pushed me out into the room, and we walked toward the throne. The room was full of guards and more elementals. They all started talking when we walked in. Once we were there, our guards pushed us to our knees. A hush fell over the crowd, and I lifted my head to see the king striding into the room before my guard pushed my head down. "No eyes on the king unless he gives you permission."

"Whatever," I said. I was getting sick of being a prisoner. I tried calling my magic, but my guard smacked the back of my head.

"Don't even try it." I wondered how he knew every time I tried to call my magic. I closed my eyes and focused. The room was bathed in a soft blue light. Some of the elementals had a stronger light, like my guard, and some had a weak light. I figured that had to do with how strong their magic was. I shifted slightly so I could see the king out of the corner of my eye. He had the strongest glow of all the elementals but woven into his blue light was a dark thread. When I looked closer at it, it seemed to pulse with its own life. The thread was small, no wider than a half-inch, but it wound through the king's blue glow and distorted it.

"Stand humans, and let me hear your reasons for invading my palace," the king called.

I stood up and looked at the king. Quickly, my guard smacked the back of my head. I looked back at the floor, but I got a good look at the king's face. Adam was right. The left side of his face was changing. One eye was a bright blue while the other was black, and his forehead was wrinkled halfway across his face. He had a streak of straight black hair on the side of his head that seemed to be changing even though the rest of his hair fell in golden waves.

Whatever was happening to their king was bad. Something evil had gotten to him, and I had a feeling if it took him over completely, the king would come for humans. I couldn't let that happen. I tried to stop myself, but I couldn't stand the thought of what he would do if he let the curse have him. It reminded me too much of the books I read on the other void users and how they changed.

"You're cursed," I said. "Why haven't you fixed it? Do you know what you could become?"

"Of course I do," he roared.

"Then fix it. I'm sure there is a way to do it. You could hurt a lot of people if it gets worse," I said accusingly.

"How do you even know about it, human? Did you do this to me?"

"What? No, I didn't do this to you. How could I? I just got here, and you have obviously been like this for longer than one day."

"How do you know that?"

"Because no one looked surprised to see you looking the way you do. If you had just been cursed, then they would have been shocked. You need to do something about it now." I looked at him, and my guard raised his hand.

"Stop," the king commanded. "My guards tell me that you said you were told to come here. By who?"

"By a water sprite. The note said to find the water sprites. I wasn't expecting to find you here."

"Why not? It's my palace."

"Well," I said, trying not to squirm. "I didn't actually believe you existed."

"What? You didn't think we were real? Where did you think you got your powers from?"

"I don't know. I haven't exactly had them long, so I'm still getting used to all this."

"Lies," my guard yelled. "She is very powerful. There is no way she has only had her powers for a short time. She wouldn't be able to control them. You remember how humans used to be without a lot of training."

The king looked at me. "Are you lying to me?"

"No, I'm not. I came here to find answers, and instead, I find elementals with a king who is cursed and might become pure evil if he doesn't fix it. This isn't exactly what I was looking for."

"What answers could we possibly give you?"

"I have no idea."

"I will give you a chance to prove that you mean us no harm. You must retrieve my staff for me. Then I will know that you are telling the truth, and I will answer your questions and let you leave."

"One more thing," I said to him. "We can't be missing for months. The guy you have locked up downstairs needs to come with us too. He's been missing for a few months, and he says he has only been here about four days."

"Time runs differently in our realm," the king said. "You can't have him. He may be behind the theft of my staff."

"Let us use him. If he stole it, then we will find out, but for now, he can be useful."

The king shook his head and paced around before finally turning to me. "Fine, but you only have four days."

"That's not enough time," I said.

"Maybe not, but if you want to go back to the human realm when you left, that's all you get. I can't change it any longer than that. Even that will be pushing it."

"We'll do it. Where do we start?"

"Hilail will set you up in guest quarters and tell you everything you need to know." The king strode from the room, and my guard stood in front of me.

"Let me guess, you're Hilail?" I shook my head. Just my luck.

"Yes," he growled. "You may have fooled the king, but I don't trust you. I will be following everything you do."

"Good, then you'll be around to help me if I have any questions. Now can you show us to our rooms?" I spun around and headed for my friends. I would have to be very careful around Hilail. He didn't seem like a bad guy, just distrusting.

I spun back around. "Hilail, please bring up Adam."

"Adam?"

"The boy in the dungeon, he will be staying with us."

"I don't..."

I cut him off. "You heard your king. We get to use him until we find the staff or until the four days are up."

Hilail sighed and then stormed off to talk to another guard. When he came back, he told us to follow him. I was surprised when he took us through the main hall and into one of the side halls. If we had to run for it, we were much closer to the entrance now, though I would rather find the staff. He stopped in front of a door and ushered us all in.

"We are all staying here?" I asked, surprised.

"There are four rooms to sleep in. This is one of our bigger apartments."

"What about Adam?"

"I don't care where he sleeps. Put him on the floor. He's your responsibility now. When you are ready to leave your room, someone will be waiting to escort you if I'm not here. Don't disobey them, or I'll send you back to the dungeons."

"What is your problem with us?" I asked, fed up with his attitude.

"You are the problem, you shouldn't be here. The shadow king will kill us all for this," he grumbled, storming out of the room.

"Well, that went well," I said sarcastically.

"Actually, I think it did. You got us a reprieve for the next four days, and if you find the staff, we can get answers and get out of here," Abby said.

"Any clues on how to do that?" Richard asked.

"None," I said. "I guess we should ask Adam first. He seemed to think he knew who the thief was."

There was a knock on the door, and when I opened it, Adam was standing there with a different guard behind him. "Hey guys, you got me out. Thanks. When do we leave?"

"We don't. Let's go sit down, and we'll fill you in."

I looked at the guard standing at the door. He was looking at us scornfully. "Can you tell us when the staff went missing, and who had access to it?"

"Why would I tell you that?"

"Because I'm trying to save your king before the curse takes over him completely."

The guard glared at me for a minute before finally answering. "You will have to talk to Hilail. He didn't give me any orders to talk to you."

I walked back to my friends and shook my head. "This isn't going to be easy."

"So we don't get to leave?" Adam asked.

"Nope. We have to find the king's staff if we want to leave."

"Well, that's easy. His daughter has it."

"His daughter?" I asked.

"Yeah, from what I overheard, she wants to rule in his place. She thinks she can do whatever she wants. She wants to go live with humans so they can worship her."

"Maybe we can get into her room or at least figure out where it is so we can look for the staff," I said.

"We could pretend to worship her," Abby said. "That might get us into her rooms."

"That's a great idea," Richard said. "While you two do that, we will try to talk to some of the servants. Maybe they will be more likely to talk than the guards."

"Hopefully."

We went to the door and told the guards we would be leaving to start looking for the staff. We had to wait for another guard since we were splitting up. They didn't want us going off on our own. When our guard got there, I grimaced. It was Hilail. It seemed I wasn't going to be able to shake this elemental. Either he really didn't trust us, or he didn't want us to figure it out. Maybe he was helping the king's daughter.

"We want to go see the king's daughter," I told Hilail.

"Sorry, she is busy."

"Seriously, or are you being difficult? We are trying to help."

"I doubt that. She really is busy. She has meetings today."

"Fine, take us to these meetings. We need to start as soon as possible. We don't have much time, and neither does your king," I said, glaring at him.

"I will take you, but she won't be able to see you. Appointments must be made in advance to see the princess."

"We'll see," I said.

We followed him through the palace, taking multiple turns to get to the area where the princess held meetings. We came to a small room where a few elementals were seated on couches, and a woman was behind a desk.

"Do you have an appointment?" she asked us.

"No," I told her.

"Sorry, if you don't have an appointment, she doesn't have time to see you." She turned back to her desk.

"Excuse me." I tried getting her attention. She ignored me. Hilail was smirking, and I was starting to feel like hitting him. I turned my attention back to the lady.

I put my hands on the desk. Immediately, Hilail moved to stop me, but I put my hand up. "The king gave me this task so you can stop. Unless I'm hurting someone, you need to let me do what I'm supposed to," I said, glaring at him. He wasn't happy, but he backed down.

"Now," I said to the lady, "I'm sure your princess would like to meet the humans that are visiting her palace. Especially since we are here to help her father."

I could tell she still didn't think it was a good idea.

"If you don't let us in to see her and her dad, the king, falls to the curse because of it, how do you think she will feel? She definitely won't appreciate what you're trying to do."

Finally, the lady sighed, got up, and went to the door. "Stay here," she told me. I waited while she went through the door and came back out a few minutes later with an older elemental following her. The older elemental glared at me before hurrying away. The door opened again, and a tall, beautiful female elemental stood there.

"Well, are you coming?" she asked me.

"Yes, your highness."

She huffed and then walked into the room with us following. "Hilail, not you," she said.

Hilail stopped. "But you don't know what they will do, princess. You could be hurt."

"Do you think I am so weak that I can't take a couple of humans down?" she asked him in a fake sweet voice.

"No, princess, of course, you could defeat them. You shouldn't have to though. That is the guard's job, and your father said to stay with them."

"That's the real reason. You don't want to disappoint my dear old dad. You couldn't care less about me getting hurt. I will talk to my father if he has a problem with me meeting them. Now go wait outside until I send them out."

Hilail glared at us, and I smirked right back at him. Someone needed to put him in his place, and the princess did an excellent job even though I really didn't like her. On first impressions, she seemed very selfish and spoiled. And from her comment, she didn't like her dad that much. Maybe Adam was right. I would have to be careful not to offend her.

After we were seated, the princess looked from me to Abby with interest. "What are humans doing here? I heard the guards saying they caught another human a few days ago. Are you here to save that human?" I didn't like the way she talked about us as if we were beneath her. Almost like we were bugs she was playing with.

"No, we aren't here with Adam. It was luck that led us to him."

"I wouldn't call it luck. Dad's going to keep you here for the rest of your lives. You will never see your family again. It's a good punishment for sneaking into our palace, though I wish he would punish you all a little more. You shouldn't be allowed to roam freely." She sounded a little too excited to punish us. I closed my eyes and scanned the area.

The room looked fine, nothing was keeping us from using our magic. Her magic was a very dark blue. It wasn't a pretty color, and I thought about how the colors were so different on the elementals even though they were all blue. It couldn't be strength like I first thought with Hilail. He was worried about the princess's safety with us, and he wouldn't be if the darker blue had to do with strength. She would be stronger than him. I would have to figure it out, but I needed to focus on the princess.

When I opened my eyes, she was studying me. "What are you doing?"

"I'm trying to figure out how to talk to you. You are the princess of the elementals. You are way above us." I tried to appeal to her egotistical side. "You are so much more amazing in person than I thought you would be."

She smiled and relaxed in her chair. "This is how we should be treated. Worshipped by all, not trapped in our cities hiding. We are the most powerful." Her voice started to sound strained.

"Yes, you are." I tried to calm her again. "Why are you stuck here?"

"The shadow king told us we can't interact with humans anymore, but that was hundreds of years ago, maybe more. I'm sure he forgot about us by now, but Dad won't hear a word of what I have to say. He makes us stay here and says we are bound by some old law of the shadow kings."

"You don't believe him?"

"Why should I? The shadow king hasn't been seen or heard since we were banished. I think he is gone, and we are stuck here because my dad is too scared to do something different."

"Why would he be scared? He seems so powerful." I tried to sound genuinely caring.

"He isn't as powerful as me. But he says we need to remember what happened last time the shadow king got mad at us for playing with humans. He supposedly destroyed everything of ours."

"Supposedly?"

"I don't buy it. I think it was a fight with the other elementals. I think the fire elementals did it and blamed it on the shadow king. They are probably out there with humanity doing whatever they want." She looked at us. "Have you seen them? Did they send you?" She had a maniacal gleam in her eyes.

"Of course not, princess. We have never seen them. At least I don't think so. Are they as beautiful as you? If they are, then I definitely haven't seen any fire elementals. I wouldn't forget that." She calmed down again. As long as I kept complimenting, she seemed to be ok.

"Of course they aren't as pretty as me, but they would still be much prettier than you humans," she said, smirking. "Why haven't you seen them? Maybe they are hiding out until their numbers are strong enough to take over. I'm sure many of them were destroyed in the fight."

"When was this fight?"

"It was a long time ago," she said.

"Why would your dad lie about the fight?"

"To control us." She stood up and started to pace. "I don't know, I just know he is. So are his guards, but I've got my own guards now. They are loyal only to me."

"Like Hilail?" I guessed.

"What? No, he believes everything my dad says. He can't be trusted."

I snorted. "I know, he's the one watching us. Not the nicest is he?"

"He's never nice. He thinks he is so smart, but he's not. I'm much smarter." She looked at us waiting,

"Oh yes, you do seem to be much smarter than him," I told her what she wanted to hear.

"I like you, humans. Maybe I will keep you here as my pets after all. I'm sure Dad wouldn't mind."

"I wish we could stay, but Hilail said we have to listen to him or our lives are forfeit, so we have to go," I said, trying not to panic. We couldn't get stuck with this princess. She clearly wasn't right in the head. "Besides, you have all those people waiting to talk to you. Maybe Hilail will bring us back tomorrow."

"Yes, I will tell him to do that. Or maybe I will have him bring you to my rooms later today. It would kill him to have to do what I say when he doesn't want to. That sounds much better. And bring your other humans with you."

"Yes, princess." I bowed, and so did Abby. We headed to the door and walked out, right into Hilail.

He wore his customary glare. "Are you all finished?"

"Yes. She wants to see us tonight. All of us."

"No."

"I figured you'd say that."

"You aren't going to argue with me?" He sounded confused.

"Nope. At least not about that." I really didn't want to go see the princess again. She gave me a bad feeling. She definitely could have taken her dad's staff.

Hilail looked at me in surprise for a second before leading us back the way we had come. Before we got to our room, I stopped in front of an open door. "What's this room?"

"It's a sitting room for the library next door. Elementals come to sit in here once they've found what they are looking for."

I peered inside. It was empty, so I walked in. Abby followed me. I looked around and saw a small couch in the corner that looked private. When I sat down, Hilail looked at me in exasperation. "What are you doing?"

"I actually want to talk to you privately. I'm not sure if my room is bugged."

"Bugged?"

"Set up so other people or elementals can spy on us."

"Oh." He didn't deny it, so I figured it was true.

"What do you want?"

"I want to know what is going on. The princess hates you, and she barely likes the king. Why?"

"I don't know."

"There has to be a reason. It might help find the staff."

"You think she did it."

"I wasn't sure until I met her, but yes, now I do."

"Why? What did she say to you? We have always kept a close eye on her, but lately, she's been very secretive, and I don't know what she is up to. Even her guards don't know what she is doing."

"I'm sure they do. There's no way she could keep things from them all, but she said she has her own guards who are loyal only to her."

"What? All guards are sworn to obey the king first."

"Well, it seems that a few of them have broken that vow."

"What else did she say?"

"Nope, I'm not telling you anything else until you tell us what you know. I'm not planning on staying trapped here forever, so I need all the help I can get."

"I'll think about it. I still don't trust you." Hilail stood up, and we followed him back to our room.

CHAPTER NINETEEN

I closed my eyes and looked for any magic that would let the elementals see or hear us. The cameras were easy to spot, but they were not like our cameras. They were magical balls that floated in the corners in an orange bubble. When I opened my eyes, I couldn't see them at all. I closed my eyes again and continued looking, trying to make it seem like I was resting my eyes.

I finally spotted a microphone hidden in a nook in the coffee table. Maybe if I was very careful, I could make a barrier around the microphone so it couldn't hear what we said. I focused my magic and encircled the microphone. I was pretty sure there would be others in each bedroom, but as long as we only talked out here, I didn't need to worry about those. We would have to talk about regular things in the bedrooms.

"I'm not sure if it will work, but it's the best I can do," I told everyone once the guys got back.

"Hopefully, it works. Otherwise, this is going to get a lot harder," Tider said.

"Yeah, I know."

"So, what did everyone learn today?" Richard asked.

"We learned that the king's daughter could have done it. She doesn't hold her father in very high regard," I said. "She talked about humans as if we were pets too. It was disgusting. We better find that staff because if she becomes the queen, she won't stay here. She will be heading to our cities to cause problems for us."

"We will find it. We got a couple of good leads today," Richard said. "There is a town behind the castle where someone could have taken the staff to be hidden."

"A whole town?" I asked.

"Supposedly, there are many towns. You will have to ask Hilail to take us to the one closest to the castle tomorrow."

"We need to find out if anyone has been out to the town recently that doesn't normally go. From what the servants said, there are very few who go to the town from the palace. They have almost all their goods brought in to their houses by their servants," Tider explained.

"Where are their houses?"

"Right next to the palace is a walled-off area filled with houses for prominent families. Getting in there is very difficult. They have guards posted at all times. That's all we found out."

"Let's get cleaned up for dinner. Remember, don't say anything in your rooms. I'm going to tell Hilail where we are going tomorrow."

I walked toward the door and opened it to see a different guard. "Excuse me, but I need to see Hilail." The guard ignored me, and I stepped out of the room. He turned and glared at me, but I kept walking.

He reached out a hand and grabbed me. "You will go back to your room and get ready. The princess wants you at dinner tonight."

"Sorry, we can't. Hilail said no."

"You will do what you're told, human. Hilail is busy, so you are now my charges." He pushed me back into the room.

"Where is Hilail?" I asked. I might not like Hilail, but he wasn't going to make us go see the princess. Plus, I was starting to believe he really wanted to find the king's staff. I didn't think he had anything to do with the theft.

The guard wouldn't answer me, so I walked back into the room and slammed the door in his face. I paced back and forth for a few minutes before I had an idea. I walked over to the microphone and took the bubble down so whoever was listening could hear me.

"Please send Hilail to me. I have important information for him." I waited for a response, but nothing happened. It was worth a shot, but since it didn't work, I had to get ready to go see the princess. We would need to be very careful. I didn't want her thinking we were investigating her. I put the bubble back up around the microphone and headed to my room.

I cleaned myself up as best as I could, but I could only do so much for my clothes, considering everything we had been through. I could hear my friends talking in the other room and wondered how they were feeling. I felt bad that I dragged them into this. They were following me, and now we might not get out of the water elemental realm.

"Hey, Sally," Abby said, walking into my room and shutting the door. She was holding some clothing out to me. "These are for dinner with the princess tonight. I thought Hilail said we can't go?"

"He did, but he seems to be missing right now, and the guard at our door is loyal to the princess. At least I think he is."

"That's not good," Abby said. "At least they gave us something clean to wear. My clothes are a mess." Abby held up both outfits. One was a deep green dress with sparkles all over it, and the other was a pale blue with pearls around the neckline. They both looked like they would be uncomfortable to wear. I wasn't a dress person. Abby was even holding shoes that matched each dress.

"Which one do you want?" she asked, holding them both up.

"I don't care. You pick which one you want." She immediately pushed the green dress into my arms.

The guys were already waiting for us. They had changed into very lightweight pants and shirts. They looked incredibly soft and comfortable, but still fancy enough for dinner with a princess.

"Wow, you guys clean up nice," Abby said.

"Yeah, you do too," Tider chimed in.

I didn't think I was going to enjoy walking in the shoes. If anything bad happened, they would be the first thing to go. I wouldn't be able to run at all.

"Sally," Richard said as he walked up to me. "You look amazing." He looked pretty amazing too, but I didn't know how to tell him that without sounding weird.

"Thanks, you too," I tried to say stammering. "I really like…" A knock at the door interrupted us before I could say anything else.

Hilail didn't even wait for one of us to come to the door, he barged right in. "What do you think you are doing?"

"What do you mean, what are we doing?"

"The guard told me you are planning to go to the princess's dinner. I thought we already discussed this." He was furious. I looked at my friends in confusion. The door to the hall was still open, and I saw the guard from earlier looking in. He must have lied so Hilail wouldn't know he was the princess's guard. I pushed the door shut in the guard's face with a gust of wind.

"Hilail, stop." He was still pacing around the room, waiting for my answer. I walked up to him and grabbed his arm. "Look at me, Hilail. We don't want to go to dinner with the princess." I decided to be straight with him. I would have to trust him if we were going to get out of this. "You need to believe me. We were told that we were going, and we didn't have a choice. When I asked the guard where you were, he said you were busy, and we were his charges now."

Hilail paled but said nothing.

"Listen, we are trying to do the right thing, and I think you might be too. We don't have to like each other, but we do need to work together. I don't want your king to be cursed either."

"Why would you care?"

"Because I'm not an awful person. No one should be cursed to become evil, and if his daughter gets to be in charge next, the whole world could suffer. She isn't planning on staying here when she is queen. She wants to live among us and be worshipped. She seems cruel enough to destroy many people's lives if she doesn't get her way. I don't want her anywhere near the human realm."

Hilail looked at me, trying to decide what to believe. I knew he believed us when he finally relaxed. His gaze moved over my friends, and then he laughed. "I have an idea. I will take you to dine with the king tonight. That way, the princess does not retaliate, and her guard can't say you disobeyed him. It should keep you out of trouble with her for a day."

"So, you think she took the staff too?"

"I don't know, but we are looking into everything and everyone. So far, she hasn't given us a reason to think she did it."

"But you still think she did?" I asked.

"Like I said, I don't know, but something is not quite right with her. She has always been spoiled, but lately, she treats everyone like they are beneath her. We may have a king, but he listens to us here at the court and respects our thoughts."

"When we talked to her, she made comments saying she didn't like her dad. She told us what she would do when she was queen. I know it's not enough to accuse her, but I think it's her. That's why we didn't want to go to dinner with her tonight."

"Is that why you said for the guards to send me to you?"

"Yes, I didn't think it worked."

"That's one of the reasons I was so angry when I got here. You aren't allowed to summon me. I understand why you did it now. I don't want you dining with the princess either," he said. "Especially if she really did do it."

"We need to go to the town tomorrow. If she was going to hide it somewhere safe and away from here, that's where we think it would be."

He looked at us for a minute before nodding. "Let's get going. I wouldn't want the king to start without you. It's bad manners, and he won't be as forthcoming if you upset him right away."

Everyone was ready to go. I saw the relief in Abby's eyes. Dining with the king was way better than the princess, at least we hoped it would be. Hilail opened the door, and the other guard stumbled. It looked like he was trying to listen.

"Duron, I am escorting our guests to have dinner with the king. The princess will have to reschedule for another time."

Duron looked at Hilail and nodded. "Yes, sir. I will let her know."

"See that you do."

"Of course, sir," Duron said. "Whatever you need."

"Come to me at the end of your shift. I want to change your schedule. You have been doing a good job, and you deserve some time off for it."

"Oh no, sir, I'm fine."

"I'm sure you would like to have a little free time to spend with your family. I insist on giving you that time," Hilail said. I turned, and the guard was still standing there watching us. He looked scared. I wondered if the princess was going to be mad at him for the change of plans.

"Why did you reward him?" I whispered to Hilail when we were further down the hall.

"If he gets time off, he isn't guarding your door. I occasionally give time off to the guards that are doing the best, so it won't be suspicious, and it gets him out of the way. I will put a guard on your door that I can trust. I wonder how many other guards the princess has on her side?"

"A lot from the way she was talking. She must be doing something to win them over."

"I don't know what. She has no real power right now. Maybe she is making them promises of power if they support her."

"I don't know. I was thinking something worse, like blackmail. That guard, Duron, looked scared when you told him we wouldn't be going with him. I'm guessing it's because of the princess. He has no reason to be scared of you or us."

"I hope she isn't using blackmail." He looked really upset. "An elemental who chooses to do bad things slowly changes into a monster. The more bad things you do, the more you want to do bad things. Usually, it ends up with an elemental doing black magic, which causes their souls to be destroyed forever. They can never come back from using black magic. At that point, the darkness takes over and causes them to do horrible things. We haven't had anyone succumb to black magic in hundreds of years."

"How do you know if you did a bad thing?"

"We all know when we've done something wrong. You can feel it in your magic."

"That must be why some of you have a darker glow around you than others."

"What do you mean, a darker glow?" He stopped in the middle of the hallway to face me.

"Some of the elementals glow a darker color than others."

"You see a glow around us?"

"Yes, don't you?"

"No. What does it look like?"

"It's just a blue glow that surrounds each elemental. I've been trying to figure out why certain elementals have a darker blue. At first, I thought it was strength, but when I met the princess, she had the darkest blue of everyone. She didn't seem very strong, so I knew it couldn't be that." I thought about it for a minute. "It makes sense. If an elemental makes bad choices, their glow gets darker, eventually turning it into a gray or black color. Kind of like the curse around your king."

He gripped my arms. "You can see the curse?"

"Yes, I thought all of you could. I mean, you knew every time I went to use my magic, so I figured you could see magic, just like me. When you use your magic, the blue glow gets stronger around your hands."

"I know when you use your magic because I can feel it building up near you. I can't see it. I've never heard of anyone being able to see it before. What does the king's curse look like?"

I explained to him what I saw, and he shook his head. "I don't know what that means, but it might be useful. I will let the healer know immediately. Maybe she can use your description to heal him."

We continued down the hall as Hilail questioned me about what else I could see. He wanted to know a lot about what the princess's glow looked like.

"What about me?" he finally asked.

"It's darker than everyone I've met but the princess. But it is still pretty light blue compared to hers, so you probably haven't done anything too bad, right?"

"Right. I've only done what I've had to do," he said.

I wanted to ask more, but he stopped in front of a set of doors and pushed them open.

"Your majesty, I present the humans for dinner."

"Hilail, I wasn't aware they would be dining with me tonight," the king said from his chair at the table. Nothing had been placed before him yet, so I knew we weren't late.

"I apologize, but I thought it would be important to talk to them as quickly as possible, and they had a lot of questions for you."

The king started to say something but shook his head and smiled. "Of course. Please join me," he said. He seemed genuine, and I wondered if this was what he was always like before the curse. If he was, it made sense why so many of the elementals in the palace liked him.

"Thank you," I told him. We all sat down. Servants came out of a hidden door and set places in front of each of us. They poured water, and then they were gone.

"What is it I can do for you?" the king asked.

"We need more information so we can find your staff," Richard said, getting right to the point.

"Who do you think did it? Who had access to it?"

"I don't know who did it and as to who had access, no one. I was the only one who knew where it was."

"Are you sure about that?" I asked.

A dark look crossed his eyes. "Of course I am, this is my house. I know who has access to everything," he growled.

"I'm sorry. I didn't mean to offend you," I said quickly, trying to calm him.

"You humans know nothing," he said. "You don't belong in this place, or at my table."

Hilail walked over and tried to talk to the king. I closed my eyes and looked at the king. The dark strand was longer than the last time I saw the king, and it was winding around his body. A small tendril floated directly next to the king's head, and I reached out with my magic to try and move it. I suspected it was influencing the king's behavior. The rest of his glow was still a bright blue, so he had to be a good elemental.

"What are you doing?" Hilail turned to stop me.

"There's a dark part of the curse trying to wrap around his head. I'm going to try to move it so the king acts more like himself."

The king was shaking his head and grimacing. "Do it quickly before it retakes control."

I gathered my magic and tried to use air to make the dark thread move, but I couldn't get the air to even touch the blue or black around the king. I walked up to the king and put my hand near his head where the dark thread was. I tried grabbing it, but it was so fine my hand went right through.

The king shuddered. "Try again, I could feel you do something."

I gathered more magic and willed the air to flow around the black strand and leave the blue alone. My magic surrounded the black strand. I tried to take it away from the king, but he cried out.

"Stop. It hurts. Whatever you are doing, stop."

I stopped immediately and waited for him to stop moving. I took the strand and tried to push it down away from the king's head. Slowly it moved further and further away from his head. When I finally got it to his knees, I stopped. I was panting and out of breath. I started to fall, but Richard grabbed me to keep me upright.

"I need to sit," I whispered weakly to him. I felt a little stronger, and with his help, I made it to my chair and flopped into it.

"Young lady, I don't know what you did, but you stopped the curse," the king said happily.

I barely had the strength to look at him. "I didn't stop it. I moved it away from your head so the curse can't influence your decisions. I can't get rid of it. I was trying to when you said it hurt. I may have bought you some time, but we still need to find your staff right away."

His face instantly changed. He stopped smiling and looked deeply saddened. "How much time do you think I have?"

"Maybe a day or two. We need to hurry, but no one is very helpful." The king looked at Hilail sharply. "Except Hilail, of course."

"What is it you need?" he asked.

"We need people to talk to us. They look at us like we are either monsters or beneath them."

"Many elementals are going to treat you that way. They think they know what it was like when we lived among you. They think they were all worshipped as gods and goddesses and they never had to work for anything. It's not true, though they won't listen to what I say."

"It's not true? That's what I thought too."

"We were worshipped, but elementals were also teachers to the group of humans we chose to share our gifts with. We worked beside them, teaching them how to use their powers for good, not for darkness. There were always a couple of elementals and humans who used dark magic and tried to use humans for their own gain, but they were easy to stop." He took a deep breath and looked away from us.

"The shadow king didn't really bother us until elementals from each group came together and started teaching humans how to use very dark magic for their own gain. When these dark magic users started destroying hundreds of lives, the shadow king finally had enough. He didn't think humans were capable of controlling magic, and he blamed us for teaching them, so we were banished. Now, a new darkness spreads across the land, trying to destroy us."

"Will you help us?" I asked, thinking about the dream I had about the darkness.

"Yes, though many will not agree with it. If you find my staff, I will help you when it is time to banish the darkness."

"Thank you. I think we will need all the help we can get. First, we must find your staff. I know you don't want to hear it, but it is looking more likely that Adam is telling the truth."

"The one from my dungeons." The king looked at Adam. "How can this be?"

"I overheard your daughter, she is not satisfied with her life here and wants to rule among the humans. She thinks you keep the elementals here over a vow with a shadow king that is not even here anymore."

"He's here. She doesn't want to believe it. Even as a little girl, she wanted to live among humans. I don't know why or who would have made her believe it is her right to do so, but I thought I talked her out of such things."

"No, she has hidden her thoughts from you. I'm sorry, your majesty, but I don't think you can trust her. We think she has done some darker magic than she should have."

"Do you have proof?" he asked, his voice gruff.

"Not really, at least not that you can see." I explained to him my theory on the darker glow coming from her. He listened and nodded quietly until I was finished.

"I've never heard of a human that could do that. Once long ago, in my grandfather's time, there was an elemental who could see our magical signatures. He said it was the most important part of us, and I think that's what you are seeing. You are describing it in the same exact way. If you think that's the case, there is a good chance it is." He looked at me. "What about my color? Is mine dark now?"

"No, you have the brightest blue I have seen, even though there is a strand of black running through it from the curse. It hasn't changed who you are. You are good. The curse can't change that, even if the curse takes you over completely, it looks like your magical signature won't be changed. It's the curse that is bad, not you."

He looked relieved. "Tell me why you came here in the first place. I still don't really know."

I told him everything about the note and how I thought I needed to come.

"The water sprites are here in this realm. They came with us when we left our homes to come to this planet. They do not like to be bothered though, and we rarely see them. I am surprised that they have been in the human realm. I didn't even know that was possible. I thought I sealed the entrances."

"There's more than one?"

"Of course, but they are tough to find. You came through the main entrance, but we used to have many ways to your realm." I filed this information away to think about later. "I will send word to the sprites to come for a meeting with you. Then we can see what they called you down here for. They know that humans aren't supposed to know of us."

"Thank you."

CHAPTER TWENTY

"I want to give you something that will help you find the staff," the king said after staring at me for a minute.

"If you have something that will help, why haven't your men been able to find it yet?" I asked suspiciously.

"Because I didn't give it to them."

"Why not?"

"By the time I realized the staff was missing, I was already being changed by the curse. It didn't want me to find the staff, but you have given me a second chance. I know I need your help."

"Why don't you give whatever it is to Hilail?"

"Once the curse fully takes me over, it will start to affect everyone around me. Those closest to me will feel it first. Hilail is my nephew, so it will come to him quickly. Our healers were able to learn that much. This curse will eventually turn all the water elementals if it takes me since they are connected to me. I can't trust that the staff will be found before Hilail starts to be affected too."

"I understand. What do you need to give me?" I asked him.

"I will show you once we finish our meal. We will need to go to a more private place. If my daughter really is behind this, she will have spies everywhere. I'm surprised you have magic. The shadow king must have spared some of you, but for what purpose, I'm not sure. No one knows why the shadow king does the things he does. He hasn't been seen in ages, but he is still around."

"How do you know?"

"I can feel him," he said. "All the elemental kings and queens are linked with the shadow king. When we swear our oath to him, we become bonded. If he died, I would know."

"Wow," I said. To be bonded to the shadow king was a pretty big deal.

"The shadow king is not bad. He did not banish us without good reason. Some of our own people made terrible choices, and we should have stopped them before they caused so much trouble. It's why we are careful not to use dark magic."

"Is there a reason why your daughter would have turned to dark magic?"

"No, she has been protected from having to do anything that would cause her to use dark magic. I don't understand what would have made her do this." He hung his head and didn't speak for a minute.

"Can you tell me anything about the elementals?" I asked, changing the subject.

"Earth, air, fire, and water are the four types of elementals. We all came from the stars very far away after catastrophes affected our homes."

"What about void?" I asked.

Void is not an element. There really isn't a name for it, which is why we called them elementals. No one knows a lot about them. When they first arrived, it wasn't in a burst of wind or even a ring of fire or ice. They just appeared one day, as if they had been here the whole time and were choosing to reveal themselves to us."

I leaned in closer. I really wanted to know more about the void elementals or whatever they really were. "What else do you know about them?"

"Sadly, not much. They were incredibly secretive, and they didn't take humans as followers like we did. I think they may have given power to a few humans, but I'm not sure. We haven't seen them since the banishing, and even then, we only saw them once every couple of years. They never caused anyone any trouble, and they were never involved in any of the fights between elementals, though I heard that they had power over life and death. That's all I know about them," the king told us.

We finished our meal, and he stood up. "Come with me."

We followed him out of the dining hall and through a door that led into an outdoor garden. I looked up and into a beautiful blue sky. The sun was shining and plants and flowers everywhere. "How is this all possible?" I asked. We were still under the lake as far as I could tell, but it didn't look like it.

"Magic," he said. "Look up again, but out of the corner of your eye." I did what he said. "There, do you see it, a slight rippling or shimmering in the air?"

"Yes, what is it?"

"It's a protective dome. Technically, we are not in your realm, but this one does push up against it. We keep protections up in case our realm and yours were to collide. Then the water from the lake would be able to get in and destroy our home. The protections are always being reinforced," he said when he looked at me. I probably looked worried thinking about all that water flooding into here.

"You have to stay in this realm?"

"We don't have to. We are not allowed to interact with humans, but as long as we stay near the oceans or rivers, we can go wherever we want. Anyone leaving has to have my permission. No one has been out of our realm for hundreds of years, except to collect the belongings of Adam after he snuck in. I thought it would be best to keep everyone away from humans. There is too much danger in someone revealing themselves to a human and the shadow king hearing of it," he said. "Come here so I can share this with you."

He walked over to a small fountain in the center of the garden. "Please put your arms out with your palms up." He put his hands over mine, and a slight tingling began in my palms. I closed my eyes and watched as the light around the king started to glow even brighter. Slowly the brightness pulled in on itself, condensing to form a small ball that glowed so brightly I could barely look at it. I opened my eyes and saw that the king was glowing.

I closed my eyes in time to see the small ball of condensed light flow from his hand down to mine. I gasped. The ball of light exploded around me. I felt tingles all over my body, and for a second, I thought I was going to be sick. I stood quietly, letting my body relax and absorb the light. Once I felt calmer, I closed my eyes and could make out a bright blue glow coming from around me.

"What did you do?"

"I gave you some of my power." I looked at my friends and caught sight of Hilail. His mouth was hanging open, probably from shock. I turned away, not wanting to face the fact that something crazy happened.

"Why?"

"It will help you find the staff. Think about where it is. You are the only one now who can find it."

I thought about the staff and immediately felt a slight sensation around my body, tugging me to the right. "I think I know where it is. I can feel it tugging at me. Why couldn't you do this?" I asked him.

"I haven't been able to get it to work since I was cursed. Now you must go and find it as quick as you can. And bring me evidence if my daughter is the one behind this. I need to know for sure."

"Ok," I told him. "We will do our best."

He led us back to the door and opened it. "Go now, before anyone else knows. Hilail, you have the crest, so you will be able to get them anything else they need while you are gone. Please be careful and bring the staff back."

"Let's go. The sooner we find the staff, the sooner we can get answers and leave. We don't want any more trouble," I said.

Hilail opened the door and took us a completely different way then we went before. We stopped at our room to change back into our clothes before Hilail led us down another hallway. It eventually led us to a double door that opened up to the back of the castle and a stable. Hilail took four horses out, and we mounted up and started riding down the only path. I was riding with Richard, and Abby was with Tider. Adam got his own horse.

I looked around to appreciate the view. Everywhere I looked, I could see waterways intersecting with the roads. The sun reflected off the water, making it look like glittery glass lay everywhere. I looked back at the castle and caught my breath. It was almost entirely surrounded by water except for a couple of roads leading away from it. A thought struck me.

"Hilail, did you ever hear of Atlantis?"

"No, I haven't. Why?"

My excitement vanished. I thought I found the lost city, Atlantis. The castle and surrounding area looked almost exactly like what I pictured Atlantis to look like.

"No reason," I told him. "It's a myth that humans have."

"I never would have thought of that, but it makes sense," Tider said. "Maybe humans made it up after the elementals were banished so they wouldn't forget them. Maybe that's why it's never been found. It was here all along, in another realm."

"Maybe," I said, letting myself feel excited again. It would be awesome to discover Atlantis, even if I couldn't tell anyone about it.

"You need to stay close to me in case we get in a fight so I can protect you," Hilail said.

"We aren't as defenseless as you think we are," Tider said.

"You've never fought one of us before."

"I'm sure we will be fine, especially if you give us some pointers," I said.

"I don't think I should be telling you how to beat my own people."

"Come on, Hilail. We need all the help we can get. There's a good chance the princess has elementals guarding the staff. We need to be able to fight them."

"Fine, I will try to help you when we stop for the night. We will need to find a place that's private anyway. That way, we can have a fire without anyone noticing us."

I was looking forward to the end of the day after an hour. My butt was sore, and my back was stiff. It was an incredibly uncomfortable ride. Once, when our horse hit a low spot in the forest, I was thrown against Richard. As soon as he grabbed me, the energy sparked between us.

He pulled back quickly, but not before Abby got a glimpse of the sparks. She gave me a look, and I shook my head. I still didn't understand why sometimes when we touched nothing happened, and other times we made sparks fly between us. When things calmed down, we would have to figure it out.

We rode for another hour before Hilail called for us to a stop.

"We will make camp here," he said. "There is a town only a few minutes ride ahead of us. I will go there and get some provisions while you get the horses fed and set out our blankets for the night. They are in the saddlebags on your horses. I will be back as soon as I can. And don't let anyone see you." He rode off toward the town.

We went through the saddlebags and pulled out everything in each one. There was some water, the sleeping bags, and the feed for horses, but that was it.

"What do we do with this?" I asked.

"No idea," said Tider.

Adam started spreading the sleeping bags out.

"I don't want to sleep outside," Abby said. "What if someone sees us. Can't we find somewhere else?"

"We can't sit out here. It's already starting to get dark, and the temperature is dropping. It will be too cold without a fire," Tider said.

"Why don't I make my shield, and we can put the fire in it with us?" I asked.

"You still have trouble with the shield when there is movement, and fire makes a lot of movement. The last thing we need is to have you exhausted if something bad does happen."

"We've all read about hobbits. Their houses are underground. Why don't we raise up a pocket of the ground for us to stay in? Then we could have a fire, and let the smoke out. We could put a hole in the roof to vent it," Abby said.

"That's a great idea," I told her. "I will see what I can do."

I called my magic to me and imagined the earth opening up to make a little pocket. I closed my eyes and watched as the magic went to work. It was beautiful to see, and within minutes it was done. It was a very rough looking space, and there was no door, but we would be inside, and we could make something to cover the way out.

Richard grabbed some wood and started a fire to warm us up.

"I'm so glad we can take a break for a while. All that riding is hard," Abby said.

"Yeah. I've never ridden a horse before. It's harder than it looks," Tider said. We all felt the same way.

"We need to eat something and then get some rest." I thought about the staff and felt the same tingle in my middle. It was still pulling me the way we were heading. "We will have to go around the town tomorrow. I don't think it's in there. Somehow it feels farther away. "

"Well, let's hope it's not much farther. We only have tomorrow and the next day to get the staff back to the king. Otherwise, we are all screwed," Adam said.

"We'll get it. I doubt they took it far. The princess isn't going to want to wait for it when she can finally use it."

"That's the thing. I don't think she will be able to use it. Only the ruler can use it. The curse isn't killing the king, only turning him evil. I think she expects him to die because of the curse. Someone is lying to her," Richard said.

"I can't believe she doesn't even care if her dad dies. How could someone become so twisted?"

"I don't know, but I don't want her guards to catch up to us, so we need to get moving first thing in the morning."

I heard a noise outside and went to investigate. Hilail was walking into the clearing with a look of astonishment on his face. "What did you do?"

"We didn't want to stay outside, so we made an area for us to sleep and stay warm." He walked inside, looking around.

"How did you do this? Humans aren't supposed to be this strong magically."

"It really didn't take a ton of magic. We only needed the ground to lift up a bit. It was pretty easy."

"Which one of you did this?"

They all looked at me. "Why am I not surprised," he said. "I received word from a loyal guard, the princess sent her own guards to your room to search for a trinket she says went missing while you were with her. She told them to look for anything else with the royal crest on it too since you are thieves and may have stolen from the king."

"Why would she do that?"

"She must have known that the king gave you something, so she sent her guards in, thinking it would have the royal crest on it since it was her fathers. It's all the proof I need that she is the one who stole the king's staff."

"I'm sorry, Hilail. I'm sure you were hoping it wasn't her." Hilail looked upset.

"Let's work on your magic," Hilail said after taking a deep breath.

"Why don't you all watch so you can help each other once you leave here? I'm not sure if these moves will help if you don't have power over water, but it's worth a try."

"Sounds good to us," we said.

We watched as Hilail started to call on his magic. It was almost instantaneous. He raised his arms in what looked like a dance position. He opened his palms, and rain started falling. He closed his palms, and the water pulled together into a large ball. It broke apart into thousands of pieces of ice suspended in the air when his hands twisted.

I closed my eyes and watched the magic. It didn't fight Hilail. It was a part of him, and it knew what he wanted with barely a thought. The magic flew from his hand to the air around us, twirling in the air to keep the ice suspended. When his hands came together, the ice started to move, one piece at a time, into the shape of a snowflake. Hilail moved his arms slowly, and the ice snowflake turned into a real snowflake. The pieces broke apart and hovered right in front of us. I opened my eyes and reached out a hand. A snowflake dropped onto it but didn't melt.

"This is amazing. You barely have to think before the magic does what you want."

Hilail put his hands into the air and pulled them apart. The snow completely disappeared. "That is what our children are taught," he said.

"Wow. You're right. We can't compete with that," Abby said, awed.

"Maybe not, but I will try to teach you some of it. Which of you has a water element?"

"I'm a water elemental," Tider said, stepping forward.

"No, you're not. You have a water element, but I am a water elemental. You are human." He frowned.

"It doesn't matter what the correct term is, you can still teach us more about having a water element," I said.

"Fine. I will show you each a move, and you repeat it but without magic. First, you must learn the moves."

We followed along as Hilail taught us the different moves. Eventually, he stopped to get some rest so we would be ready for the morning.

In the morning, we woke up and grabbed a quick breakfast before stepping outside.

"I want you to show me what you did to create this, but this time uncreate it," Hilail said to me.

I closed my eyes before directing my magic toward the earth. The ground caved in and slowly knit itself back together. It didn't look any different from the rest of the area.

"Is that good?" I asked.

"You have a lot of magic, but you are still fighting it. Next time ask the magic to come to you willingly. It will be faster and easier to use."

"I will try. Thank you," I told Hilail before getting on the horse with Richard. Hilail gave us warm cloaks that he bought from the town. We all had them on, but the hoods were down. If anyone approached, we would put the hoods up to cover our faces.

We skirted around the edge of the town, staying far enough away that no one could see us but close enough that we wouldn't lose as much time. We got back on the road again on the far side of town and were able to pick up the pace.

Suddenly, I felt a tugging sensation around my stomach. "We need to change direction," I yelled up to Hilail. "It's this way." I turned the horse to the left and set off. The tugging sensation kept getting stronger until I felt like all my stomach muscles were being pulled apart. Finally, the tugging stopped, and I looked around. We were on top of a giant cliff face. A few more feet forward, and we would fall off. The rest of my group rode up behind me.

"Where is the staff?"

"Below us," I said quietly.

CHAPTER TWENTY-ONE

"I don't think there's a way down." I looked out over the cliff to see a vast ocean below us. There was no path leading down, but that didn't stop Hilail. He pushed his hands out, and part of the ocean rushed toward us. Before it hit the cliff face, it froze, turning into ice steps.

"We will have to be very careful, so we don't slip, but I think there will be a cave down here that we can get into," Hilail said.

Hilail and Richard went first with the rest of us following. Tider went last in case he needed to help one of us if we slipped. Halfway down, Abby saw a cave in the cliff. Hilail used his magic to create a walkway to the entrance, and soon we were all standing on dry ground.

"Well," Adam said, looking around. "We found a cave that might have the staff in it. How do we find it from here?"

"We will have to look for it," I said.

We hiked forward, trying to figure out where we were. I knew we still had to be close to the staff since it wasn't tugging at me. Our tunnel split into two, and we quickly went left. Tider used a rock to scrape a mark into the wall near the tunnel we were going down.

"Good idea," I told him.

"I don't want to get lost down here."

We hit another split in the tunnel and decided to go left, but Adam stopped us.

"Look at this," he said, pointing to the wall where the tunnel went right. Scratched into the rock was a small wave, no bigger than my thumb. "I think the cave is marked so her followers can get here without getting lost. I didn't look at the last one, so I'm not sure."

"I saw this on the last one but didn't think anything of it. I figured it was a normal scratch, but now I see the wave. We should follow this tunnel and see if the next one is the same," Tider said.

We agreed and set off with more determination in our step. At the next split, we looked for the wave and found it on the left tunnel. We kept following the wave until we finally came to a tunnel where we could see a faint light at the end.

"I don't see anyone, but we better be careful," Hilail whispered. "I think it opens up after that turn."

We started walking into the tunnel, trying to be as quiet as possible. We made it to the turn and peered around the side. I looked out into a vast cavern. All around the edge were torches, and in the center was a giant chest surrounded by a lake of water. I knew the staff was in there. I went to step forward when Hilail grabbed me.

"Stop," he whispered. "There are elementals in here." He slowly pointed to one of the shadowy areas. I stared for a few seconds and was about to look away when I saw a slight movement. I couldn't tell what it was, but something was definitely there.

We stepped back into the tunnel. "What do we do now?" Tider asked.

"How many do you think there are? Can we take them?" Richard asked quietly.

"Give me a second to look. I might be able to tell how many there are," I said.

I peeked back around the corner and closed my eyes. I looked at the same shadowy spot again and saw a faint blue color. I wasn't sure why the color was so faint. I scanned the rest of the cavern and saw three more figures, all with the same faint blue color.

The one I was watching shifted and moved silently toward the torches. I gasped. They weren't weak. Their colors were a faint blue because the rest of the magical signature was black, so I couldn't see it in the dark. I moved back to my friends.

"We have a problem," I told them. "There are four elementals, and they have been doing dark magic. Their signatures are almost completely black."

"We need more help. Let's leave, and I can go for back up."

"We can't, Hilail. We need that staff now. Your king doesn't have time to waste. We won't get back to him in time if we don't act. We may already be too late," I said.

He looked torn. "I don't know if we can fight them all."

"We don't really have a choice. We have to come up with something."

"Hilail, you can take one on by yourself, right?" Tider asked.

"Yeah, but there are four."

"Abby can stay here so she can heal us, and the rest of us can keep them distracted until you get yours down. Then you can come help whoever looks like they are having the most trouble and so on."

"That could work. You will have to be very careful though. These elementals are probably trained in combat and won't be trying to keep you alive."

"Let's do it," Adam said.

"Wait, one more thing." I reached into my bag and pulled out the black vials Mr. Connor had given me. "These are the bomb potions. Only use them if you have to. Mr. Connor said they affect about a five-foot radius, so make sure it's clear before you throw it." Everyone nodded, and I handed them out to Adam, Tider, and Richard. I kept one for myself too. "Be careful," I whispered.

We looked back around the corner, and before I could say anything, Hilail slipped out into the cavern. He went to the right, so we went to the left, keeping our footfalls silent. Before we made it to the first elemental Hilail launched his attack. Adam and Tider turned to the nearest elemental and start attacking too.

Richard turned as another elemental came running toward us and shot a blast of air at him. The elemental wasn't expecting it and tumbled backward but got up immediately and headed for Richard. I was about to help him when I saw the last elemental sneaking up on Hilail.

Hilail had no idea he was there, so I called on the water in the lake to grab the elemental and trap him in place. It worked for a few seconds, but he broke free and started toward me. I pulled more water from the lake, trying to stop him. I pushed the water at him, and he stopped advancing. He moved into one of the forms that Hilail had shown us, and I jumped to the side, right before an icicle impaled me.

I made an ice shield around myself and held it there while icicles of all sizes hit. I took a second to look at everyone else. Richard was using air to keep the elemental's attacks from hitting him. He flew above the elemental and used wind to pick up rocks to throw.

Tider and Adam weren't doing too bad either. Adam was attacking with fireballs. The elemental kept using water to put the fire out, but it was distracting him enough that Tider was able to hit him with jagged pieces of ice. I turned to Hilail. I watched as he called water from the lake to swallow up the elemental he was fighting. The water swirled around and lifted the elemental, trapping him in a bubble of water. The elemental could breathe, but Hilail had made long ropes of water to tie his hands and legs.

My shield made a loud groaning noise and was starting to crack when the barrage of icicles stopped. I quickly fired my own icicles at the elemental, but he dodged them easily. He was definitely trained in combat. He was too fast for me to hit, but maybe I could outthink him.

Before I got the chance, Hilail was at my side. "Are you ok?" he asked, panting.

"So far, but this guy is fast," I said as I dodged another icicle.

Hilail started throwing magic at the elemental. I stood in awe for a minute, forgetting we were in a fight. Hilail and the other elemental fought with raw power. Hilail used water on the ground to throw the elemental twenty feet in the air. The elemental pulled water up from the lake to cushion his fall.

A large explosion behind me caused me to jump. It was from Richard. He used his potion, but he still looked like he was having a lot of trouble, so I ran to him and joined the fight.

"What do we do?"

"Try to hit him with a stream of water until he hits that pillar. Then I can use air to keep him there."

I did as Richard asked and pushed a stream of water at the elemental. I kept at it until he was finally up tight to the pillar. Richard pulled air to gather around the elemental. It swirled faster and faster, forming a small tornado. The elemental was trapped against the pillar as long as Richard could hold the magic there.

"Go," he said to me. "Help the others. I can keep him here for a while."

I ran over to Tider and Adam and saw that they had everything under control. Their elemental was already weakening from having to continually put out Adam's fire and fight Tider's water magic.

"Good job, guys," I yelled as I ran for the staff. As I got closer to the lake, I froze an area to walk across to get to the chest. I was opening it when an explosion rocked the cavern. A hole opened directly above me, and the princess jumped down. She used water to slow her fall and landed only a few feet from me.

"What are you doing?" she screeched. "You are ruining everything. I will kill you for this." She threw a blast of water at me that swept me off my feet. The water tried to drag me under, but I pushed it away with my magic and looked at the princess.

"Why would you want your dad dead?" I shouted at her and dove to the side as she tried to hit me again.

"He is weak. We need to rise to the top again. We should be the rulers," she yelled, trying to blast me apart.

I knew I wouldn't be able to reason with her, so I put all of my energy into the fight. While she continued trying to hit me with water and ice, I slowly started making the ground a couple of inches beneath her sink. The ground was steady enough for her to stand on, but I kept working at it, making a deep pit for her to fall into. Once I thought it was deep enough, I let the last few inches crumble. She tried to jump out of the way, but I used water to push her down.

As soon as she fell in, I started closing the hole up around her. I left her head free so she could still breathe, but the rest of her was covered entirely. I made sure to pack the earth in tightly so she wouldn't be able to get out. She was still able to use her magic though and tried to hit me with a massive wave of water. I jumped out of the way, but she sent the wave as a distraction. Right behind it was a piece of jagged ice that ripped through my shoulder.

I screamed in pain, and she laughed. She threw another icicle at me. I tried to dodge but couldn't get out of the way, and it tore open my arm. I was barely able to stand from the pain. I was losing my hold on the magic that kept her down too. She was using water to help pull the dirt away from her. I tried to stop her, but I fell to my knees and couldn't get up. I heard a yell and looked toward it. The princess was unconscious. Richard had run up and hit her on the head with a rock.

He ran to me. "Sally, are you ok?"

"Yes, I'm fine," I tried to say, but it was very weak.

"Abby, come here. Sally needs you."

Abby came running and dropped to her knees next to me.

"What happened?" she asked, looking at Richard. "I don't think I can heal her." She had tears in her eyes as she stared down at me. "I just finished healing Tider. He was hit pretty badly too," she said.

"You have to try," Richard said.

"Potion," I whispered to them. "Give me the potion."

"I forgot," Richard said. He rolled me over a little and reached into my bag, grabbing the red vial. He held it up for me to see and helped me drink it. Within minutes my skin and muscles started to knit back together. I was still woozy but already felt a lot better. I stood up and looked around the cavern. All the elementals we were fighting were tied up.

"Will that hold them?" I asked Hilail, pointing to the rope.

"Yes, it's a special rope made to contain elementals. Once it is on, it nullifies your powers. They won't be going anywhere. I just need to tie up the princess."

We waited while he tied her up and then walked over to the chest. I opened it and looked inside. The staff was on top of a pile of other things that looked valuable. I reached in and grabbed it. A fission of power snaked up my arm, and the staff started to glow the same bright blue color as the king.

"How did you do that?" asked Hilail. "Only the king should be able to use it."

"I don't know. Maybe I can use it since he gave me some of his power."

"We don't have to walk back to the palace. We can go there right now," he said.

"How?"

"Think about where you want to go and who you want to go with you. The staff will do the rest."

I looked at the staff doubtfully.

"It will work," Hilail said. "Come on, we have no choice, we don't know what condition the king is in. This gives us the chance to make it back quickly."

Hilail was right. We needed to hurry, or else the king might not make it.

"Fine, let's go. What do we do with all of them?"

"Picture them coming with us. The staff should transport us all."

"Everybody grab hands just in case. I don't want anyone getting left behind. Hilail grab the princess. She needs to make it back so the king will release Adam."

We all grabbed hands, and Hilail threw the princess over his shoulder. I looked at the staff and thought about all of us going to the palace. I pictured us standing in the throne room, and the next thing I knew, I felt lightheaded, and we were back at the palace.

I heard a small shriek and saw one of the servants run out of the room. I looked around. We were not a pretty sight. We were bruised and bloody, and we were carrying the princess. It didn't look good.

The king came striding in. "What do you think you are doing? You are making a mess of my palace. What did you do to my daughter?" he roared, making us all flinch.

"She is fine, sir, just unconscious," I said, trying to calm him.

"You will all rot in cells for the rest of your lives. Guards," he called.

I closed my eyes and looked at him. The curse was almost completely wrapped around him. He needed to hold his staff.

"You sent us to get your staff, remember?"

"I don't need or want the staff," he yelled. "That staff is a curse. It makes us weak when we need to be strong." I could hear the guards getting closer.

"Good," I said, "because we couldn't find it." My friends looked around, confused. I had put a shield of invisibility around it as soon as the king started yelling. I knew he wouldn't want it if the curse was too strong.

He looked surprised. "You didn't find it?"

"No, we found the princess fighting with an elemental that did this to her. She wasn't the one to blame, but the guy said he was going to use the staff and get rid of you and her."

"Who was this?" the king yelled.

"I can't tell you."

"Why not?" he screamed in a rage.

"It's one of your guards. I don't want him to know that I told you. He might run, and then he could cause you trouble."

"Why are you helping me? I told you that you were going to rot in a cell," he said, looking at me suspiciously.

"I like your daughter. She doesn't deserve somebody beating her up to get to you." I was making things up, trying to get him to believe I wasn't a threat.

"Fine, come here and tell me who did this."

I took a small step forward, and the staff almost became visible. I couldn't let him see it. I concentrated on keeping the staff invisible and took another step. Then another. I was sweating by the time I made it to him. "I'm sorry, sir. I was hurt pretty badly, and it is still hard to move."

He looked at my clothes and nodded. "Now, tell me."

He leaned in. So did I, but then I started to fall. He grabbed me to keep me from falling into him, but instead of grabbing my arm, I thrust out the staff, and his hand closed around it. His whole body bent backward, and I was thrown from him. I landed in a heap next to the column I was thrown into. I could barely breathe, and I struggled to stand. Everyone else was thrown back too, even the guards who were entering the throne room. I looked at the king and watched as magic swirled around his body.

The staff let out a vibrant blue light that grabbed the curse and smothered it. Soon only the bright blue light surrounded the king. I blinked and looked at the king again. I could see the light without closing my eyes. I looked around and saw everyone's magical signature faintly.

"Sally." The king walked over to me. "How bad are you hurt?"

"Fine," I managed to say.

"Healers," the king called for them to help me.

The healers arrived quickly. I could feel them using their magic to heal my body.

As soon as I felt better, I opened my eyes and tried to stand up. One of the healers pushed me back down. "You need to rest for a little bit," she told me.

"But I need to talk to the king."

"You will have plenty of time for that."

I tried arguing, but Abby leaned over me. "Sally, you need to do what they say. You could have died today. Twice. I think your body deserves a bit of rest."

"Make sure the king knows it wasn't Adam."

"Don't worry, Hilail is giving him the whole story."

I laid my head back down and fell asleep.

It was dark when I woke up. I didn't hear any noise, so I quietly got up and threw some clothes on. Someone had changed me and taken all my bloody clothing away. They replaced it with the same style clothes as before. I wasn't going to be able to sleep any longer, so I headed out into the hallway. I didn't want to wake my friends. I walked toward the throne room, hoping to find the kitchen along the way. I was starving and needed something to eat. I hadn't had a good meal in a couple of days.

I walked into a room and was shocked to see a servant up already.

"What can I get for you?" she asked.

"I'm not sure. I was hungry and thought I would try to find the kitchen to see if there was anything to eat."

"I can make you whatever you would like."

"Glorian makes a wonderful breakfast," the king said from behind me.

"That would be great," I told him.

"We will be in my dining quarters," the king said to the elemental.

"I will bring it to you when it's ready," Glorian replied.

"Come," said the king. "We have much to discuss." I followed him back to his dining hall, and we sat down while we waited for food.

"I figured you would be up early and hungry enough to search out food. I'm glad I wasn't wrong."

"What happened after I fell asleep?" I asked.

"The healers brought you up here and let you rest."

"What about my friends and Adam and Hilail? And what about your daughter?"

"Your friends told me what happened. I spoke with each one of them, granting them something special for helping break the curse. Adam was also given a gift. He is free to leave. Hilail is either sleeping or more likely back at work. As for my daughter, she is locked up. I will have to choose a different successor. I would like you to tell your side of the events," he said.

I told him exactly what happened, not leaving anything out. At some point, someone brought me food, and I ate while I talked. I figured the king could forgive my manners. When I finished talking, I looked down and continued eating my breakfast.

"Sally, you did a good job. I have a gift for you when you are finished eating."

"Wait, you need to take your magic back," I told him. "Thanks for letting me use it. I never would have found the staff without it."

"I will not be taking the magic back. It is yours now."

"What? Oh no, I can't take that," I tried to tell him.

"You need to. This whole thing has shown me that we need someone else to have the power of the staff. It can't be a water elemental. They are all connected to me, so anything that happens to me happens to them. I need an outsider that we can trust. You are perfect for it. If anything ever happens to me, you will know, and you can help us again. Besides, it helps you with your magic. I'm sure you noticed a few changes?"

"I guess." I wasn't sure what to think about everything, but I was glad the king trusted me. And I had noticed changes. Like being able to see magical auras without my eyes closed for starters.

"Now that that's settled, let's move on. For helping me, I want to give you a gift. Name what you want, and if it's in my power, I will do it for you. Take a few minutes to think about it," he said.

"Can you help Abby's dad? He is under a curse that the Pulhu..." I trailed off as he shook his head.

"Don't worry about Abby's dad. She asked for the same thing. I gave her a potion to help him ward off this curse. We know of it, and it is extremely cruel. These Pulhu need to be stopped. If they are willing to use a curse like that, then there is probably nothing they won't do, including killing innocent people."

"I don't know how to stop them," I told him.

"If you are who everyone thinks, then the darkness is coming, and you will have to defeat it. When you win, these Pulhu will be finished too. I am guessing that the returning darkness is what has made them act the way they do. Some people are so filled with greed and lust for power that it only takes the smallest push for them to jump into black magic. I'm sure the darkness has reached out to find those weak enough for it to control."

"There is nothing else I can do?"

"Don't let them get you. We will be there when you need us most. Use my power to call me when the darkness arrives. My elementals will come to help."

"Thank you."

The king reached into his pocket and pulled out a small, black, velvety box.

"I thought you might have trouble coming up with something you wanted. I had a spell put on this last night for you." He handed me the box, and I slowly opened it. Nestled on a cream-colored silk cushion was a luminescent pearl. It was the biggest pearl I had ever seen, and the color was amazing.

"It's beautiful," I told the king.

"Yes, but that's not what makes it special. It is enchanted to give you your reward when you are ready. All you have to do is hold the pearl in your palm and say what you want out loud. If it is possible, the pearl will light up and break into a million pieces, leaving you with your gift. These are very hard to make, so please don't lose it."

"I won't," I said, still staring at the pearl. "Thank you. This is amazing."

"I have one more thing to show you. You said the water sprites brought you here, and I believe I have figured out why." He led me through an open doorway and out into a garden surrounded by water. It was stunning. There were water sculptures everywhere.

Every plant that grew in water was in the garden, and the water itself danced and sparkled over everything. It almost looked like a play. Water would shoot out of one fountain and hit a stream of water from another, forming rainbows. I could hear the sound of tinkling bells and stopped to listen. It was beautiful, but then everything went silent.

I looked at the king. "What happened?"

"Wait for a second."

Suddenly out of all the plants and even from in the water, sprites started pouring out. They circled me, and some even landed on me. I was trying to look at all of them when I lost my balance and fell. The king grabbed my arm and helped steady me. The water sprites tittered at me disapprovingly.

"I'm sorry."

"Hello, everyone. This is Sally. She is the one who lifted the curse."

The sprites clapped and laughed and flew around me faster. One of them came right up to my face and studied me. She looked just like the one from my dream.

"How are you?" I asked.

She tilted her head from side to side and then spoke slowly to me in ancient. "Thank you for helping us. Without you, we would have been lost."

"What did I do?" I was confused. I hadn't even seen the sprites till now. How could I have helped them?

"You stopped the curse. From what we can tell, the curse was put here in our garden long ago, but it was hidden from everyone. No one could see it or even sense it. When the king's staff was stolen, the curse came to life and was able to get to him. We were trying to slow it down, but it was overpowering us."

I was following her down one of the paths while she talked. She stopped suddenly and pointed. In the middle of the garden was a circle of dead grass. It was almost ten feet across.

"The curse kept growing and was killing everything it touched. We almost lost two of our own when they tried to get inside the circle to attempt to stop it."

"I'm sorry your friends got hurt. Are they all right?" I asked, worried about such small beings.

"Yes, they are," she said, smiling. "You have a kind heart. That's why we were sure you could help. We knew the king would be awful because of the curse, but we thought you would still care enough to help, and we were right."

"It was you who left the note?"

"Yes."

"Why couldn't you tell me?" I asked.

"We are not allowed to interfere with humans, especially in something as big as the prophecy. As it is, what I did could get us in trouble, but I didn't feel I had a choice."

"How would you get in trouble?"

"The shadow king."

"I don't think I like him," I said.

The water sprite laughed. "You don't have to like him. You just have to listen to him. He makes the rules, and we follow or at least try to. He did it for good reasons. Humans and magic don't always get along so well."

I tried to protest.

"Look at the Pulhu," she said, and I shut my mouth. She was right. If the Pulhu didn't have magic, they wouldn't be as much of a threat.

"Even elementals can make the wrong choices, like the princess and her followers, though it doesn't happen often. It will get harder and harder for the Pulhu to control themselves, and many will choose to follow them the closer the darkness comes. You will need to be very careful. I will be with you from now on. We have talked and decided you need one of us to help you. I was chosen for this task."

I stared at her blankly, not truly understanding. "Unless you would prefer someone else," she said crestfallen.

"No, no, I am definitely happy you will be with me. I'm just not sure how to process this all. It's a lot of information," I told her.

She laughed again. "We will talk later," she told me and came to rest on my shoulder.

"Come now. It's time for you to meet with your friends and head back to the human realm," the king said. "The Pulhu will be after you when you get back. You need to get somewhere safe quickly."

CHAPTER TWENTY-TWO

The king walked me out to the hall and said we would meet in thirty minutes to go home. I went back to the room and woke my friends up. We headed down to the hall that would lead us to the entrance.

The king and Hilail were waiting for us. We followed them down to the archway, and the king began to chant in the ancient language. "Go," he said when he finished chanting. We jumped through the arch. I looked back one last time and watched as Hilail and the king disappeared. I swam up through the water and quickly climbed out.

"Hey, guys. What are you doing? I thought you wanted to search this area," Gary said.

"We already did," Richard replied.

"You just went down there. You couldn't have searched very hard," Gary said skeptically.

"They found what they were searching for. I'm Adam. Who are you?"

"What? How? Who?" Gary asked, shocked.

"This is Chet's missing grandson. We were down there for a while, but the water elemental king moved time back for us. Otherwise, we would have been gone months. Time moves differently there. We need to leave. The Pulhu are coming, and we can't let them catch us here. We don't want them to find out where the elementals are," I explained to him.

"How do you know that?"

"Trust me, and let's go."

We ran for the path back to the car.

"Wait," shouted Gary. "If they really are coming, they will come from that way. We need to take a different route."

"You're right," I said. "Do you know a different way?"

"Yes, but it's going to take longer. We need to stay closer to the shore and then cut inland. Hopefully, that will throw them off our trail."

"Let's go," I said. We walked past the lake and headed along the shore, keeping a steady pace. It would be easy to break an ankle on the loose stones if we ran.

Soon we saw storm clouds gathering behind us.

"It's the Pulhu. Keep going," Gary said.

We picked up the pace. I almost lost my footing a few times but managed to right myself before I fell. I looked back and saw the storm clouds getting closer. Lightning started to crackle across the sky, pointing in our direction. Soon it would be on top of us.

"We are aren't going to make it," Tider shouted over the roaring wind.

Gary left the shore and turned inland. There was no cover, and as we reached the top of a hill, I looked back and saw a group of people running toward us.

"They've seen us. There's no chance of getting past them now. We need to fight," Tider said.

"Not yet," called Gary. He opened his phone while running and spoke into it. "Back up is on the way. They will meet us in ten to fifteen minutes. We need to keep going until we meet them, then we can fight."

We stopped talking and focused on running. All I could hear was our labored breaths and the wind rushing past, bringing the storm closer. At the top of the next hill, I could see two figures running toward us.

"Gary," I yelled, pointing in the distance, "is that our backup?" I asked with a sinking feeling in my gut.

"Yes, that's them," Gary said.

"That's all?" I couldn't stop myself from screeching. "We can't fight them with only two more people."

"Trust me, they are the best we have, and they are the only ones close enough to get here. Everyone else is thirty minutes or longer away. We're lucky I have been keeping these two nearby."

"Keep going," Adam yelled. I looked back and saw the Pulhu coming. Somehow they were moving faster than us. They had to be using magic. At this pace, they would catch us in a few minutes.

"We need to fight. Get to the next hill. We need the high ground, and there's a small lake on the other side of the hill so you can pull more water magic if you need it," Gary yelled.

"What about the storm?" I asked.

"Don't worry. One of my guys can try to counteract it, but we need to get the one controlling it out of the fight as fast as we can."

We turned around once we were on the top of the hill and watched as the Pulhu closed in. There were over a dozen of them. I looked up as the storm stopped moving closer. One of Gary's guys had a strained look on his face. I figured he was fighting the weather, and I looked back at the Pulhu. I noticed a guy toward the back that had a strained look too.

"There," I said, pointing. "That one with the green shirt. He's the one controlling the weather."

"I'll take him out," Gary shouted. "Everyone else, give them everything you've got."

The Pulhu were close enough to start hurling magic at us. Gary and the other security guy quickly moved forward to fight. I watched as Gary used earth to batter a member of the Pulhu while the ground fell out from under another one.

The other security guy threw fireballs at three of the Pulhu. He was able to hurl the fireballs faster than the Pulhu could stop him. It kept them busy, but there were still a lot left. They turned their attention to us and started forward.

I didn't even see the first one throw a blast of water at me. I flew through the air and landed hard on my back. The wind was knocked out of me, but I got back on my feet. My friends were now fighting the Pulhu with everything they had.

I pulled my magic toward me and did the same moves that Hilail taught us. We would need all my power, and after having Hilail help us, my water magic was the most powerful. The water came naturally to me, and I let it know what I needed it to do instead of forcing it. The water flew away from me and quickly engulfed one of the others. A little air bubble formed around his head so he could breathe, but he was no longer a threat as long as I had the energy to hold him.

I could barely even feel a pull on my energy, and I silently thanked Hilail for teaching me a little about how to use my water element better. I turned to the next guy and saw a blast of fire leave his hands and head straight toward Abby, who had her back turned while she tried to heal a cut on Tider's arm.

"No," I yelled. Water flew out from the lake and swirled around the flames, smothering them right before they hit her. The man turned to look at me and grinned triumphantly.

"You are ours now," he yelled to me.

"Never," I yelled back and sent a wave over him. When it settled back down, he was still standing there grinning, steam rising off of him.

He threw fire at me. I dodged to the side at the last second and flung a rope of water at him. It grabbed his legs first, causing him to fall. Then it wound around his arms and upper body. Once I was sure he couldn't escape, I checked to make sure the other guy I stopped was still in his bubble of water.

I breathed in relief when I saw that he was. There were only a few more Pulhu left. The rest were immobilized. Gary finished off his two and was now fighting a different guy. The two he had fought were covered in dirt, and they looked unconscious.

Our security guy had also beaten two of the Pulhu and was working on a third when the air behind the Pulhu shimmered, and three more people suddenly stood there. They looked around at everything happening, and then the guy in the middle looked directly at me. I knew him. He was the guy at the airport. He pointed at me, and the other two with him turned their attention to me.

"Guys," I yelled. "We have a problem. Richard, it's the guy from the airport."

My friends looked at the newcomers, and Abby turned white. "That's them. That's the guy that questioned me. Mr. Damon." She was trembling. I felt a rush of anger toward the man that hurt my friend. I looked back at the guy and saw a cruel smile on his face. This guy needed to be stopped.

"Don't worry, Abby. We won't let him touch you again," I told her. I turned toward the guys. "Tider, Richard, we need to stop that guy," I said, pointing. "He hurt Abby." They both looked at Abby and saw how scared she was.

"We won't let him get anywhere near you," Tider growled.

We didn't have any more time to talk. Adam was trying to take care of two of the Pulhu, so there was no one left but Tider, Richard, and myself to deal with the newcomers. I wasn't sure we would be able to beat them. The guy to the right pushed his hands out, and a wall of dirt flew at Richard. Richard used his magic to create a mini-tornado that took all the dirt and threw it back at the man.

As the two of them fought, the man on the left went for Tider using air to lift Tider off the ground. Tider sent icicles through the sky. One hit the man on his leg, and he lost his concentration. Tider fell out of the sky but used water to slow his descent. As soon as he landed, he was throwing ice at the man, trying to find a way to stop him. It took only a few seconds for all of this to happen, but I was so caught up in it that I didn't realize Mr. Damon was moving closer to me.

Abby yelled, making me snap my head around, and I threw a protective barrier around both of us as Mr. Damon sent lightning down for me. Shocked, I looked at him, and he smiled again. I wanted to be sick. He looked super creepy.

"You can't protect yourself from me," he said, sending more lightning to hit my shield. I was pretty sure I could hold the shield for a while, but then he put his hand right on the shield and began murmuring. My shield started turning a gray color and began to fall to pieces. It would only last another minute.

I grabbed Abby's hand. "Run to Gary. He's almost done with that guy so he can protect you."

"What about you?"

"I'll be fine," I told her.

I looked around one more time. Richard and Tider were both still fighting. They were struggling to beat this new group of Pulhu. They were much stronger than the first group that attacked us. Gary and the security guys were still fighting too, and Adam looked to be in pretty bad shape. I was on my own. As soon as the shield fell, I pushed Abby in the direction of Gary and turned to face Mr. Damon.

"What do you want?" I asked him. "Why won't you leave me alone?"

"There is something different about you. I will figure out what," he said.

"There is nothing different about me. You have had people following me since I got to school. You would know if something was different." I was hoping to keep him talking so my friends could come help me with him.

"That's just it, no one has seen anything, but the teachers seem to be trying to protect you. You must be hiding something, and it's my job to find out what."

"Who do you work for?"

"Come with me willingly, and you will find out. You can be on our side. The right side."

"I don't think so. Your side is definitely the wrong side. You want to hurt people without magic."

"Once they learn their place, no one will get hurt."

"Their place?" I was having trouble controlling my temper, and I started to pull my magic to me.

"They are inferior. They don't deserve to tell us what to do. We will rule over them, and they will do as they are told." Mr. Damon paused. "I can see that you aren't convinced. Obviously, you've spent too much time around them to understand." He threw his hands up, and a cage of lightning started to fall over me. I pushed a water bubble over my head and rolled out of the way as the lightning hit. Steam covered the area between us, and I took a second to try to figure out what to do. He was much stronger, and he knew what he was doing. I needed to keep him occupied until someone could help me.

Another blast of lightning hit my water bubble, and a burst of wind lifted me off the ground and carried me high into the sky. Mr. Damon lifted himself off the ground and hovered in front of me, his hands crackling with power.

"Are you done with this now? Are you ready to come with me, or do I need to knock you out?"

"I will never come with you," I told him. I tried to call water to me so I could get away from the swirling wind, but something was blocking it. I could see the same grey color that had been in the elemental's dungeon strung through the air around me. The only spot that wasn't covered by it was where Mr. Damon was standing.

I strode forward. "I said I will not come with you. Now let me go," I yelled as I walked up to him.

I needed my magic, or he would be able to take me wherever he wanted. As soon as I was within arms reach, I could feel my magic again. I couldn't pull enough water out of the air to do much damage to him, so I called on wind instead. I pushed air out at him in a concentrated burst, and he flew through the air, barely righting himself.

I flew out of my prison of wind and quickly headed for the ground below.

"Sally, watch out," Abby yelled.

I turned around and saw Mr. Damon behind me. He was gaining ground and had what appeared to be a coil of lightning in his hands. If he got that thing around me, it was going to hurt, a lot. As he reached me, Richard flew up. Tider used water to raise himself up to my level too. Thankfully we were almost over the lake, or there wouldn't be enough water for him to get this high.

"We need to do this together," I said. "He's too strong."

"On three," Richard said. "One, two, three." We all pushed our powers right at Mr. Damon. Tider threw jagged fragments of ice that spun in all directions, and Richard used the wind to push the pieces even faster. I called water to create a barrier behind him so he wouldn't get away. I didn't want him to get killed, but I also didn't want to be killed or kidnapped.

Mr. Damon threw up a shield to block against the ice, but he couldn't stop it all. I saw him flinch as a few pieces got past his barrier and cut him. I could see blood dripping from his face, and he looked as surprised as I felt. Tider and Richard managed to hurt him. They were stronger working together than Mr. Damon. Maybe we had a chance after all.

"Quick, we need to push him toward the ground. Gary is waiting for us. He can help hold him," I said.

We tried using our powers to grab Mr. Damon. I made coils of water. So did Tider, and Richard used air ropes, but each time we thought we got one on him, he would use his own magic to break free. We only managed to pull him a few feet when he suddenly burst up through the ropes and flew across the sky. He stopped as we went after him and put his hands up and chanted something. The air shimmered, and he disappeared.

I looked down and saw that the rest of the Pulhu were still trapped below us. All except the two that had shown up with Mr. Damon.

"Where did they go?"

"I don't know. I thought we had them trapped," Richard said.

We landed on the ground next to Abby and Gary. Abby was bent over somebody, and as I came around her, I saw it was Adam. He was covered in cuts and bruises, and blood soaked his shirt.

"Will he be ok?" I asked Abby as she healed him.

"Yes, though it will take a few more healings. I've healed all the biggest wounds," she said after most of his wounds healed.

"Are you able to walk now, Adam?"

"Yes, but what are we going to do about all these guys?"

"I will take care of it," Gary said. He stepped away and opened his phone.

"The rest of the security will be here in a few minutes, and they will deal with this. We will wait for them. We have a transporter on hand. She will take you back to the haven."

"You have a transporter, and you didn't tell us. We didn't need to do this hike every time?" Abby asked.

Gary laughed. "She just got back from another important job, so she's pretty worn out already. She agreed to transport you guys because of how much activity you are attracting. But after that, she's probably going to be out for at least a week."

"What's a transporter?" I asked.

"It's someone who has the ability to transport people anywhere they want to go. It's rare, and transporters are massively protected. The Pulhu would love to get their hands on them. Thankfully, only one or two work with the Pulhu. The rest work for us."

We followed him down the hill and waited for everyone else. Gary took us right to an older lady who wore a frown.

"Are these the ones I need to transport?" she asked.

"Yes, they need to get to the haven right away."

"Come on, kids," she said. "I only have enough energy to get you all back to the haven. Sorry, Gary, but I can't take you too."

"That's ok, I have stuff to do here anyway. I'll see you back at the haven. Don't get into any trouble while I'm gone."

"We won't," I assured him.

"Alright, everyone, grab hands so I don't lose anyone, and whatever you do, don't open your eyes or let go."

I grabbed Richard and Abby and watched as everyone else did the same, including Adam. I closed my eyes, and it felt like the ground fell out from under me. I felt Abby try to let go of my hand and gripped her tighter. I couldn't open my mouth to say anything as wind tore through my hair.

I clasped their hands tighter and squeezed my eyes shut until I felt the ground come up to meet me again. I fell to my knees and carefully opened my eyes. I still didn't let go of my friends. I wanted to make sure we were safe first. I looked around and saw that we were right outside the haven. We had all fallen to our knees, and Abby and Tider both looked sick.

"Sorry, kids. It's a tough first ride. Come on. We need to get in the haven. I can only transport right outside of it. We have protections up so the Pulhu can't transport inside, but it keeps us from doing it too," the transporter said.

CHAPTER TWENTY-THREE

My mom and dad came running over to me and scooped me up into their arms. "Are you ok? They told us what happened and that you were being transported back here."

"I'm fine, Mom. We all are," I told her.

She looked over my friends, and her eyes landed on Adam, whose clothes were still covered in blood. "Oh my goodness, are you ok?" she asked him.

"I'm fine," he assured her as healers rushed up to check us over.

"We haven't met you yet," my dad said.

"I'm Adam, a friend of Sally's." He shook their hands.

More people kept arriving, and soon a large circle of people were surrounding us, asking lots of questions about what happened and why the Pulhu were after us.

The leaders of the haven pushed their way through, and I was surprised to see Mrs. Sullivan with them. "Everyone, go back to your day. These kids need to rest. We will find out what happened and let you know. Until then, there is nothing to worry about. You are safe here."

"Mrs. Sullivan, how did you get here? Why are you here?" I asked.

"After I heard what happened, I came immediately to make sure you were ok. You've had a lot of excitement," she said, looking us over. "Why don't you get cleaned up, and we will meet in an hour to hear what you have to say?"

We agreed and made our way to our rooms to get ready. My parents were reluctant to let me out of their sight, but I promised them I would be safe in my room taking a shower. I told them to come back in half an hour, and then we could talk for a few minutes before we met Mrs. Sullivan. As much as I wanted to spend time with my parents, I really needed to get the blood and sweat off of me.

I went directly into the bathroom and started to take off my clothes. When I was taking off my shirt, I noticed a couple of rips in the fabric. I checked the rest of my clothes and saw the same thing. Around each tear in the material was a thin smear of red. It had to be blood. I was getting cut up in our battle. I didn't notice, and I must have healed really fast.

After a long shower, I felt more like myself. My friends were already waiting for me, and we sat down to talk about what we were going to say.

"We can't tell anyone about the elementals," I quickly said. Everyone agreed.

"Let's tell them we went to the lake and were swimming when we met Adam. Then when we were leaving, the Pulhu showed up and chased us. It's close enough to the truth that no one should question us," Richard said.

"What about Gary?" Abby asked. "He knows what happened."

"I already talked to him. I called him before I got in the shower to make sure we were all saying the same thing. He agreed not to tell anyone about the elementals. He doesn't want the Pulhu to get that information, and he doesn't trust everyone in the haven after the Macie incident."

"Good."

"I'm going to see my dad before we meet Mrs. Sullivan," Abby said, heading for the door.

"Of course, Abby. Let us know if it works. Our fingers are crossed." I really hoped the cure worked so she could get her dad back. "You'll have to find us. We will talk to the council first. That way, you have more time."

"Thanks," Abby said, darting away.

"Hello, Mr. and Mrs. Abeneb," I heard her say as she left the room.

I turned toward the door. "Hi, Mom and Dad." I walked over to give them a big hug.

"The Pulhu want you badly, Sally. We want to know why."

I hung my head. I really couldn't lie to my parents. "I can't tell you everything, or they could use you against me. Please don't ask me to. The Pulhu think I'm super powerful and want me on their side or out of the way."

"You are going to do things that are dangerous, aren't you?" Dad asked. "I know you, and you won't let someone do something bad without a fight. Sally, please let people with more training handle this."

"Don't worry, Dad. I'm going to stay safe in the haven and the school for a while. This was too much excitement for me." I smiled at him.

He gave me a hug and smiled sadly. "You aren't going to stay safe there forever, are you?"

"No, I'm not. I'm sorry, Dad. It has to do with the stuff I can't tell you about. Trust me. If I didn't have to do it to keep myself and other people safe, I wouldn't. You know I don't like to do anything dangerous without a good reason."

"I know. That's why your mother and I trust you. Otherwise, I would keep you locked up here with us. Promise you will try to be safe."

"I will, and besides, I have my friends with me."

"Yes, you do. All of you need to stay safe," Dad told us. Mom came over and gave me a hug.

"You need to get down there now, or you will be late," she said. "We will see you when you're finished."

I walked down to the council room with my friends. Everyone was already there.

"Where is Abby?" asked Mrs. Sullivan.

"She went to see her father," I told her. "She should be down soon."

"I see." Mrs. Sullivan smiled. "Richard, I sent you over here to help protect Sally, and I see that you were needed. Can you please tell us what happened."

Richard explained everything to the council without interruption. When he got to the part about Mr. Damon, they all leaned forward, listening intently. Once he finished, they asked a bunch of questions. Then they turned their attention to Adam.

"You have been missing for months. How did you get here?"

"I have no idea. I remember going to the bay to look at the ruins, but then I can only remember darkness. When I finally came around, Sally and her friends were surrounding me, asking if I was ok. I was hoping you could explain what happened to me," he said. It was a good idea to ask them, they would be trying to figure out what happened instead of questioning him more.

Abby burst in the door with a big smile on her face. "Abby, come sit down, we were just going over what happened. Is your father ok?" asked Mrs. Sullivan.

"He is doing great." I could tell she wanted to say more, but she couldn't. There was no explanation for how she got the potion, so she gave it to him in secret. Hopefully, they would think one of their healers fixed him. "He seemed much better. Whatever you are doing for him must be working."

"That's wonderful, dear," an older lady on the council said, smiling at Abby.

"Everyone has already gone over everything, Abby. Was there anything you would like to add? Anything you can think of that your friends may have forgotten?"

"No, I don't think so," she said. "Most of the time, I was with Sally or Gary. I'm not very strong in magic."

"Then I think we can end this meeting. Does anyone else have anything to say?"

I stood up. "I actually wanted to ask you something, Mrs. Sullivan."

"What would you like to ask, Sally?"

"Can Adam come back to the school with us? If he wants to? He was a big help during the fight, and if he has more training, he would be even better." I looked at Adam. I hadn't asked him about coming back to school. I thought of it while we were sitting here.

"If you want to," I said to him.

He looked at me and then at all of our friends. "I think I would like that. I probably need more training. I was beaten up more than anyone else. I would like to be able to take better care of myself if anything like that ever happens again."

"Let's hope it never does," said Mrs. Sullivan. "I would love to have you at our school if you want to come, and if it's ok with your grandfather. He will be here soon, and you can talk to him about it then."

"Thanks." Adam looked excited, and I hoped he would be able to come with us. I was sure Chet couldn't wait to see him and would want to spend some time with him first, though. For Adam, it had only been a few days, but for Chet, it had been months of worrying.

"You are free to go, but you can't leave the haven. Let's not take any more chances. Ok?"

"Yes, Mrs. Sullivan," I told her.

"Sally, you will be leaving in three days to come back to school. We have a transporter who is going to take you directly there, that way the Pulhu won't have a chance to get to you. I will be going back with you too. Everyone else, I will see you at school in a few days." Mrs. Sullivan dismissed us, and we walked out.

"That was a lot easier than I expected," I said.

"Yeah, it was almost like Mrs. Sullivan knew we had done something, and she didn't want the rest of the council to find out," Richard said.

"She might know. She may have expected something to happen, which would explain why she sent you out here to help me."

"If she doesn't trust the council, then we probably shouldn't either. The fewer people we trust, the better chance that no one finds out anything we don't want them to know," Tider said.

"I agree," I said. "I'm going to find my parents and hang out with them for a while," I told them.

"Me too. I want to spend time with my dad now that he is normal again," Abby said.

"Be careful, and no leaving the haven," Richard called after me.

"See you later," Tider and Adam called.

I headed right for the dining room, where my parents said they would meet me. I grabbed some food and turned to look for them. They were waiting at one of the tables. I walked over and gave them both a kiss on the cheek. "Thanks for being the best parents ever," I said.

"What's that for?" Mom asked.

"Everything. I know this has been a crazy year so far, and you've supported me through all of it. I appreciate it," I told them.

"We will support you through whatever you need. As long as you aren't doing anything illegal, of course," Mom said, laughing.

"I wouldn't ever." I laughed too.

They knew me so well. My parents were my rock, and I was going to enjoy spending time with them. The next few days went by in a blur. I spent most of the time with my parents, but occasionally I would see one of my friends and chat with them for a few minutes.

Chet came up to talk to me the day before I left. He walked right up and wrapped me in a big hug.

"Thank you for finding him," he whispered. "He told me everything once he was sure you had already told me who you were. Without you, he would probably still be stuck there."

"I'm glad I was able to help. I hope you don't mind that I asked if he could come back to school with us."

"I already told him I think it's a good idea. If I had forced him to go to the haven school, he might have been able to get away himself."

"Did he say he wants to come?" I really wanted him to go back to school with us. I wasn't sure why, but I knew we were going to need him.

"Yes, he did. That's why I'm here today. I'm dropping off his stuff. He's going to fly out with the other two boys, Richard and Tider, this afternoon."

"I forgot that they are leaving today. I don't leave until tomorrow."

"Come visit me anytime you're in the area or let me know, and I'll come here." Chet gave me one last hug and headed off to find Adam.

"Who was that?" my parents asked, coming up behind me.

"That was Chet, Adam's grandfather."

"He looked pretty happy with you."

"He thinks it's because of me that Adam was found."

"Was it because of you?"

"Maybe," I told them. They were still gently probing for information, but only if I willingly gave it. One day I would tell them the whole story, but not until I was sure they would be safe.

"Let's go enjoy the rest of the evening. You will be leaving tomorrow after breakfast, so this is our last night for a while," Mom said.

We spent the evening watching movies and eating pizza and snacks. I didn't want to leave my parents, but I wanted to get back to school. I had a lot more to learn if I was going to be able to beat the darkness. In the morning, I got everything ready before heading down to find my parents.

We had a nice breakfast before we walked to the front of the haven.

"I love you, Mom and Dad," I said, giving them a big hug.

"We love you too. Be good at school, and stay safe. Make sure you call us every night."

"Don't worry, I will. I'm going to miss you." My mom had tears in her eyes, and so did I.

"Come on you two. No crying or you'll make me cry, and then how am I going to be able to work with everyone. They will think I'm a big blubbering mess," Dad said, trying to make me smile.

"Thanks, Dad," I said, laughing.

Mrs. Sullivan walked up with a man I hadn't met before. "Mr. and Mrs. Abeneb, Sally, this is Jordan, our transporter. Are you ready to go?"

"Yes, Mrs. Sullivan," I told her.

"It's nice to meet you, Jordan," my parents said. They told me they loved me one more time before I grabbed Jordan and Mrs. Sullivan's hands and shut my eyes. This time I was ready for the ground to drop out from under me. I kept my eyes closed and waited for everything to stop spinning. When it did, I was in front of the school. I was surprised that this time, I stayed on my feet.

We walked into the school, and I breathed a sigh of relief. I felt safer here than anywhere else. "Thanks, Jordan," I told him.

"Anytime," he replied.

"Go get some rest and let me know if you need anything. Don't forget, classes start next Monday," Mrs. Sullivan told me.

I walked up to my room and sat on my bed, grateful to be back. I couldn't wait for my friends to arrive and the new semester to start. I heard a noise and whirled around to see the little water sprite sitting on my pillow.

"Hi. Where have you been?"

"I've been with you the whole time, but I couldn't let anyone see me. It wouldn't be good for the Pulhu to see us together. Then they would know that something is different about you."

"I think they already know. I used water magic around Mr. Damon. Now he knows I have two powers."

"That's ok, now you can use water and air whenever you want since they already know."

"That's true. So do I need to do anything for you? I'm not sure how to take care of a water sprite."

"You don't have to take care of me," she said, laughing. "I can handle everything myself, but if you need me or have a question, ask, and I will answer what I can for you. Now, are you ready to start a new adventure?"

"A new adventure? Already?"

"Look on your dresser," she said, grinning.

I walked over to look. A piece of paper sat there written in the ancient language. "Find the sylphs as quick as you can. If you don't find us by summer, we will be lost to you," I read out loud to the water sprite. "I guess that's our next adventure."

She smiled.

Other Books by H.M. Sandlin

Elemental Seekers Series
Lost Tides
Guarded Skies
Buried Embers

SNEAK PEEK

GUARDED SKIES
BOOK TWO OF ELEMENTAL SEEKERS

I searched the library, trying to find information on sylphs. Before coming to this school, I didn't even know what a sylph was, and I still barely had an idea. I knew they were air spirits, but that was about it. Somehow, I had to find them by summertime. It was already February, and I hadn't learned anything new. The internet wasn't helpful. All I could find were articles from the sixteenth century and on. I needed something that went back much further than that.

"Have you found anything?" I asked my friend Abby.

"I found a section over here that might be helpful," my other friend Richard said, walking out from behind the bookshelves. He was carrying a large pile of books.

"Hey, Richard. I didn't even realize you were in here. I thought you had class."

"Mr. Connor had to finish my master class early. He got a text message and said he had to go. I tracked down Abby and decided to help. By the way, how did your meeting go with Mrs. Sullivan?"

"I didn't get to talk to her. She got a phone call and said we would have to talk later. Something urgent came up that needed to be taken care of."

"What are the chances that both Mr. Connor and Mrs. Sullivan had something urgent come up at the same time?" Richard questioned.

"I would say pretty slim," Abby spoke up.

"So would I," I agreed. "There's no way they both had emergencies at the same time. Something must be going on."

"We should go find out what," Abby said.

"I don't think that's a good idea. What if we get caught?" I didn't want Mrs. Sullivan to be upset with us. She didn't say anything about what happened over Christmas break when we were visiting the Ireland haven, but I didn't want to press our luck.

"What if it is about the Pulhu. You need to know if they found anything else out about you," Richard said.

The Pulhu are a group of elementals that are trying to kidnap me. We think it's because they know I'm a powerful water elemental. After I was almost captured in Ireland, they found out I controlled two elements, so they have even more reason to come after me.

My friends think I'm part of an old prophecy because I can use all the elements, including void, but I'm still not sure. All I know is that someone left me a note telling me to find the sylphs, so that's what I'm going to do.

"I'm sure Mr. Connor will let us know if something is wrong. Besides, I talked to my parents last night. There haven't been any problems with the Pulhu since I left," I said.

"I still think we should check it out," said Abby.

"I don't know. Sally is probably right," said Richard. "Mr. Connor would tell us if something was wrong and if Mr. Connor knows what's going on, so will Mr. Merrem. He will definitely let us know if we have to worry."

"That's true," Abby said. "He's not worried about following the rules if it puts someone in danger."

"Good, then we can stay here and try to figure out where the sylphs are hiding."

Richard divided the books up that he was carrying, and we all sat down to look through them. I was lost in the book I was reading and didn't realize someone else had walked into the library until Richard's chair scraped against the floor as he quickly stood up.

"What do you want?" he asked.

I turned to see who it was and recognized Sean, the jerk in our class who thought he was better than everyone else. I was pretty sure his family was involved with the Pulhu too.

"I came in to see what kind of filth was in here. I can't say I'm surprised to see you. And I see all your friends are here too."

Slowly I stood up. "What do you want, Sean? We are busy."

"Doing what?" Sean tried to pick up Abby's book to see what she was reading, but Richard moved forward, causing him to stop in his tracks.

Sean glanced nervously behind him but continued to talk. "I want to know what you are doing. You guys are up to something. I can tell, always whispering and hiding in the library. When are you going to learn that you can't hide from me?"

"We aren't hiding from you," I said. "Honestly, I couldn't care less about what you think we are doing. Now leave us alone."

"Don't worry, Sally. Soon you will see things my way," he said with a small grin. It made me flinch, and he smirked. Something was off, but I couldn't figure out what.

He looked over his shoulder again, and I thought I saw a flash of color.

I could see faint magical auras with my eyes open ever since the water elemental king had given me some of his power, but I wasn't seeing anyone else's magic but Sean's. I saw the flash of color again.

I closed my eyes and looked around the room carefully while Richard talked to Sean. He must have realized what I was doing because he was keeping Sean's attention off me. With my eyes closed, I looked behind Sean. I could see two muddy green magical signatures, and as I turned my head, I saw another one creeping closer to Richard. I looked behind us and saw one coming toward me. They must have found a way to hide their signatures and become invisible. I opened my eyes and grabbed Abby's hand.

"What is it you want, Sean?" I interrupted. I was squeezing Abby's hand, trying to warn her.

"What I've always wanted, you and Richard to switch sides."

"Yes, but why are you pushing the issue now?"

"Because I've figured out how to make you see reason."

"Sean, we will never side with the Pulhu. You don't seem to understand that," Richard started saying, but I cut him off. I walked forward, dragging Abby with me, and stepped up to Richard.

"What is it you think you have figured out?" I reached out with my other hand and grabbed Richard.

"Oh, don't worry. I will show you," he said menacingly. I saw him start to raise his arm and immediately threw a shield up over us. Vials of foul-smelling liquid hit the shield with a hiss, and we watched as the liquid ran down the side of the shield before disappearing. I wasn't sure what was in the vials, but it looked bad.

"What? Where did they go?" Sean asked what appeared to be an empty room.

"They have to be here somewhere," a voice said from behind us, but when I looked there was no one there. I closed my eyes and saw the dark green and brown signature.

I shook my head when Abby went to whisper something. I didn't want them to hear us. I could keep us invisible for a long time as long as we didn't move a lot, but if Sean found us and started hitting my shield with magic, it would eventually burst. Richard whispered a word as quietly as he could and then looked at me.

"We should be fine now. I put a silence bubble around us so they can't hear us."

"What did they throw at us?" Abby asked.

"I don't know, but it didn't look like something we want getting on us," I said, grimacing.

"It had to be a way to control us, like how Mrs. Ravenis was controlling Abby's dad. Remember, Sean said that he found a way to get us on his side. That's the only way he would ever be able to do that. None of us would join him willingly," Richard said.

"What do we do now?" Abby asked.

"Sally, can you hold the invisibility spell if we move very slowly?"

"Maybe, but not for long. Not long enough to get to the door."

"We don't need to get to the door. We only need to get out of their way so they don't run into us."

I turned to look at Sean. He moved down the aisle and was standing in front of the door, blocking our escape. I closed my eyes and tracked the other people with him. One of them was standing at the base of the stairs so we couldn't get upstairs and go out that way.

The others spread out around the library and were shooting bursts of magic down the aisles trying to find us. It was a good thing they didn't know that we couldn't move quickly and stay invisible at the same time.

They must have thought we had an invisibility potion like they did and scattered as soon as we used it. They didn't even try to hit the spot we were standing in. Eventually, they would come back to this spot when they couldn't find us anywhere else.

"Why haven't you found them yet?" Sean yelled.

"We are looking," someone yelled back. "We will find them."

"You better, or my dad is going to be angry at all of us."

"Come on. We need to try to make it to the elevator," Richard said.

"We can't use the elevator, they will hear it," Abby replied.

"We don't need to use it. We only need them to think we used it. When they all run upstairs, we can make a break for the door and get out of here."

"Do you think they will fall for that?"

"There's only one way to find out."

"It might be our best chance of getting out of here without a fight," I said. "It will take us a few minutes to get there though. Hopefully, we won't run into them first."

We started to inch forward. I closed my eyes and concentrated on the gold strands of magic trying to flow into my shield. For some reason, every time I tried to move while invisible, these gold strands of magic would try to seep into my shield and disrupt it. I still hadn't figured out a way to stop them so I could move quickly. We only made it halfway down one of the aisles leading to the elevator when I heard Sean.

"I think they are over here," he yelled. "I can sense magic coming from that side of the room."

I looked at Abby, and she shook her head. We didn't know Sean could detect magic. There were a lot of elementals that could detect strong magic, but Sean had to be extra sensitive to pick up on my magic. I was barely using any, and what I was using wasn't powerful magic.

"Which aisle?" someone yelled.

"I don't know. I could only sense it for a second. Check all of them. Quickly."

"That's still a lot of aisles," the other person grumbled.

"We need to move quickly," Richard said, "or they will find us."

We crept forward, trying to move as quickly as we could, but I was having a lot of trouble controlling the gold strands. We could hear the people looking for us a few aisles over, and we hurried even more. I was sweating by the time we finally reached the elevator, but I didn't let the shield drop.

"Everyone get as close to this corner as you can. I will hit the button, and then we need to stay as still as possible when they come over here to look."

"We are ready," Abby said.

I reached out, pressed the button, and squeezed into the corner with my friends. I closed my eyes as the elevator opened and dinged, alerting Sean. Immediately, I saw the greenish-brown signatures of two people come running down the aisle. The elevator doors started to close, and I watched as the figures ran as fast as they could. The doors shut as they made it to the elevator.

"We missed them. They are headed upstairs. Hurry," they yelled.

Sean came running down the aisle. "How did you miss them?"

"We were at the other end of the aisles. We couldn't get here in time."

"Get up there now," Sean yelled. "Don't let them get away. Rafael, guard the door up there. I'm on my way."

Sean turned and headed toward the stairs with the other guys but turned back and stared right at us. I didn't breathe, and after a few seconds, he shook his head, turned, and ran to the stairs. I let out a sigh of relief

"Now's our chance. Let's go." Abby tried to take off for the door, but I grabbed her.

"No, we go slowly for now. The closer we get to the door without them seeing us, the better chance we have."

ABOUT THE AUTHOR

H.M. Sandlin is a stay at home mom of two daughters. She loves to read, garden, and run. She lives in Rock Hill, South Carolina, but grew up in New Jersey.

Lost Tides is her first novel, and she enjoyed writing the beginning of Sally's story. She has continued writing Elemental Seekers and is now working on book four. No matter what she has going on, she always finds time to write when inspiration strikes.

H.M. is also writing a new adult series called The Guardianship, and she has a few other books in the works. To stay up to date on news from H.M. Sandlin check out her website at https://hmsandlin.com/

Made in the USA
Middletown, DE
05 June 2020

96656133R00123